House of the Deaf

Lamar Herrin

UNBRIDLED BOOKS

Unbridled Books
Denver, Colorado

Originally published as an Unbridled Books hardcover
First paperback edition, 2006.

Library of Congress Cataloging-in-Publication Data

Herrin, Lamar.
House of the Deaf / Lamar Herrin.
p. cm.
Hardcover edition ISBN 1-932961-11-9
Paperback edition ISBN 10: 1-932961-28-3
ISBN 13: 978-1-932961-28-7
1. Terrorism victims' families—Fiction. 2. Fathers and daughters—Fiction.
3. Americans—Spain—Fiction. 4. Basques—Fiction. 5. Spain—Fiction. I. Title

PS3558.E754H68 2005

813'.54—dc22   2005017274

1 3 5 7 9 10 8 6 4 2

Book Design by SH • CV

First Printing

House of the Deaf

This book is dedicated with love to my son, Rafael, and my daughter, Delia, who have exceeded all my hopes.

But no one dies in the right place
Or in the right hour
And everyone dies sooner than his time
And before he reaches home

—*Reza Baraheni*

House of the Deaf

W hen Ben sensed they were getting close, he signaled the taxi driver to let him off. Calle Isaac Peral, a strange name for a street in Madrid, but for some reason names were important to him, and he wanted to get them right. He paid the driver and tipped him fifty pesetas. Deliberately, as though stepping off terrain, he continued on foot, passing a travel agency, a photocopy center, a cafeteria with pastries in the window, a fitness center and a book store. Across a narrow side street was a large gray hospital, Hospital Militar Generalisimo Franco, that occupied much of the next block. Then a pharmacy, a bar advertising *comidas caseras*, and a marble-faced apartment building.

If he'd been back in Lexington, Kentucky, where he lived, he would not have been able to identify the neighborhood he was in by the foot traffic he saw along the street. He saw plenty of student-aged people, some of whom might have been Americans. But this was a mainly middle-class street, filled with office workers or technicians of some sort, midrange businessmen and civil servants. Older women rolled shopping bags behind them, on their way to or from a market he neither saw, heard nor smelled.

He came to Plaza de Cristo Rey, where two other streets intersected.

The first he crossed without incident. The second was broader, and he stood with the crowd, waiting for the light. The streets were full of small flashing cars, driven bumper to bumper. Threading their way among them were kids on unmuffled motorbikes, which made a drilling din. He smelled the motor exhaust, and he smelled again and again the same soap or cologne scent— some combination of lavender and lemon, with a chemical edge.

He was on the outskirts of the city, before it gave way to the university. Beyond lay the sierra, the mountain range that bounded the table land; the sky was a bright, scoured blue.

The light changed.

On Paseo San Francisco de Sales Ben saw a boutique, Miss Jota's, and a children's clothing store with an English name, Neck and Neck. Beyond them he could make out a string of banks. But peering up the street he must have veered to the side, for he jostled a passerby, a young man, perhaps thirty, whose eyes, in the instant he fixed on them, were of a brown so light they appeared golden. There was no anger in them, no irritation, just an aged and alien luster. Every other time in his life Ben might have apologized—*lo siento,* the Spanish said—but he felt no need.

He allowed the young man to step around him. By the time he got where he was going he had made contact with two others, brushes, really, but solid enough to feel flesh on flesh. He was not sorry. The Spanish sounded like a chorus of well-trained, shrill and heckling jungle birds. When an American boy and girl passed they sounded like puppy dogs in comparison, yapping with a sunny fair boding. It was all in the voices.

He was not here to make fanciful comparisons.

Before he entered the building—brick and concrete and relatively nondescript for a country not averse to making a display of itself—he stood facing the street and allowed his weight—and the weight of his emotions—to settle over his knees. He was forty-eight. He was blond and balding and too fair-complexioned for this sun. His traveling had taken him as far west as Hawaii and as far east as London, where he'd spent a week. He'd felt at home in both places, where all foreignness was kept behind glass.

He had inherited wealth. People had died so that he might be standing here without a financial care in the world.

Inside the door of the building was an iron gate, and in order to be buzzed through he was asked to identify himself. The voice—a woman's—spoke to him first in Spanish and then in an accented but carefully enunciated English. He hesitated, surprisingly reluctant to reveal his name. He identified himself as the father of a student.

There was a doubtful pause, followed by a brief buzz, just enough to let him enter. Two students, both girls, passed him on the stairs. One was heavyset and blond, and the other had frizzy black curls. The curly-haired one looked East Coast; her companion Midwest and corn-fed. They had book bags, and he assumed they were going to class. The first said to the second, "I'm like, 'Tell me you're a *torero* and I'll scream.'" The second, trailing heavily along, said, "That's *so* Spanish!"

He came to a door with a bronze plaque. *Centro de Estudios Norteamericanos.*

In the director's office he discovered the woman who had buzzed him through. *"Buenos dias, "* she greeted him with what he could hear was operational cheer. He was struck by her beauty, above all by the warmth in her eyes, which seemed so at odds with the falsity in her voice that he went on guard. The warmth was such that he might have stepped into a greenhouse that housed this single extraordinary bloom. He reminded himself: she was a functionary, assistant to the person he had come to see.

Yes, the director was in. Did he have an appointment?

She knew he didn't. Amazing—she could speak these rehearsed phrases and look at him that way.

From almost three years earlier he remembered a director's name. He said, "Is Madeline Pratt still the director of the center?"

If Madeline Pratt was the director, he knew her as an American in permanent residence here, hired by a consortium of choice American universities. He had had no contact with her.

"Sí, senor, " her assistant said.

3

"I want to see her," he said with a cool directness. "I have come a long way."

"And you are . . . ?"

"The father of a student."

"Please, could I have a name?"

At that moment a door to his right opened, and a woman stood there with considerably less aplomb than her assistant, also requesting a name.

There was a brittleness about her, an upright, gray-lined brittleness. Her hair was cut short, the dulled color of cornhusks, and it was shot through with gray. She wore a loose-fitting *campesino* blouse with a matching skirt, but her sweater gave her away. It was a mix of fall colors, even though the month was May and the day was heating up as they stood there. The sleeves were pulled up to the elbow, exposing sinewy wrists. She wore two copper-colored bracelets. The earrings were made of bronze, short dangles of an Aztec design. He thought of Hernando Cortez: with his single-mindedness and handful of soldiers, horses and dogs, he'd burned his boats and given the world these earrings. He looked Madeline Pratt in the eye and said he'd like to talk to her in her office alone.

She had a pleasant, practiced smile she could replace with a matter-of-fact one, which told him the facts would not be to his liking. The eyes were hazel, more green than brown, and he didn't doubt she could turn their natural kindness into something administratively cold.

She showed him into her office. Stepping around her, he picked up the uninviting scent of some herbal mixture. Her walls were decorated with photographs of Spanish cultural monuments—a cathedral altarpiece, coated in gold, a pool reflecting Moorish arches—and there were prints of Spanish paintings, none of which he could identify. One was of two young women, perhaps a century ago, at a beach. They were standing beside the billowing cloth of a bathhouse. The clothes they wore were diaphanous, their hair was, the light that bathed them was a pale diffused yellow.

"Sorolla," the woman beside him confided. She'd caught him off guard. He stiffened, and she added, in a measured, marveling voice, "Has anyone ever painted the Mediterranean like that?"

He turned to her and they exchanged a look.

"If you'll tell me your son or daughter's name, I'll do my best to help you."

He paused. He had a name to give, a name to give up, and in that single lucid interval he knew he should keep the name and take it home with him. He had a home. He had a daughter in college, with no desire to go abroad, who loved him.

"Michelle Williamson," he said, adding before the name could register, "you might not remember, she was only here for a month before she was killed, and that's been almost three years now."

Stunned, Madeline Pratt sat down behind her desk. "Of course I remember," she half-whispered.

"When she was little we called her Mick, sometimes Mickey Mouse," he went on, giving it all up, with a flat grudging vehemence in his voice he couldn't control, "but she probably hadn't been here long enough to get to the nickname stage."

Madeline Pratt lowered her eyes to her desk and shook her head. There was a single framed picture on her desk that he could only see the back of. He checked the urge to reach out and turn the picture toward him, but promised himself he would see it before he left this office. It was, he understood, a way of moving ahead, making these small daring promises to himself. He added, "But come to think of it, she would never tell you that nickname. We teased her with it, and she didn't like to be teased."

Madeline Pratt raised her head and said, "I'm terribly sorry, Mr. Williamson. I don't know what to say to you."

Her eyes were moist. They were large in their sockets, the hollows beneath them were washed out. She looked utterly unresourceful. What was a woman like this doing running a program responsible for the safety of fifty students a year?

"That's okay," he said. "I'm sure you said it all to her mother when she came to bring the body back. I stayed home. I had no desire to come to Spain. Spain didn't interest me in the least."

"Yes, I remember your wife well. I was astonished at how well she bore up."

"My *ex*-wife," he corrected her. "Not many marriages will last after a thing like that."

"No," she allowed, but only to do him the courtesy.

He didn't want the courtesy. His ex-wife, Gail, would never do that, but he didn't want his ex-wife either. She sold real estate now and was enormously successful because she had a talent for disarming you with her honesty. It was a talent she'd developed, a strategy: here's what's going to drive you crazy about this house, but here's where the balance tilts slightly in your favor. She'd kept a balance sheet on her marriage in a similar way until the balance tilted against him, against it.

He'd once loved her, her beauty and the freshness of her outlook, her mind, her very being, until that freshness had hardened into something brusque and hurtful. That was before their daughter had been killed. Gail had put on weight too, and in the name of that hardened freshness, she knew how to throw her weight around. After the divorce she'd told their daughter that her father was a fool. No one could be such a romantic sap about a woman looking the way she looked now. No one she'd want to be married to. She'd gotten a divorce, and had actually told their daughter that. Annie. Their surviving daughter.

Then he told Madeline Pratt what he did want. It brought a flinch to her face and a start to her eyes. "I want you to take me where it happened," he said. "I understand it's not far from here. I want to stand there," he was more emphatic now, speaking from the unsounded depth of his desire, "where they killed her."

She took a moment to compose herself. She drew a deep steadying breath, which she made no attempt to disguise. "I could show you on the map," she conceded. "But I shouldn't leave the office. I have someone coming in."

He didn't believe her. "They're still killing people, aren't they?"

She hesitated. "ETA?"

He hated the anonymity of the initials, that uppercase shield. "Yes, the Basques," he said impatiently, "ETA."

"ETA only represents a tiny minority of the Basque people."

"Those who want Basque independence."

"Yes, but not even a majority of those."

"Only the most violent."

"Yes, only the most violent. The fact is, the Basques are prosperous, and most prefer to remain part of the Spanish state."

"Yet they permit the presence of ETA on their soil," he reminded her. "They don't get rid of it."

In her forbearing half-whisper, Madeline Pratt said, "Because they are afraid."

He was vigilant. He would not join her in her forbearance. "Are you afraid?"

"Of ETA?" Again she hesitated. She tried to assume a professional bearing. She was going to yield to him. A director of an American study abroad program was going to yield to a distraught parent. Somewhere it was written: parents who feel their children are lost to them, lost on foreign soil, should be treated with the utmost consideration, babied if that's what it takes.

She nodded. "If you live in Spain for any length of time, you get used to the threat of ETA. You learn not to think about it and to go on with your life."

She bit back a tiny grimace. *You go on with your life if you're still alive.* She should not have put it like that.

Suddenly it became clear to him what she was going through. He would be willing to bet that she had never lost a student under her supervision before, under any circumstances. Surely that was a director's worst nightmare, and at that nightmare's darkest depth, to have lost a student as his daughter had been lost . . .

His heart went out to her.

He couldn't afford any more excursions of the heart.

Reaching across the desk, he turned her photograph to him. She sat back from him, erect, soldiering through this bad moment, perhaps a little appalled. The photograph was of a teenaged girl, her husk-colored hair cut short, her face reddened by the sun, her chin, her nose, her hazel eyes, the green muddied with brown. He didn't know whether he was looking at her at a daughter's age or at a daughter destined to become the woman he saw sitting here.

He turned the picture back around. He sat back. He put it to her squarely. "Take me there. Show me the spot. I won't ask any more of you, and I won't be back."

She shook her head. "It won't mean anything. There are dozens of parks like that one in Madrid."

"All with a Civil Guard headquarters?"

She chose not to answer him and, stepping to her office door, spoke to her assistant instead. Her name was Concha. Madeline Pratt spoke in Spanish, but he understood that she was telling her assistant what to do in case a certain argumentative woman who housed their students showed up before she could return. Concha smiled at him as they left the room; in return, he thanked her, although she would never know for what. He was thanking her for her Spanish eyes, the eyes of the song that when he was a boy he had sat beside his mother and sung. They had sung through stacks of sheet music, the whole romantic songbook. To her credit, when she had closed the piano lid, his mother had trapped the romance inside, where it took on the mustiness of the old ivories, the old felt hammers and pads. Ben thanked Concha for showing him her eyes. They were real. They had nothing to do with the world.

In the hall he asked Madeline Pratt, "She lived here, didn't she? Where did she live, upstairs?"

The director nodded. "Now not as many students do. More live with families. But your daughter chose to live by herself. She said she was here to learn."

Her tone was detached, informative. If they were going to do this, would he allow her this tone?

She continued, "She went running every morning. She was running that morning. But you already know that."

He did, but he wanted to know everything. He wanted her to skip nothing. He nodded, and they descended that last flight of stairs, pushed through the iron gate and stepped onto the street.

Where, two years and eight months earlier, September the twenty-ninth, his daughter, Madeline Pratt's program member, Michelle Williamson, turned left and ran up this street. She ran along the sidewalk her father had walked down, only she ran earlier in the morning. How much earlier? Between seven-thirty and eight. Before reaching Paseo San Francisco de Sales, the street where her father had jostled that passerby, she turned left up a narrower street, Calle Domenico Scarlotti, and ran uphill, a gradual incline. She passed office buildings and apartment buildings and a small hotel, the Mindanao, where he might have taken a room. There were three upscale restaurants and a jewelry store—they were quickly leaving the student scene—and two beauty salons. After four blocks, Domenico Scarlotti deadended in Calle General Ampudia, and there, before an elegant furniture store, she turned right and ran past apartment buildings in whose glassy façades she might have observed herself, had she not had her attention turned to more important things. On Paseo San Francisco de Sales she ran past that string of banks her father had noticed from down the street, closed at that early hour. Directly ahead she came to a plaza that turned out to be a small park, Parque Santander, where cypresses and sycamores and locusts grew and short gnarled trees she would have known the name for and her father didn't. Paths led off into the park. A runner could either piece these paths together or use the broad sidewalk that surrounded the park as a track. The trick would be to cross the heavily trafficked streets and reach the park without breaking stride.

She would know the trick. She had been running in this park for a month. It was where she came.

When the light changed, Madeline Pratt led him across the street. He saw no runners at this late-morning hour. No students. But he put his daughter there; he allowed her to appear before him. The gold of her hair was drawn up in a ponytail. She ran with her upright carriage and measured stride. She wore light-colored shorts and shirts—pale greens, blues, oranges, pinks—clothes he'd never seen darkened with sweat. She wore her timer's watch with the black band. She didn't wear headphones. She would hear the world around her, as well as see it, smell it, feel its crunching give under her feet.

On her face Ben saw an expression of great diligence, as though she were monitoring all her vital signs at once.

He followed Madeline Pratt into the park. Tables were set out before a concession stand. Two women whose small children played on some teeter-totters were having coffee. These were working-class women—at least the jeans and featureless tee-shirts they wore indicated little interest in clothes. They wore no makeup; their hair did not look combed. There was a dry itemizing tone to their voices, with a hint of some grievance. He asked Madeline Pratt to have coffee with him. When he offered to bring the coffee to her, she cautiously corrected him. Even in such informal sur-roundings they would be served.

He had what she had, a *cortado*, an espresso with a splash of warm milk. One sugar.

Fate had brought his daughter here. For the last month of her life she'd run around this park, and there on the far side, beyond bushes and trees, he lost her to view. He believed he could hear her then, a sort of whispering pant, like a sound she made in her sleep, but she wasn't calling him to come drive away the spooks of her dreams. She was simply on the dark side of his moon.

He had no idea of the expression that had appeared on his face. But when Madeline Pratt said, "I can't let you do this," she was clearly more concerned for his well-being than her own, and he didn't want that.

"Take me there now," he said. "I want to stand on the spot."

A building occupied the entire side of the block, tan-colored stucco alternating with columns of brick; it was four stories high, its two visible corners dominated by guard towers. There was a guard booth at the driveway leading in. From the sidewalk where he stood he estimated the distance across the street to where two Civil Guards patrolled their stretch of sidewalk at sixty feet. The Civil Guards were dressed in a darker, denser green than army green and carried machine guns slung over their shoulders. Sixty feet was the distance separating a pitcher from a batter. As a teenager he had pitched. These two Civil Guards might have been teenagers themselves. They had fresh bony faces that looked struck from the same Spanish mold. They had vigorous eyebrows and hair along their upper lips. The predecessor of one of them had not survived. Ben asked Madeline Pratt where, and she moved them farther along the sidewalk, up from the headquarters' entrance. When she stopped, he estimated the distance between them and those two patrolling boys now at ninety feet, or the distance between home plate and first base. As well as Madeline Pratt could remember, his daughter had died here. There was a tree just inside the park, one of those low gnarled trees with what looked like carob pods hanging from its limbs. He could see how the bark had been blown away. What remained of the tree looked indestructible. The car loaded with dynamite had been parked almost directly across from the entrance where the two Civil Guards patrolled. And the blast had caught her here.

"What kind of car?"

Madeline Pratt had newspaper clippings from that day. As documents pertaining to the center she'd felt obligated to keep them. He could consult the clippings.

But she must have remembered the car.

She nodded. It was a Seat Ibiza. She looked up the street and raised her hand and pointed at an unexceptional white car wedged into a parking spot.

"Like that one," she said.

It was a hatchback model. It had no trunk. There would be a storage area for luggage, but anyone peering in . . .

"And other than my daughter and that Civil Guard . . . ?"

"Two more people were slightly injured, and there was a lot of shattered glass. But I hope you'll believe me when I say it was truly miraculous that there were no other casualties. I know that's small consolation."

"It's been two years and eight months since it happened. Look around. If you didn't notice that tree, you'd never know. That building looks like it never got touched."

"They had to rebuild some. They put up a plaque beside the door."

"I don't want to see it. What does it say? Does it even mention her?"

Madeline Pratt bowed her head. "No," she whispered, stage-whispered in the traffic noise, the noise of concentrated human habitation, "it's what they always say when a Civil Guard is killed, that he died for the glory of his country."

Todo Por La Patria.

Ben stood where she'd positioned him. The pavement had been littered and swept and rained on hundreds of times since his daughter had lain here. Each horn that blew, each motorbike that drilled by, took some of her with it. He looked back along the diagonal to the headquarters' entrance. The two Civil Guards were hardly on alert; they chatted with each other, rocked back on their heels, and cradled their guns idly, like something they'd been told to hold on to for the duration of the day. He looked from them on another diagonal to where that white car was parked. As far as those boys knew, it too could carry explosives. It could wipe out Madeline Pratt and Ben Williamson where they stood, or the vagaries of the blast could reach the Civil Guards and countless others, instead, and leave the two of them unscathed.

"They didn't catch them, did they?" he said.

Madeline Pratt shook her head. "They have a phrase they use in the press. *Desarticular comandos,* which means they disband a group of four or five terrorists operating in Madrid. Another *comando,* or another team, comes in from the Basque country to replace them. The authorities try to pretend otherwise, but it's not really a matter of a particular person and a particular crime. . . ."

"Why?" he asked. "Why do they pretend otherwise? So they can show that justice is being done?"

"Yes, you know . . ." and she forced herself to look at him out of that desolate dead space around her eyes, "for society and especially for the families, so that they can get some sense of—"

He stopped her. She was going to say "closure" or something equally cruel in its banal right-mindedness. "Closure" would have been a bomb blast out of that white Seat, and it hadn't come.

He smiled at her. He wanted her to take away this smile and study it, take it to heart. He saw her eyes widen and begin to glisten. She was a tall woman, almost his height, and he could feel the shakiness in her knees. "Go away," he told her. "Go back to your students. It's been long enough. Erase Michelle Williamson from your mind."

When she wouldn't leave, he insisted. After she'd taken a few steps he called her back. "My daughter, when that car blew up, she was running away from the blast, wasn't she? She was almost safe on first base."

When Madeline Pratt didn't know what to say, he dismissed her entirely. He waved his hand in front of her face. She was so brittle-boned he could have crunched her into a powder, except that she deserved better than that, bereft of one of her most promising students through no real fault of her own.

L̲ate that afternoon Ben Williamson sat in El Parque de Buen Retiro watching the evening's promenade. He was off the main thoroughfare, where, in addition to the promenaders, performers staged their mime and puppet and juggling shows, beggars begged, and teenagers ran amok. He was sitting in a formal garden of trimmed hedges and conical bushes whose leaves had the metallic glossiness of holly. Along the axis of this garden couples, mostly his age, walked arm in arm. It was quieter here. Behind him was a basin where a single jet of water spouted. There was a stone gate down to his left, imposing enough to be an official portal, and beyond it lay a building belonging to the Prado Museum. Out of the ruckus of that main thoroughfare, up to his right he heard guitar music competing with a violin and human voices singing for their supper, all amplified, yet strangely remote. He heard the delicate splash of the water in the fountain behind him and the footfall on crushed stone of the deliberately pacing couples.

He watched the couples, observed them closely as if he were recording his own heartbeat, his rate of respiration. Gentlemen in suits and gentlemen with canes seemed right, just as women dressed in tasseled shawls did. The evening was growing cool. But he saw more jeans and khaki and even exercise suits than he did elegant attire, and more running shoes and cheap versions of Birkenstock sandals than polished leather. But regardless of how they were dressed and out of what period of Spain's history they seemed to emerge, as they paced by him it was as if he were being introduced to an elemental rhythm that was the social equivalent of his heartbeat, his breath-taking. People paired off and lasted the years so that they could come here in their middle age and round out the course of their lives. If he wanted to think of it that way.

He drew a breath, and, arms linked, one couple replaced another. His heart beat, and to the music of that drum, the feet paced by. The water spilled back onto itself and rose again. The smells were the prickly unsweetened smells of an orderly procreation.

If he wanted to think of it that way.

Or he could think of it as lockstep. The pacing as penitential. The procreation a mockery. The fruits of their labor were up on that thoroughfare living by their wits.

Until a bomb went off.

Here in the Park of the Buen Retiro.

What Madeline Pratt didn't know was that Ben Williamson had spent days reading about ETA. Days he'd gone to visit his daughter Annie in college, he'd slipped into the library, found a carrel and pulled books down off the stacks. ETA—Euzkadi Ta Askatasuna—Basque Fatherland and Liberty. The only insurgency that Francisco Franco hadn't been able to wipe out. Insurgency was in the Basque blood. One summer, in an effort to disrupt Spain's tourist trade, ETA had planted bombs at random in favorite beaches on Spain's *costa azul* and *costa del sol*. They'd buried the bombs in the sand. A German had had the bad luck to spread his towel over one.

Why not here? Blow a hole in Spain's generational chain. Here, this potbellied *paterfamilias* and his hobbled wife whose ankles turned in her shoes.

Or this next couple, younger, much more attractive, she tall, blond, still with a coltish lift to her knees, and he sporting a jaunty handlebar moustache. Both stylishly dressed.

One couple interchangeable with the next? He remembered what Madeline Pratt had said about "disarticulating *comandos*." The futility of putting a face on what was essentially faceless. His daughter had had blue eyes, the blue of a mountain lake—he had seen the very lake in Wyoming's Grand Teton National Park—but with a subtly tightened, puzzled look about them, as if at any moment that blue water were about to freeze. A mouth that was pensively pressed shut; a pert point to her chin. Across her temple there was a blue vein that gave her away, pulsing when she was otherwise composed. An eyelid also sometimes twitched. He too had had a twitching eyelid, but the time he'd called her attention to it had led to a rebuff. A twitching eyelid meant nothing. They had taken her away from him before he'd been able to find something that did mean something. He could see her now, far more clearly than when she had been alive, but she, of course, was her own shield. She'd died on her shield.

Sitting there, witness to a procession he was ineligible to join, but, nonetheless—as his heart beat and his lungs filled—in a processional state of mind, all he could tell himself was that he'd need a face—one of theirs. He'd need a face to make a fair exchange.

II

As big a pest as her father could be, Annie had always considered him capable of a serious act. Her mother no longer did, and that, as far as her father went, was the difference between them. She didn't know why she felt that way—she could cite no evidence—but every time she and her mother got in a discussion about him, that was the position Annie took. And they talked about him a lot. Her mother rarely visited her at college, whereas her father came often. After all, he was responsible for her education—it was the only financial demand her mother had made of him during the divorce. But her mother called. Her mother lived on the phone—luring house-hunters her way, proposing deals, closing deals. She had Annie on speed-dial on her apartment and cell phones.

Annie could speak frankly to her mother, who wasn't one of these easily offended sorts. Her roommate Valerie's mother was like that, every phone call was an exhausting dance around what could and couldn't be said and in exactly what tone. Annie could say, "Don't call me for the next three days, I'll be studying for a test," and her mother wouldn't. She had boyfriends—her current boyfriend was a blue-blooded Bostonian named Jonathan who regarded her Kentucky upbringing as exotic—and when she told her mother she'd be out of reach for a while, it was like a code phrase they had. Annie would be spending time with her boyfriend, and her mother was not to call. When she did call she didn't pry into how her daughter's little romantic idyll had gone. They understood each other— since her sister's death, it was only natural that her parents would take extraordinary care with her. But in her mother's case it represented no effort. It was how she was. Gail Williamson cared, she cared enormously, but she had absolutely no capacity for devotion. And that suited Annie fine.

The only disagreement between them concerned her father. Her mother considered her ex-husband negligible, and Annie didn't. Time had passed him by, and Annie, with nothing to back her up, begged to differ.

She believed her father was lonely. He'd lost both his mother and father. His brother, Charley, lived in California and showed no interest in coming east. Her father had had a wife, and then he hadn't. He'd had an older daughter, and then he hadn't. But he still had her, his younger daughter, and he came often, even though he tried to stay out of her way. Once she'd seen him when he hadn't bothered to tell her he was coming; it was as if he were haunting the campus. "He's lonely, Mother," she'd said. Her mother had answered, "Nonsense. I offered to fix him up with one of my clients. They would have suited each other fine. At the last moment he backed out and nearly cost me a sale."

Annie wondered about the ethics of that from any angle at which she cared to examine it. But her mother had an ease with ethics that could almost win you over.

"I haven't heard from him in more than a month," Annie confided to her mother during their latest phone call.

"Now that you mention it, neither have I. Are you worried?"

She wasn't, but that last time he'd visited he'd behaved strangely. They'd had dinner together. They'd talked about nothing in particular, then out of nowhere he'd made a comment about digging in to face the day that was sure to come, and she'd thought he was referring to some paper she was putting off writing, or upcoming exams. She'd laughed in his face. Then she'd kissed him good-bye. But he hadn't left. Friends had seen him in the library, squeezed into one of the stack carrels, and once in the Government Department, standing before a professor's door. Her sister had been a government major, with a concentration in international relations. The irony of that had struck Annie as criminal in itself. Maybe her father had gone to her sister's professor to protest that at long last something had to be done.

When she'd called his hotel for an explanation for his behavior, she was told he'd checked out. The programmed voice of the man who told her that left a cold empty space in her ear.

She was annoyed with herself, that for her last communication with her father she had laughed in his face. And she was annoyed with him, that he would make her regret her laughter, that he would force her to accuse herself of laughing out of place.

She liked to laugh. Her laughter was like her trademark. When Michelle was alive her laughter was sometimes her only means of expression; then, when Michelle died, it was as if she were being forced to defend her laughter. Now she laughed every chance she got. "Digging in to face the day that was sure to come" was certainly worth a laugh.

Yet in spite of herself, and especially in spite of her mother, she still considered her father capable of a serious act.

"I want to see him, that's all," she explained to her mother. "I miss him."

After a puzzling pause, her mother said approvingly, "Well, good, good for you."

Then her mother began to tell her about Rennick Road. This was a road running out of town that Annie didn't know. It was barely a mile long, and at least half of the land was taken up by what used to be a small dairy farm but was now given over to the raising of goats. Apparently in Greek and Arab restaurants there was a big city market for goat meat. But Annie had to imagine looking out over a pasture; instead of goats she was to see popcorn popping. Seemingly unprovoked, and from a standstill, the little white kids would leap straight up, and it was like watching corn pop. All over that pasture—pop, pop, pop!

Each time they talked, it seemed, her mother had a tall tale to tell. She'd just served up a pasture of popping kids.

Well, on that short road, last week, her mother had closed on three houses, two as a buying agent and one as a seller. She attributed her extraordinary success to the goats. She'd personally taken the two buying families to the goat pasture on a sunny day, and the fleecy white kids had performed. The kids—*Homo sapiens*, now—had gone crazy. She'd made sure the buying agent for the house she was selling did the same. People, against their sensible best judgment, were so easily won. A boiler could be about to go, water damage all over the house, and goats on a sunny day could make them forget it. What does that tell you?

"What?" Annie replied. "That people like goats?"

"No, sweetie. That people are still children. Appeal to the child in a buyer, and you've got him. But it can't be just anything. We're not talking an old rope swing hanging from an oak tree. People have calluses on top of calluses just trying to stay alive in this world. It's got to be something mysterious, powerful, but something as fresh as spring."

Annie said, "Was there a boiler about to go, and was there water damage all over a house?"

"Please! The pasture of popping goats was a bonus. The houses were all first-rate. They'll pass inspection like that."

Her mother snapped her fingers. Her mother was a great finger snapper. Annie could hear it over the phone, and she could hear it in her mind's ear. Time to get going—snap! I want that bed made up like this—snap! Let's cut the shit, it's over—snap! The popping goats and the snapping fingers, and she realized that in the midst of the tall-tale telling she hadn't stopped thinking about her father.

She said, "I know you divorced him, but you have to stay friends. Friends look after friends—"

Her mother cut her off. "Annie, that's enough about your father! I divorced him because I didn't intend to stagnate with him. I've told you this a hundred times. It had nothing to do with love. The kind of love your father believes in doesn't exist—it never did. That doesn't mean I'm going to stand by and watch him walk off the edge of the earth, if that's what you're saying. To be honest, he'd never find a way to get there. . . ."

"Where? The edge of the earth?"

"Anywhere beyond his beaten track!" There was some impatience in her mother's voice now, and some heat, which Annie knew not to take personally. Unless she were taking her father's side. "I wasn't going to stay with him just because he lost a daughter. I lost a daughter. I wasn't going to stay there and match his loss against mine. There's a law of survival, you know. And if you don't, there's nothing they can teach you in that university worth a damn. I wasn't going to let Ben pull me down, Annie— although 'pull' puts it too strongly. Not Ben—"

She stopped her mother there. "Give it a rest, Mom. Okay? Dad's doing what he has to do."

As usual, her mother handled her daughter's occasional flare-ups of temper by marking off a cool distance on the phone. Then she said, "Oh, really? And what might that be?"

"He's seeing me through school."

He's doing his court-ordered duty, nothing more or less, her mother might have replied. And Annie might have responded, You demanded it of him as a way of making clear how badly, how catastrophically, he had failed with Michelle.

Her mother asked her about her boyfriend, Jonathan, instead, and if Annie were being honest she would have admitted that Jonathan was beginning to bore her. It was either Cambridge or the Cape, and when the heat was bad, it was the family estate on Mount Desert Island in Maine. These were all places that Annie had in store. He, in turn, wanted to see the horse farms around Lexington. Calumet. Then, if she could show him a moonshiner . . .

She heard her father say it again. Your friend Jonathan sounds like a fellow who has yet to dig in to face the day that's sure to come.

She winced and laughed at the same time. Her roommate, Valerie, who had just walked into the room, heard what might have sounded like a snarl and shot Annie a look. Valerie's looks were always larger than life, more often than not exaggerated wrenchings of her features. Annie gave Valerie a look that backed her off.

Her mother said, "More intelligence than maturity, it sounds like to me. Once he grows up he might be something to call home about. You will call home, won't you?"

"Of course."

"You did say he was a handsome devil, didn't you?"

"Did I?" She decided to include Valerie, who might be sulking from that last look. The fact was, Valerie was a dear friend who had been Annie's roommate both in the dorm and in this apartment, and whose family life, if it didn't include the death of a sister, did include a mother who had overdosed on sleeping pills and was not above threatening to do it again. Valerie's father was hanging on for compassion's sake, although Valerie would not have blamed him if he'd left. If he left, Valerie would inherit the whole of her mother. You could divorce a wife, but mothers lived off your blood.

"Valerie," Annie inquired, "my mother wants to know if Jonathan is 'a handsome devil.'"

"He's a step up from that sleazeball you had before. Tell her that."

Annie told her mother that Valerie said Jonathan was an improvement on his predecessor, nothing more.

It was time to get off the phone.

She said, "I've got a lot of work coming up—exams and stuff. Probably best not to call." After a pause she added, "Hey, that's great about the three houses. They used to have goats and cows on the Arts Quad, did you know that?" There was another pause, calculated, measured, not her intention. Then she said, "Call if you hear from Dad." She insisted, "Call then."

When Valerie asked her what all that had been about, Annie shook her head. Would she believe a herd of goats popping like popcorn over a field? Valerie bugged her eyes. Annie said she was going to class.

All her classes were on the Arts Quad. She had to cross a narrow gorge on a footbridge. Once on the quad, she could position herself in the right opening between the old stone buildings, half-covered with ivy, and let her eyes sail out to the horizon, where the glacially formed lake the university was built above took its first jag toward the west. It jagged east and west on its way north for forty miles. It was, in one spot, said to be six hundred feet deep. She frequently came here and looked at the lake before attending classes. It was a way of clearing the head, straightening the spine. It was also, as far as she could remember, the only tip her sister had given her about how to meet the rigors of the university. "Rigors" had been one of Michelle's favorite words.

Beautiful, spectacular, sure, but as an act of self-discipline, learn to see through all that. Then you're ready enter the classroom and not be distracted by the pretty phrases. If the professor has anything to teach you, that's when you'll learn.

Annie had been a freshman here when Michelle had begun her junior year abroad in Spain. They had not overlapped by a single day.

She was trying to pay attention to what her teacher was saying about the six causes of the Spanish-American War, a Catholic culture about to be replaced by a mercantile Protestant one, but it was mid-May and a lilac bush was in bloom whose scent was pouring in through an opened window. She closed her notebook and quietly slipped out the back door.

Her sister had died, her father had gone through a disorienting divorce, and Annie had survived with her friends, her health, her intelligence intact. And her beauty. Michelle had not been beautiful. Her defense system was so elaborately wrought that any natural warmth she might have had was smothered, though in unguarded moments she'd let it show. They'd had canaries in the house, and tropical fish, and more than once Annie had surprised her sister sitting before the cage or aquarium with something like wonder in her face. Once—only once that Annie could remember—Michelle had invited her sister to share it. They'd sat together and watched. The canaries would hop from the floor of their cage, where the feeders were, to the top perch in one nervy zigzagging ascent. The guppies or black mollies or angelfish would swim placidly along, then suddenly describe darting arabesques. Michelle's face in those moments shone with the iridescence of the fish and the canaries' yellow glow.

Stripped of her defenses, her sister had had her beauty.

Where did her defenses get her, anyway?

Blown away.

Annie was alive on this lovely spring day. Tall, graceful as a dancer, warm-complexioned, tints of auburn in her hair. She wore no makeup. Her eyes were dark, but not bold, not forbidding. They scared nobody away.

Lips moist, teeth white. The face of somebody who laughed.

She had started to cry. She went and sat in the obscuring shade of an Arts Quad oak.

Curiously, she'd never blamed the people who had set the bomb and denied her another chance to get to know her sister. In her art history class she'd learned that the cornices of buildings built three and four hundred years ago were falling all over Europe. Pedestrians were sometimes killed. The Old World was crumbling, and those who frequented its streets ran the risk of falling with it. That was what had happened to her sister. The Old World had fallen on her. The Old World was more dangerous in that way than the New, but this oak could fall too. If it did she would join her sister, and their father would have no one left.

Her thought had taken a turn. Life and death were such fragile, flickering things, such whims of the moment, such accidents, that all the records we kept of them were the biggest joke of all. We recorded history to keep from laughing, out of sheer terrified disbelief, at ourselves. This oak, for instance, made mockery of anybody who sat with her back to it pondering the meaning of life, and of what belonged to whom. My life belongs to me. Then, poof! What life? What you? The oak had been planted when they'd cleared the Arts Quad of its goats and cows. That had been at least one hundred and twenty years ago. It had seen how many generations of students into the grave? Administrators? Trustees? Presidents? And the university owned it? She laughed, inside, on a deeper register. Someone sitting at her side might have heard it as a growl. It would be an honor to be killed by this oak tree, she thought. Just to be worthy of this oak tree's attention would be an honor. This noble oak. Sprung from a tiny acorn. What a joke.

Its bark hurt her back. She pressed against it, mortifying the flesh, as monks and nuns and other religious fanatics did when they failed to have God's attention. Her tears had dried and her eyes felt parched with the heat of an unaccustomed anger. She remembered something her sister had told her that suited her mood. They were in Michelle's bedroom, where Annie had gone to return a sweater she'd not really had permission to wear, and which didn't fit her in the first place. She was two years younger than her sister but had experienced a gangly spurt of growth and was already taller. Michelle accused Annie of having taken the sweater without her permission, and Annie, defiantly, put it back on and showed Michelle how woefully short it was in the arms. In her memory, it barely came to her forearms. It was tight in the shoulders. Buttoned up, it made it hard to breathe. It was some pale indeterminate color between beige, tan, gray and green, and quite simply, it was like being wrapped up in her sister's skin. Annie took it off and flung it on the bed. She stood there with her superior stature to see what her sister would do. Michelle took her time hanging the sweater back up in the closet. Then she turned and said, "You know what you are?" Annie didn't, but she knew not to bite at her sister's question. "You're their backup daughter. You know what that means? You're the daughter they've got left over in case something happens to me. The backup daughter," she repeated in a quieter, more private voice, clearly savoring the phrase.

It wasn't her sister's meanness—Annie was used to that—it was the private pleasure Michelle took that caused Annie to lash out.

"That's just you! That's just something you like to hear yourself say!"

Still savoring her pleasure, Michelle said, "I didn't say it. Mother did. Mother was ready to stop with me, but Dad talked her into having you, just in case." Then Michelle turned to her closet and ran her hand along her clothes. "There's nothing in here that fits a backup daughter. Try the Salvation Army or someplace like that."

Annie didn't doubt that the phrase originated with her mother. She could hear her mother saying it now. Michelle could be forgiven, at that uncaring age when she could be expected to latch on to anything with an authoritative ring. But the sentiment Annie recognized as coming from her father, the foreboding. The world could crush you—an Old World cornice or a New World oak—and suddenly you would have nothing left. He no longer had Michelle, and he no longer had his wife. He had her, Annie, his backup.

He would not have put it that way. He would have said, Please, give me more life.

A book bag hit the dirt beside her. "It's been realpolitik from the start. If students in the '60s had known anything about American history they wouldn't have felt so disillusioned."

"Saltonberg?" she said.

"You left before he got to the good stuff. If we're good at getting our innocence crushed, it's because we defend our ignorance like nobody else."

"I've heard it all before."

"Carolyn . . . whatever her name is, the blond that sits on the front row . . . hadn't heard it. She took offense. She took offense 'mightily.'" With his Tennessee accent, he gave to the word a deep oratorical roll. This was her friend Chad, whose last name she couldn't remember, so she called him Chad the Volunteer. "And Saltonberg told her she was proving his thesis for him, like any good American she was defending her ignorance, and he asked her if she would mind standing as his example. You didn't see her come storming out?"

"Wanna get something to eat?" Annie said.

They crossed back over the gorge to Collegetown. She had a bagel with cream cheese and a carton of some juice mixture. While she ate, she got Chad to tell her about his town, Murfreesboro, and about his family. His father sold Buicks in town and had had the foresight to grab the Honda franchise when that was tantamount to desecrating the American flag. Thanks to Hondas—who bought Buicks anymore?—Chad was able to get out of town and come to this elite spot. Laughter. No sisters? No, a spoiled little brother and the mother who spoiled him. Scandals? Not really. A cousin who was gay. During a summer visit he'd come on to Chad, and Chad had let him. Really? Yeah, Chad had always liked him, and to be frank, he wasn't exactly sure what it was they did. A single laugh. Really? No shit? Chad was young at the time. He was young now. Blow job, what did it mean? She sized him up. He was smart, clear-eyed, a face of such balanced proportions it'd be easy to draw, a shock of light brown hair on his forehead, unhidden, she decided. To top it off, a voice from home. Did he like it? He was amazed to see his cousin rooting down there, too amazed to get hard, much less to come.

And she was amazed to hear him go on like this. Southern boys didn't talk about sex as freely as Northern boys did. She had her mouth open on a single soundless laugh. "Wild," she said, and discovered she had put her hand on his leg under the table. When had she done that? And when had she reached up high enough to feel him go hard down a pants leg? But that was where she found her hand. Amazing. As if she were rewarding the loyalty of the family dog, she patted him there. Thanks for cutting a class. For coming to lunch with her. For telling her his stories. Out on the street, he wanted to take her to his apartment, which wasn't far away. She followed him there. She'd begun to feel ghosted and guided by a not unfriendly intelligence, and she was curious to see where it took her, of the array of possibilities, which were the ones she had in store. It crossed her mind that if she wanted to conjure up her father after more than a month's absence, this might be a way. Over there, across the street. Under that tree. Inside that doorway.

It was noon. It didn't matter. She'd draw him out of hiding. He was in the closet. Under the bed. Behind the bedroom door. Having been warned, her mother wouldn't call.

III

Sabino Arana—a mysterious man. He'd been jailed by the Spanish government, charged with sending a letter of congratulations to Theodore Roosevelt for liberating the Cuban slaves from their Spanish masters. He considered Spaniards lazy, violent and drunken, a threat to the purity of any people they came into contact with; the Catalans, who, like the Basques, languished under Madrid's rule, he considered godless. Arana himself was a devout Catholic, a sort of neo-Carlist. He espoused nonviolence. He believed the Basques were God's chosen people and that their language was the language spoken in Eden before the fall.

They had been granted a "collective nobility" long ago; that meant, to a man, in their mountain strongholds, the Basques were a noble race. The fact that that title had been bestowed on them by a Castilian king for their defense of the Spanish realm didn't bother Arana. Occasionally Castilian kings could be made to see the light. The Moors had never penetrated the Basque country; no Jews had. They had a blood that wouldn't mix. A language only they could speak. The young men banded together and made periodic retreats to the mountaintops overlooking their towns. There they held their virile exercises and communed with God.

Searching for a face, Ben Williamson remembered Arana, a mystic, a holy fool, but a politician too and the founder of the largest political party in the Basque country. A pacifist. A fascist, if there ever was one.

He had not seen a face. College texts drawn off the shelves rarely contained photographs.

Basques were said to have a special cranial formation, and, it was true, a certain rare blood type. They were all black-haired, black-browed, with deep-set eyes and pronounced jaws. That was not a face.

When Franco rose it was to liberate Spain from the atheists, ideologues, soulless state planners. Yet he bombed the Basques savagely. Hermann Goering wanted to give his Luftwaffe a trial run before Germany attacked Britain and the rest of Europe; Franco pointed to a small Basque town and said, "There. It shall be a lesson to separatists. In its ruins, their shrine. You have my permission to make it disappear." Guernica.

Ben had seen the painting. He had stood before it in the Museum of Modern Art. At the time it was an obligatory stop on his tour of the city. He'd come with his wife and two girls, when they were small. Yet only he had felt obliged. The museum guide had explained that the painting was to remain here, in the land of the free, until real freedom was restored in Spain. He remembered the guide's almost quipping and partisan aside: since Spain had never been a free country, it was hard to imagine just what Picasso had had in mind. And too late to ask him since the exiled Spanish master had recently died. The chances were *Guernica* would be here in MOMA for years to come.

After the great visceral howl that came off the painting had died down, what Ben remembered was its playfulness. He would not remember it being painted in blacks and whites and grays. He would swear it was painted in the primary colors of a child.

ETA was born when the commander of the Allied forces that had rid the rest of the continent of fascism, but had failed to do so in Spain, came to Madrid to extend an approving hand to Franco in his stand against communism. Ben didn't remember this. He was far too young. He didn't really remember Ike, except as a sort of cloudy grandfatherly visage hovering over the country during the first years of Ben's life. Ike came and shook Franco's hand, and separatist Basques, who had been waiting for years for the Allied hero to give them their D-Day, split from the dominant nationalist party and became an armed insurgency.

He had read that and had no reason to doubt it. Nineteen fifty-nine. In that year, that cloudy grandfatherly visage had looked down on his daughter. But a cloudy grandfatherly visage was not a face.

The books agreed that Franco had used the Basques to set the rest of Spain an example. The Galicians, the Valencians, the Mallorcans, the Canary Islanders, the Aragonese and especially the Catalans might entertain separatist ambitions, but once they saw what Franco did to the Basques, they'd have second thoughts. Municipal government, education, taxation, labor, the appointment of officials down through the ranks, the running of the ports, the prisons, the policing of the streets—everything of any importance was controlled by Madrid. The Basque *fueros,* special rights granted centuries ago by some Carlos, Felipe or Ferdinand, and which, as far as Ben could tell, had mostly to do with the levying of tolls in and out of the region, were suspended. The use of the Basque language was outlawed, although certain folkloric customs were allowed to continue. Boys and young men could still band together in groups of five or six—*cuadrillas,* they were called—and swear a loyalty oath. They couldn't be kept from forming their mountain-climbing clubs and climbing to the tops of their mountains. Nor, once there, could they be kept from airing their grievances in the language of their choice, or from plotting.

In the green valleys, beside rushing rivers, the businessmen who chose to accept Madrid's terms prospered, while on the mountaintops, where Franco's police and Civil Guard couldn't be expected to climb, clandestine organizations were born.

In God's eye, ETA was born.

In Sabino Arana's eye.

The purist. The pacifist.

The organization would splinter, of course. There would be personality clashes and clashes of ideology. Those who sought any sort of accommodation with Franco's Spain were termed *españolistas*. There was a Marxist group that thought along international lines. Those who continued to subscribe to Arana's vision were interested only in a nation of pure-blooded Basques. Given the effects of immigration—there had been an influx of poor Castilians to work in Basque steel and lumber mills—you were considered to be pure-blooded enough if one of your grandfathers was.

On the top of a mountain, of course, everything might seem pure.

On a clear day, from the top of a Basque mountain, you might imagine you could see all the way to a Madrid park, around which ran a girl with a golden ponytail.

Memory began, Ben believed, in 1970, his first year in college. In addition to all the civil rights turmoil, and information and misinformation coming out of Vietnam, he vaguely remembered something about a trial of ETA activists in the Castilian city of Burgos. The books he read at his daughter's university would tell him that the exact number of activists was sixteen, that two were priests and several more ex-seminarians. There were two women. One of the defense attorneys managed to get on the record that Spanish police had tortured his client, and with the court looking on, scars were displayed. Before they were banned from the proceedings, members of the international press got the word out. Nevertheless, all sixteen ETA members were found guilty, and three were sentenced to death. A general strike followed in the Basque country. Sympathy strikes were called in various countries. Dockers refused to unload Spanish ships. There was an act of self-immolation. Reading brought it back to him. He began to recall his first impression of ETA, and it was of bravery, and the heroism of self-sacrifice, and the glorious legitimacy of their claim to self-determination, and even of their special character, something of their larger-than-life, mountain-rimmed apartness, as if the Basques really were a tribe of superior beings. Strong, noble and steadfast down through the years. Licensed in a way inferior beings weren't. In a manner of speaking, pure.

He remembered the Basques and ETA, and then he forgot about them. Later he'd hear something about a bomb going off in a supermarket, killing dozens, and a news report that stuck with him for a while about a woman out walking with her five-year-old daughter who was identified as a disaffected ETA activist and was gunned down by her erstwhile comrades, with her daughter looking on. That image stuck with him for a while; then he forgot it too. He assumed the people who had killed that woman and bombed that supermarket and the people who'd opposed Franco and to whose cause he'd once thrilled were not the same.

The truth was, he forgot them all. He didn't know if ETA had succeeded in its intentions or not. Or if it had gotten the best deal it could and, like everybody else in this impure world, had compromised.

He was in his midforties and felt older than that.

He had not lacked for money, not really. He'd made modest amounts of it buying and selling properties of diverse sorts. He'd been consulted. Without having a real specialty, certainly not a profession, he'd been a conduit; things had flowed through him. His father had built up the family fortune with a road construction company, which he, Ben Williamson, except for one summer spent shoveling blacktop, had never taken part in. But when his father died in his midsixties of a well-deserved heart attack, Ben's mother, instead of selling the business as she'd been expected to do, hung on to it, hired a manager she could trust and watched it prosper.

No one had thought she could do it. She had been known as the heart of the party. She was the woman who gathered all the other partygoers around the piano and made them sing. On those midweek evenings when the next party was still days away, she might run through a few chords on the piano, and, regardless of where Ben was in the house, those chords were as good as a summons. They sang songs of a deep dark yearning—"When day is done and shadows fall I think of you"—and they sang twilit songs with a melancholy lilt—"We were sailing along, on Moonlight Bay"—and they sang songs to make your foot tap—"Just direct your feet to the sunny side of the street." Some nights they sang through the songbook, and on some songs his mother might break away and sing harmony to her son's melody. It was always a thrilling moment because he never knew when she was going to do it. The effect was as though he suddenly had another person sitting at his side, someone keeping pace with him but hanging just out of his reach, a potential match when the distance closed and the two voices sounded as one; someone who was no longer a mother.

"We could make believe I loved you. We could make believe that you loved me."

He was young when she first sat him down on the piano bench and taught him these songs. How young? He sang with her before his voice changed, and he sang with her later when his voice had dropped an octave. Her voice was narrow in its range, and there were times he was afraid she wouldn't be able to hit a high note, that the song would shatter and it would all end. He dreaded singing "Indian Love Song" for that reason. There was a high yodeling note she could reach but, he worried, wouldn't be able to sustain— "I'll be calling you . . . oo . . . oo . . . ." She insisted they sing it too, he taking the Nelson Eddy part, she the Jeanette McDonald. That he and his mother would be calling their love back and forth to each other, as though from mountaintop to mountaintop, didn't embarrass him. His father might be reading the evening paper in his living room easy chair, and he might give his paper a crackling snap. Upstairs, his older brother might slam a door. Their mocking disapproval didn't bother him. He was afraid his mother's quavering voice in that upper register might come apart. He was afraid there would be a final croaking note, and then she would fold up the sheet music, close the songbook, and bring the piano top down. It would be over.

His father died when, hands on, he was unable to open a tar-stuck valve on an asphalt spreader down at the yard and his heart exploded in his chest. His brother he rarely saw. Charley had gone west to college, caught the current of things out there, and made his fortune being a Californian. His mother made a go of the business and succeeded to a degree her husband hadn't. And when her sense of things told her the times were about to turn, she sold the business for a handsome price. Then after informing her older and never unsuccessful son what she was going to do, she gave Ben, her companion in song, a significant part of that handsome sum. Outright. He immediately called Charley, and Charley laughed his qualms away. Charley said he'd earned it. All his mother really said was that he'd spent too many years bouncing around from job to job. She knew he wasn't poor, but here was enough money to allow him to do what he really wanted to.

Which was?

To "stagnate," his ex-wife would claim. It was her favorite word. She gave to its pronunciation a sort of bog-like gloom. With enough money Ben Williamson would become a bog unto himself. Give him some more and that bog would become quicksand.

His mother died a year after Michelle was killed. She too from a heart attack, also without warning, while she was having her morning coffee. She'd had no history of heart trouble. She couldn't have been expecting it. Nonetheless, she'd had the presence of mind, as her body failed her, to place her coffee cup back in its saucer and move her breakfast plate aside before lowering her head to the table. She'd been alone. A friend who'd found her told him that she had died with her eyes sweetly shut and a smile on her face. He doubted the smile. His mother must have experienced a wrenching pain in her chest, but by the time he had driven there—a distance of over one hundred miles—the mortician had already gotten his hands on her and Ben didn't know what with her parting expression she'd been trying to say.

He took his ex-wife's point. She talked of a bog; he could feel himself going vague. He had a special sense for the mystery of things, but he was too soon overwhelmed. Defending himself, he could say the mystery was not supposed to be explained away. He could accuse not himself but those songs—the stardust of those songs. Smoke was supposed to get in your eyes. By nature, some things were unfathomable: "How deep is the ocean, how high is the sky?"

But he lacked lasting power, a fierce finishing attention, the knack of knowing when he was about to betray himself.

With money his mother had given him, he'd sent his older daughter to Spain, assuming that a group of Basque men and women once implacably opposed to all things Spanish no longer was. He'd lost sight of them. His attention had wandered. They'd become part of his blur. They didn't exist.

Too late, the books told him otherwise. He read squeezed into a student's carrel in his daughter's university. These carrels were reserved, and more than once he believed the student whose carrel he occupied had come and gone, preferring to study elsewhere rather than embarrass him. Whoever she was, she was a reader of Romantic poetry, for those were the books lined up on the shelf over the desk. He had been taught Romantic poetry in high school by a woman who had scanned every poem to death. He remembered the daffodils, of course, and a poet who wandered lonely as a cloud. And a single line: "I have been half in love with easeful Death." He didn't know who had written that, but, in its quiet candor, it was like the most intimate of whispers in his ear. It didn't matter who had written it. An English Romantic poet had, and all English Romantic poets, he knew, had died young.

Michelle had just turned twenty-one. She had wanted to improve her Spanish. She had wanted to concentrate on international relations. She would have gone to Spain even if he'd sat her down and forced her to read every word in the books he'd come to two years and eight months too late.

In the ultimate analysis, ETA's quest no longer corresponded to political realities but to psychological needs. A Basque's need for a grievance was as elemental as his need for water and air. The psychological gave way to the spiritual, the mystical: there was, it was claimed, a sacramental side to ETA's violence. In addition to provoking the average man's outrage, each death achieved a moment's transcendence. All the deaths together aspired to some sort of collective transcendence there on a Basque mountaintop. They expressed a violent yearning for God.

Ben had read that.

That massive supermarket bombing he'd vaguely recalled had taken place in the Hipercord in Barcelona. Twenty-three had died. That woman out walking with her five-year-old daughter was named Dolores Gonzales Catarain. Her nickname was Yoyes. Her hometown was Ordizia, province of Guipuzcoa. ETA had executed her in front of her daughter, not because she had informed on them or betrayed the cause. She had just wanted to quit.

He'd read until he couldn't anymore. Then he had flown to Spain.

With nowhere to go—he had no interest in being a tourist—Ben went back to Parque Santander. He found the small gnarled tree and placed his hand on the spot where the bark had been blasted away from the grain. The tree, he judged, would heal itself, made of tougher fiber than he or his daughter. He couldn't tell if the two Civil Guards cradling their machine guns across the street were the same as the day he'd stood there with Madeline Pratt. He looked up and down the street for a Seat Ibiza. The one he found this time was a sun-dulled red. He stood on the spot and closed his eyes. But he was not waiting for the car to blow up. He was telling his daughter good-bye. In some ways he might also have been speaking to his mother. I miss you. I love you. I'm sorry I didn't know you better. I wish it didn't always have to end like this. We travel a hundred miles or halfway around the world and stand on the spot. The spots are always empty and busy with life.

He felt his anger coming back; more than the injustice, it was anger at the everydayness, the ongoingness. He opened his eyes and for a moment willfully took on his role as obstruction. He forced people to veer to either side, and he got some looks, which he returned. Step aside? It'll take another one of your bombs to blow me away! Then the tension went out of him and his knees sagged. He closed his eyes again and stood like some martyred saint in the heat. He told his daughter good-bye. He said, I won't be coming back. What's the point?

She answered, After two years and eight months? Don't go so soon.

He shook his head.

She said, What took you so long?

He said, It's the way I am.

But he did come back. He slept in snatches in his hotel room just off Paseo del Castellana and was up and dressed before dawn. From his window he could look out on a statue of Neptune standing as upright in his chariot as the trident he held at this side. This was the Palace Hotel, whose bar Ernest Hemingway had frequented. In fact, the same travel agent who'd booked his flight had booked his hotel, which was running a special offer for American tourists in Hemingway's honor. In honor of the first or last drink the famous author had had at the bar? He never found out. He watched Neptune rise with the dawn, then went back at precisely the hour his daughter Michelle had gotten up to run around the Parque Santander, as if it were her private jogging track. Madrid at that hour was still fresh and clear, scented by its strong coffee and just-baked bread. It had yet to be fouled by exhaust. Stepping out of the cab, he had a moment's perspective, down Paseo San Francisco de Sales, all the way to the Sierra del Guadarrama, whose rugged granite escarpment seemed a cloudy emanation of the plain. The air tingled with a promise he might have believed in then, two years and eight months ago. He stepped into the park and sat at one of the tables close to the concession stand. The stand was not open. Mothers had yet to take their children to school. He sat waiting to see if his daughter or some other American student who could call her to mind began to run around the park.

He saw Madeline Pratt instead. She was pacing in long thoughtful strides with her arms folded in front of her, her hands slipped into the sleeves of her sweater. Her head was half-lowered and her whole being was so inner-directed that he couldn't escape the impression that she was performing a penance of some sort. He didn't follow her around the park. She left his field of vision and then approximately ten minutes later entered it again, at which point it became clear she was walking laps. It was possible this was her form of exercise. While exercising, was she expressing her solidarity with all victims of ETA and acknowledging her lapse for the one student of hers that ETA had killed? That too was possible.

He watched her pass before him three more times, the sun a bit higher in the sky for each lap, casting the gray and the cornhusk yellow of her hair into an indeterminate mix. She walked stooped, visibly tiring, he thought.

He waited for her to come back around one more time. He intended to get up and join her on her last lap around the park. He wanted to thank her for her efforts, and he wanted to express how much he resented her taking his place. He wanted to shelter her from the heat that was already building in the air. He wanted to accompany her back to her office, where he could consult the clippings she had collected about his daughter's death, and he wanted to bask in the warmth of her assistant Concha's eyes.

The Spanish eyes of a song.

IV

There was a song Annie had played for her father. No, that wasn't exactly how it had happened. She'd been driving his car and had left a tape in the tape deck. Between the bank and his house, or between the club and his house, or simply driving around the block, he'd listened to one song on the tape. He'd asked her about it, and on the tape deck in his kitchen she'd played it for him again.

"Give me one reason to stay here and I'll turn right back around."

He wondered if you had to sit down and reason things out point by point nowadays. His reasons, hers, then you looked not for a preacher but for an arbiter. Could you outargue your opposite number? On the strength of that, would she fall into your arms? He wondered. He asked her if her generation still believed in Romance. He tried to make his voice sound incidental. But to her it seemed to come out of a puzzling hush.

She really didn't know what he meant by the word. It wasn't love everlasting; it wasn't youthful love fading into a long pastoral twilight that never ended. As a little girl, she could remember watching her father and her grandmother sitting side by side on the piano bench singing their "gushing oldies," she called them. But what she remembered best was the way her father turned the pages of the songbook once Grandmother Louise's hands were no longer so quick. He turned them on the beat, with a poise and precision that were uncharacteristic of him.

Her father had turned the pages with devotion.

Romance?

As a substitute for what? she'd asked

He'd nodded his head as if he'd understood her question exactly, then he'd shaken his head, sadly, as if no answer were available. He'd given himself a kind of rousing and rueful grin and played the song over, moving to the beat.

"Give me one reason to stay here and I'll turn right back around."

With no reason not to, he'd left, and she didn't know where he'd gone.

She'd finished her exams. There'd been a moment when she'd stood in her apartment, with Valerie waiting for an answer, and added up her options. She could stay there—the apartment was paid through the summer—and do advance reading for her fall classes. She could take the research assistantship her psych professor had arranged for her. There was a job in New York as an intern in a human rights organization that suited her major perfectly. She could go to New York City and do that. She could go to Boston, then Cape Cod, then Mount Desert Island in Maine with Jonathan, free of charge. Chad the Volunteer wanted her to visit his Tennessee town.

Or she could go home, to Lexington, which was finally what she decided to do. Jonathan insisted on driving her there, seven hundred miles south. In passing he'd see a horse farm or two and they'd swill good Kentucky white lightning from a moonshiner. She'd let him take her. Jonathan had seen to it that they'd gotten a late start, and they'd had to stop in an Ohio motel. She had let him make love to her. He had a carefree insouciance about everything he did, and he was nimble for such a tall man, masterful, really, when it came to the things of the world—she'd give him that. But once he was inside her it was as if he sank to her bottom with an adoring groan. Was that Romance? She'd seen the best of him and there really wasn't a worst, so the next morning she claimed he'd gone far enough out of his way. She insisted he drop her at the Greyhound station in Columbus.

She had keys to the front and back and side doors of her father's house, the basement door, the garage, which stood apart, and the car inside it. The house was empty. It smelled of a mustiness so keen she knew it had been empty for some time. The few plants in the sunporch looked dead, but she watered them just in case. She carried her suitcases upstairs, where she had a room. The bed was too small; her feet hung over. It had been their joke—that her father, when he'd bought the bed, was thinking of his little girl. Or—no joke and never spoken—he'd been thinking of Michelle, who was considerably shorter than her sister. Annie said she didn't mind and slept with her feet hanging over the end.

But she had minded—so much had changed, ended or never been.

She took her father's room, where the mustiness included him. The smell of his hair on the pillow, the distant trace of his soap, cologne and shaving cream. Out of his closet, caught in the fabric of his clothes, a woodsy, nutty smell that had begun to go stale. Pictures of Michelle and Annie were scattered around the room. She turned them all over. There was one of the four of them—her mother included—that, as chance would have it, had caught them all with expectant expressions on their faces, all to varying degrees pleased. The picture had been taken at the start of a family vacation. She remembered them singing and her father remarking that this was a rare occasion in a family like theirs and he wanted to make a record. He had set up the camera on a tripod, set the timing device, then jumped into the picture himself. She was not yet ten—could she trust her memory? Her mother should have been fidgeting, and her twelve-year-old sister glowering off at the horizon. Why weren't they? Remarkably, the picture singled no one out. She was beside her father, but beside her sister too. Her father looked proud and relieved—he looked at peace. There was something dreamy in her mother's expression, as though she were already basking in the sun. Her sister looked almost demure, no hint of the single-minded ambition that would take control of her and get her killed. And she, Annie, was happy to be one of them, happy to be included, a child of good fortune, the smallest in line to inherit the greatest good.

At first she let the picture stand.

Unpacking, five minutes later, she turned it over with the rest.

Annie stayed there three days without contacting anybody, her cell phone still turned off, inserted into a dresser drawer. One morning while she was still in her father's bed, a lawn boy came to cut the small lawn and to pull some weeds, but he was done in less than an hour. The phone rang a number of times, but the message machine picked it up. Not one of those calls was from her mother. No recording that said, "Just checking, Ben, to see how you are. A friend to a friend. Stay in touch."

No one came to the door.

When the tape on the message machine ran out, she disconnected the phone. Apparently her father had had mail and newspaper delivery discontinued. Nothing was left to sour in the refrigerator, although she'd found pasta and vegetables in the freezer. He had not rushed off on the spur of the moment, expecting to be right back.

She felt no urgent need to find out where he'd gone.

On the fourth day she went out herself. She got into his car and drove around town. She had to drive a while to get to where they used to live, and partway there she gave up. Last thing she wanted to see. The city had expanded rapidly the past few years, and she drove through mall-centered neighborhoods she wasn't sure had been there the year before. The state university, which had been a forbidden—and forbidding—place for her when she was growing up, seemed institutional to her now, more like the grounds of a state hospital than a campus. She drove downtown, where color-coded signs had been erected so tourists could stay on the right trail. There was a historical trail that would take you from the old slave market to the Henry Clay house. There was a funkier bluegrass trail. A trail led you from horse farm to horse farm. The city had been smartly packaged, and these trails were like its bows. She could understand why her mother sold so many houses here. Annie drove out to an amusement park and a dance pavilion where she'd hung out during her senior year in high school. Closed. Open on the weekends. She realized then that she didn't know what day it was.

Her mother worked out of an office in a converted Victorian mansion with a wraparound veranda that said, We take care, we're grounded, we sell houses that last. Her mother was not often there. Real business was being done in gated communities out beyond the belt. These communities had names with the words "crossing," "ford" or "pond" in them, as if only when you'd crossed a creek or brought your stock to water could you consider yourself home. Annie had to laugh. If she were alive and sitting at her side, Michelle would have said, Why do you let it get to you? That's the difference between us, Annie. Don't you see it's not worth your time? Thinking there was always a difference between them, Annie might have answered, I let it get to me because I like to laugh.

Her mother was visible from the shaded street that Annie drove down. Her office had a big bay window that gave onto the veranda, and there she sat at her desk, filling the window; unless there were some funhouse imperfections in the glass, in the four months since Annie had seen her, her mother had put on weight. Her blond hair looked wildly thatched, as if in the rush to do business she hadn't combed it that morning, or as if she were trying for some middle-aged spiky look. The side of her face, her cheek, had lengthened like a chop. Annie decided it was the glass. Or it was her own uneasy motion down the street.

Her mother was busy on the phone. Dealing, Annie thought. Or talking to a daughter who wasn't talking back.

It occurred to her that she was doing to her mother what her father was doing to her. Disappearing, but hovering within conjuring range.

Annie sped up and drove out of town. Tacking around the horse farms, she turned off the air conditioner and let in the broad, heavy, overripe Kentucky heat, which always seemed to be carrying a trace of river mud. She drove along twisting country roads until she got to crossroad stores doing a side business in night crawlers, minnows and crawdads. The gas pumps were relics. On the way she kept an eye out for Rennick Road, where for one fabulous day fleecy white kids had popped like popcorn over a pasture. She didn't believe it for a minute.

Good, she heard Michelle say. It's time to get serious.

Annie told her sister to shut up.

She drove past her old high school, like a small desolate city now with its once imposing four-story main building and its array of fire-coded out-buildings angling in. She thought of Patty Hendricks, her running mate in their junior and senior years and, with the voice of her sister still in her ear, thought, That's exactly who I want to see.

She drove back to her father's house and plugged in the phone. While she was at it she retrieved her cell phone from its dresser drawer. If they wanted to call her, now was their chance.

No sooner had she graduated from high school than Patty had married a boy named Brian Paul. She was four months pregnant. Patty's mother had wanted her to have an abortion. Brian Paul had wanted the same thing. His parents had wanted the grandchild. Patty's father, who might have cast the deciding vote, had abandoned the family long before. Patty had come to Annie, and Annie had told her to do what *she* wanted to do, remember-ing that from all reports bringing up a child at their age was a bitch. Patty had narrowed oval eyes, gray-green. A flattened nose, a thin mouth. She looked a little Asian. She was short, shorter even than Michelle, so short that when she and Annie went out together they formed a vaguely disqui-eting team. Boys didn't know where to look; it was as if the two girls were out to catch them off balance.

Patty had had the child, a girl, Elizabeth—Brian's family had begged for the name. Her husband had turned out to be a spoiled shit, which An-nie had known all along. He'd thrown a childish fit and hit Patty, who had hit back. When she divorced him she took back her old name, Patty Paul being more than she could stomach for another day. She was trying to get her daughter's name changed to Hendricks too. But that had turned her former allies, Brian's family, against her. Some time ago, Annie had written Patty a letter but had never had a reply.

In the phone book, in small, unflinching bold print, she found "Hendricks, Patty and Elizabeth." That was Patty.

Annie did not call. During the half-hour that she had been back in the house, no one had tried to call her. She copied down the address, a street she didn't recognize. Out of his glove compartment she fished her father's map of the city. It lay beneath a glossy, oversized envelope. She laid her cell phone on top of the envelope, still turned on, and closed the glove compartment. Its ring might or might not be audible above the motor noise.

The address was a walk-up second-story apartment in an area of town out beyond the cheapest student housing. She had almost reached the top of the exposed stairs when the door opened and Patty appeared with her daughter in her arms. Patty was still small. Her shoulders were bony, she looked haggard around the eyes and mouth, her teeth were yellowed. She'd chopped at her dull blond hair, which had once had a silky wave she'd practiced drawing over her face, and it had grown out unevenly. Elizabeth was big; the baby was going to dwarf her mother. She was squinched up in the sun, already beginning to cry.

Patty said, "Legs."

It was her nickname for her friend, and she said it as if Annie was one of ten people she might expect to see climbing her stairs, not high on the list but no surprise either.

Patty's nickname was "the Pistol," which her father had given her when he was still around. "She's hot as a pistol, that girl." Annie couldn't stand it, but Patty didn't seem to mind.

Annie called her by her name. She was hoping to be invited inside, where Patty with her irreverence and her zealous partisanship would talk Annie out of her funk. It wasn't going to happen.

"You got a car, right?"

Annie nodded. "My dad's."

"Come on, then. Brian will be looking for mine."

There was no baby seat, of course, in her father's car. They tried to strap Elizabeth in the back, and she let out a ripping wail. So she rode up front with her mother, a pacifier in her mouth. Annie heard the baby's breathy suck, and then, before she had a chance to start the motor, she heard the muffled admonishing ring of the cell phone in the glove compartment. With the motor on and idling, the ring was like a subterranean vibration.

"Leave it," she told Patty, who was curious. Maybe Patty thought Brian had her number wherever she went.

"Where to?" Annie asked her. "You mind telling me what's going on?"

Patty motioned them forward, then, once Annie had started picking up speed, she squared around in her seat, the baby for the moment deadweight in her arms.

"Brian claims I'm denying him visitation rights. He claims he has a right to see his daughter even if he can't take her out alone. He was going to take me back to court. Now he says he's going to take the law into his own hands. I know Brian," she added with a bitter, wise flattening to her tone. "Brian doesn't give a shit. He doesn't give a shit about Lizzie. It's his family's making him do it. Brian would grab her and hand her over to them."

"That'd be kidnapping."

"Since they talked me into having the kid, they think it's theirs. They think that gives them some kind of rights." She pressed her mouth shut.

"'Proprietary' rights. If that's what they're claiming they're full of shit, legally and—"

"'Proprietary,'" Patty repeated, letting the word slide professionally off the tongue. She looked down at her baby and said it again. "'Proprietary.'" She removed the pacifier from Lizzie's mouth and said, "Now, let's hear you say it."

The baby took a couple of questioning gulps of air, whimpered once, then screamed.

Patty plugged her mouth and said, "Stop for some orange juice. That's what she likes. That's what she needs."

Annie pulled into the first convenience store she came to. When she returned with the orange juice, Patty informed her, "Your mother called. She said to stop playing hide 'n' seek. She said, 'You sound like Patty Hendricks,' and I said I was. She asked me how I was and where I was living. I think she wanted to sell me a house. She asked about the baby, and I said Lizzie'd be all right once she had her OJ. She asked if it was safe to assume that since she was talking to me on her daughter's cell phone that her daughter was back in town, and I told her it was safe. That's when she said to stop playing hide 'n' seek."

"I wish you hadn't answered," Annie said.

"I always liked your mom." Patty was pouring the orange juice into a plastic cup she'd taken from a bag containing Pampers and other baby accessories. The baby was drinking from the lip of the cup, not from a nipple. She had to be coaxed to it, but once she'd started she drank the half-cup Patty had poured her and demanded more. Lizzie had strawberry-blond hair. It was Brian's hair color, except Brian's hair just looked rusty. She had Brian's suspicious cold blue eyes, too, and a tight little dimple. Anything of Patty there? Patty had small, perfectly shaped ears, with lobes she'd never had pierced. Crazy, she'd never had her ears pieced. Both she and Annie had gotten tattoos, Annie's a small, bruise-colored rose on her right hip, Patty a "he loves me, he loves me not" daisy on her left. But she'd never had her ears pierced. From the looks of it, that was all she and her daughter had in common, the perfectly shaped, unpierced ears.

Annie didn't need this. Patty didn't either. Annie wanted to say, Turn the kid over to them for Christ's sake.

Instead she said, "Mom's all right. I'm just not ready to deal with her now."

Patty said, "Wanna take a trip?"

The baby let her weight settle in Patty's arms and then went to sleep. When Patty stretched her out in the back seat she didn't wake up.

"A road trip. Whaddaya say?"

"Is Brian really after you?"

"He says he's on the way. He says when I least expect it."

"If you're scared you should go to the police."

"Do I look scared?"

"You looked pissed."

"Let's let him chase us for a while. Why not?"

"We could take a ride," Annie said.

"Legs, if all I wanted was a 'ride' I'd find somebody else to take me."

"You didn't find me."

"No, but I'll tell you what. I thought about you these days. Maybe I was thinking about your sister, getting blown up like that. You're like, I can't take any more of this shit, and it's like you're waiting for it to happen to you. You never think it will. People get hit by lightning. A tornado picks up a trailer with a whole family in it and drops it three miles away. I saw that on TV. Won't happen, can't happen. But all you know is something's gonna explode. Happens to someone you know means it's getting that much closer."

"You didn't know Michelle, not really."

"She was the sister of a friend of mine. She got blown up. When I felt like it was going to happen to me, I thought of her. So that means I'm thinking of you. I'm thinking before you go off and conquer the world you're gonna come find me. Next thing I know you're knocking at my door."

"I didn't knock. I didn't get the chance."

"I knew you were there."

"When did you get to be such a spooky little thing?"

"If you need 'em to survive you'll grow eyes in the back of your head. I read that in a book. Got any tapes?"

Annie lifted her elbow off the armrest, which swung open to reveal a compartment. She knew her father kept things in there.

"Tracy Chapman?" Patty groaned. "We gotta listen to 'Revolution' all the way to the Gulf?"

"Is that where we're going?" Annie said.

Twelve miles due south was a small lake where they used to go with groups of friends, and Annie drove them there. Midafternoon, it was still heavy and hot, and the coolness coming off the water never quite made it up to where they sat in the flickering shade of a poplar tree. But there was grass there, and Patty unfurled a small blanket where she set out water and juice and a jar of applesauce and an extra Pamper and some swabs. It turned out Lizzie could walk, and she stumbled around their patch of grass in veering headlong rushes that reminded Annie of drunken boys who would never accept a steadying hand and who were always going to kick somebody's ass. Soon Patty had reached her limit. She said, "Watch her a minute, Legs, will you? I gotta cool off."

Patty stripped off her jeans, panties, undershirt—she wore no bra— and stepped out of her sandals. It was too hot for fishermen, and what had once been a small sand beach was now just mud. The water level was down and the surface filmed with algae, which gave off a dank, clinging smell. Annie watched Patty wade out into it, so white, so boyishly bony and so small and sagging in the breasts that Annie almost cried out in protest. Patty went under, and her little unendearing daughter suddenly sat down at Annie's side and appeared to be staring out at the water with her. Patty came back up, her whiteness a stark pallor, like something you see at the back of a cave, and little Lizzie began to smile with her mouth wide open and to wave her hands and coo. She appeared to be calling out to her mother. Ma-ma-ma something, sitting like a little sultan robed in her baby fat. Her mother waved back and stepped up onto the mud. Except for some heaviness in the thighs, Patty was all bone.

Annie didn't even see the yellows and greens and the dark dot of that daisy tattoo. Had Lizzie taken that too?

"She likes you," Patty said. "You like your aunt Annie, don't you? She'll never sit still for me like that."

Aunt Annie told the truth. "I don't know why."

No sooner had Patty sat back down beside her friend than Lizzie rolled to her feet and began to waddle away. Patty caught up with her. They went down to the water and Patty coaxed her far enough in to get her feet wet. They squished mud together. They picked up objects from the shore. Patty taught her words, "stone," "leaf," and then Annie heard "crawdad," and watched Patty touch the crawdad shell she'd picked up, lightly, to Lizzie's skin. At Lizzie's age Annie would have screamed bloody murder, but Lizzie began a sputtering laugh. Patty touched herself with it, then touched her daughter's fat little leg. She inched the shell up the leg, and Lizzie never stopped laughing. Patty was laughing too, and before it was over she'd touched them both all over their bodies. It was like some curious—and crazy—initiation, as strange a thing as Annie had seen, and when Patty held the crawdad shell up to Annie to see if she'd like a touch too, Annie screamed, "You bring that thing up here and I'm gone!"

Patty laughed and threw the shell in the water. Lizzie, of course, began to cry. Even after Patty had fed her daughter the applesauce and given her some more orange juice, even after she'd coaxed her to take a nap there on the blanket, in the shade of the tree, Annie could still smell the crawdad on her friend's fingers, and over both the mother's and the daughter's skin. It was that smell of shell death, an emptiness that had once housed life and never would again.

She lay back herself. She dreamed of Michelle, or of a sister self, who was stalking her around an empty house. The house was like her father's except that the sunporch off the living room seemed to open out onto some vista like the lake. Her sleep was light. As her sister drove her from room to room—"You can't stay here. He's gone, don't you see! This is house-breaking, this is a crime!"—Michelle's ultimate objective seemed to be to drive Annie into the lake. But Annie would not go out there. She tried to say the word, "I have 'proprietary' rights," but it was as if she were a child and two syllables were as far as she could string her sounds. At the door to the sunporch she turned to make her stand, and it was not Michelle she saw hounding her out of doors, it was the fat little toddler Lizzie, swollen to a truly destructive size. She was making a wreck of the house, and as Annie reached out to fend her off, it was the smell that drove her back. She complained, "Where's her mother, she needs her Pamper changed," but that wasn't the smell she smelled.

Annie woke up, the dream slow to wear off, still upset with her friend for letting her smelly daughter run amok.

But it was Patty who got in the first word. "What are they afraid of, Legs? If they're afraid we're gonna fuck around on 'em I could understand it, because we will. But say we don't. Say we're as faithful as the six o'clock news. They got us where they want us and they're still scared shitless. Why is that?"

Annie had been dreaming her dream and Patty had lain there entertaining her thoughts. Somehow it came to the same thing. Annie closed her eyes again. "Men?" she murmured.

"No, not men. Gorillas. Of course, men. Take Brian," Patty went on, slipping back into her ruminative tone that was strictly for show. "When he catches up with me, if he doesn't have a gun or a knife in his hand or something about ten times the size of his dick he's gonna stand there and holler and not do a goddamn thing. I'm like, let him blow out, and he'll turn around and leave and hate himself until he begins to build up steam again. What's your opinion on that?"

"My opinion is that women get beaten to death every day and some men like using their fists. Maybe it gives them a satisfying sense of contact, I don't know. These women are called 'battered women,' and they're the ones who're scared. I'd be scared. I'd go the police."

"No, you wouldn't, Legs. No one's gonna lay a hand on you."

Annie was up on an elbow now. She found Patty up on her elbow, three, four feet away. She remembered sleepovers they'd had. They'd shared a double bed—most often in Annie's house—and had lain like this, gossiping sometimes 'til dawn.

"Probably not his kid anyway," Patty confided.

Annie let out a savvy, mock-incredulous, half-guffawing laugh. "Then who is the father?"

"One of four," Patty replied.

The three or four feet separating them suddenly seemed like inches to Annie. She lay back and closed her eyes.

"You don't believe me," Patty stated flatly.

"You don't believe yourself."

"Mike Conklin, remember him?"

"One of the four?"

"The longest shot. Brian's next to the longest, but he's ahead of Mike, so that should make him feel better. Then there's—"

"I don't want to know," Annie cut her off.

"What's the difference? They're all like little boys. They shoot off in you, then run and hide and wait to see which one'll get caught with his pants down. Brian was always slow to zip up, so it's Brian who's running around trying to find his kid." Patty gave a snorting laugh. "Lizzie's mine. She's got four fathers, which is the same as having none. I'm all she's got."

Word for word, Patty's breath was in her ear, and Annie opened her eyes. She said, "I knew you back then. You weren't sleeping with four boys at the same time. I would have known if you were. Mike Conklin went to our church. I went out with Mike Conklin, not you."

"Only once. Like I said, a long shot. You jealous?"

"Wherever you're coming from, Patty, go back. Start again. DNA tests will tell you who Lizzie's father is—"

"She's got four! It's a goddamn miracle, a freak of nature! I'll have to explain it to her some day."

"Brian's her father."

"For the record."

"That red hair, that dimple . . ."

"Because of some red hair and a dimple, Brian gets to be the father? No fucking way!"

"No," Annie said, "because one of his spermatozoa got to your ovum at the optimum time and nobody else's did. Those little sperms and those little ova have a mind of their own."

"Smart-ass college kid," Patty muttered.

"You never fucked Mike Conklin. Admit it."

"He tried to roar and beat his chest when he came. Don't quite know what he was trying to prove."

"Not Mike Conklin."

A car drove in and parked beside Annie's in the dirt lot just behind the row of trees. Patty stiffened beside her and didn't look back, but Annie could see that there was a couple in the car, the woman with a blond bouffant head of hair and the man with his dark hair slicked back. They were smoking and listening to some twangy country music; then they cut the motor and the music off and Annie heard their own twangy voices, the woman's querulous and high-pitched and the man's close to a snarl. They'd come here to look at the lake and have their argument. They could have had it sitting in the back booth in some rancid roadhouse, but they'd decided on the lake. If they stuck to type, they would never get out and sit by the water.

When had she become such a snob?

Patty wasn't waiting around. She'd woken Lizzie, who started to cry, like a bitter, morose commentary on the whole afternoon. With quick, practiced motions, Patty changed Lizzie's Pamper, whipping her daughter around. She made no attempt to fold the blanket. She stuffed it and everything else into the bag. The wet Pamper she threw at a trash can up by the trees and missed. She didn't go back to make good on her toss; neither did Annie. The arguing couple settled their differences long enough to regard the three of them with mutual hostility as they got into the car. Patty gave them their hostility back, and if she hadn't had the still sleepy Lizzie crying in her arms would probably have gone up to their window and demanded to know what their fucking problem was.

It was the old problem, getting older by the minute.

The heat was all over them now.

Annie and Patty got into the car and ran the air conditioner to the top.

Tracy Chapman. Demanding one reason to stay here. Just one, and it better be good.

At a McDonald's, coming back into town, Patty asked for a Big Mac and some fries. They pulled up to the order station with its menu and mike only to discover that the drive-through service was closed for repairs. Annie parked and went in to bring out the food, and while she was standing in line she had a presentiment. She got back into the car, handed over the fries, the Big Mac and the Coke, and Patty was in an entirely different mood. She was wistful, almost in tears. Lizzie seemed to have been mastered by her mother's mood and was quiet. "Let's hear it," Annie said.

"Your father called. He said he was all right. He said he was taking a break. He didn't want you to worry. Then he said he hoped your exams went well and your summer plans were working out. When he asked who I was and I told him he figured it out and said he hoped your homecoming wasn't a disappointment. He said he loved you. He wasn't crying, but he was sort of spaced and he forgot he was talking to me. He promised one day before long you'd be back together again. But he said 'we.'"

Patty stared at Annie, confronting her through her near-tears. "You don't know how lucky you are to have parents like that," she said. "You just don't know. Your mother calls, then your father does, and what do they want? They want the same thing. They want you with them. I mean it, Legs. Where do you get that kind of luck?"

Annie drove her friend back to her walk-up, where Brian wasn't waiting for her. No one was. Then she drove away.

He didn't leave. On the recommendation of a desk clerk at the Palace Hotel, Ben took a room in the three-star Regina Hotel, close enough to the Paseo del Castellana that he could sit there in the evenings. He didn't go back to Retiro Park. Those promenading middle-aged couples might pass by him to the rhythm of his breathing and the beat of his blood, but it was as if they belonged to an exclusive club. He found he preferred a café on the esplanade of the Paseo del Castellana, where couples of all ages passed while beyond them six lanes of traffic surged by.

He began to read the Spanish newspapers and was surprised at how quickly his college Spanish came back to him. He stayed away from international news, and especially from anything his own country might be up to. He read about Spain, he read what the Andalusians were doing in Seville, the Valencians in Valencia, the Catalans in Barcelona, the Galicians in Santiago de Compostela. And he read about the Basques. He tried to follow the latest developments in the Basque quest for ever more freedom, but he was increasingly drawn to the photographs. When ETA members were arrested in France or by the Civil Guard in Spain, or when they were deported from one of the Latin American countries where they had been granted sanctuary, a photograph appeared. These were mug shots. They were cold, stark, straight-ahead and expressionless. The men, or the occasional woman, were black-haired, black-browed and white-skinned. Sometimes there was a fixity in the eyes, a look of some wildness mastered and trained to a task. But these were photographs of men and women behind bars.

Or photographs of the dead. A bomb exploded before it could be planted in a car. It had gone off in the faces of the bomb-makers, and the photographs showed what they'd looked like before. Young. Black-haired, white-skinned. One had a trace of a smile, so faint it was like something caught from the air. It told you nothing about the person on whose lips it had landed. The hometowns of these young men, openly sympathetic to ETA, declared them *hijos predilectos,* which Ben took to mean, "favorite sons."

Still, faceless faces.

Those days, ETA killed a council member from Seville and his wife. They were shot in the backs of their heads as they strolled home on a balmy evening after a late supper. The photographs the newspaper printed were from a happier time. Perhaps at a party, he caught in a convivial moment; his youthful wife with her mouth open on a breathless smile.

These were faces as Ben knew them. He tried to call his daughter during that time, just to let her know. He got her unfortunate friend.

A block up from his hotel was a long oval-shaped plaza, somewhat flattened on one side, which was known as the Puerta del Sol, "the gateway to the sun." It was said to be the center of Spain. There was a statue of a king on a horse there, a scaled-down fountain and a puzzling sculpture of a bear reared up on its hindquarters eating berries from a tree. But mainly there were people circling that oblong plaza in a steady stream. Ben walked with the crowd—Latin Americans, North Africans, Sub-Saharan Africans, swarthy immigrants from Eastern Europe, sunburned Brits, tall blond tourists from Germany and Scandinavia, and Spaniards, of course, from all corners of the country. He was not used to such a heady mix. For a while it exhilarated him, and he let himself be borne. But when his mood turned it was as though this stream of humanity he rode were the dirty water of a city, and as it circled the spot—this epicenter of the center of Spain—it was about to go down the drain.

He walked back down Calle Alcala and sat at a café on the esplanade looking out at the six lanes of traffic along Castellana and at couples promenading with or against the traffic's flow. The foreignness of it all held him off even as it teased him into wanting to see more. The masses were one thing, but there was an intimacy to the foreignness too, there was, it seemed, an intimate coded rightness to the way people behaved. He was curious about the code. If he bothered to look closely he could see it all around him. Demitasses of coffee were sweetened and swirled and brought to the lips as if they were tiny chalices; between puffs smokers employed their cigarettes like gesturing batons. There came a moment when the coffee was almost drunk and the cigarette smoked that the two were placed side by side, as if in some mysterious communion.

That was the way it was done. But even as it drew him in it held him off, and he sensed that there was no end to it. There was no such thing as an incidental act; it was all part of some elaborate arcane ceremony. When it became too much for him he'd walk back up to the Puerta del Sol until the flux and filth and endless human wreckage of it all would send him back down to the café he'd chosen, El Gijon, where he could simply sit and observe.

He'd read the papers, looking for a face.

He'd watch the white-jacketed waiters pouring wine, always with their free arm folded behind their backs.

It was only a matter of time before he found himself sitting beside Americans at the Café Gijon and eavesdropping on what they said. The Americans were both women, roughly his age, and there was a third, a man with a ruddy face and wiry gray curls and an accent Ben judged to be Irish, although he hadn't spoken much. One of the women was telling the other about a trip she and her husband—the Irishman, Ben assumed—had just taken to Zimbabwe.

The other woman was sitting diagonally across the tables from him. She was red-haired and freckled, the freckles faded and the red hair muted with strands of gray. When she saw that Ben was listening too, she began to share her reactions with him. The three mortal dangers of paddling a canoe down the Zambezi River? The red-haired woman shuddered and smiled and shook her head. She might have winked.

The first danger was the hidden snags and treacherous currents, which only the experienced guides could pick out in time. The second was the hippos, noncarnivorous, it was true, but who loved to overturn canoes and crunch them. They seemed to work in tandem with the third danger, the *very* carnivorous crocodiles, for as soon as the hippos overturned a canoe the crocs would cruise in. But they represented a mortal danger only up to a point. Sometimes they might settle for an arm or a leg.

For a moment Ben did his best to quit listening and to pick up on the white noise of the traffic at his back. He went back to his newspaper. The woman doing the talking was too interested in drawing the story out and too much in love with the sound of her own voice. But then she began to talk about the animals themselves, and her voice changed. It took on a dramatic hush, it became sobered and subdued, in a way depersonalized. The first night, she admitted, she'd been scared. Water buffalo had plodded among the tents. Families of hippos had waded by at the river's edge, making their three-toned chuffing sound, on a descending scale, that was like a scheming melodramatic laugh. There'd been lighter scampering sounds, like something running right up your spine. But the next night, she said, something had happened.

"I lay in the tent and just gave way. The hippos were out there. There were lion roars too, and something that sounded like a chain saw cutting into wood. We were told that was a leopard. Garret was already asleep. If Garret got taken by lions he'd only know about it when they were picking his bones clean. But I lay there, and there came a moment when instead of being terrified by it all I realized that we were on the scene because the animals had decided to let us be. . . . And when I say 'animals' I mean the big ones, not monkeys or baboons—you should see the mounds of shit they left. We'd go off with our little shovel to do our business and it was a humbling experience to do it beside what an elephant had done. . . . The animals were the masters and we were these powerless little intruders and they'd decided to let us be. Once I understood that, instead of being menacing, that hippo sound became restful—a hippo lullaby. The lions called back and forth, and then the lion roars blended into the night and you felt . . . sleepy and protected, I'd almost say 'secure.'"

She paused and looked around. In the process she looked to her right, right at Ben. She had a sad, entranced expression in her eyes. She wore expensive jewelry, a necklace of amethysts, more amethysts at the ears, her eyes shaded and her hair permed. She did not look as if she'd ever in her life camped beside a river or shat beside a mound of elephant dung.

"Am I making any sense, Paula? There're no animals here, so we have to go back. Gar's seen enough of it, but you'll go with me, won't you? It'll be like those spring breaks we took. Instead of Florida and the beach and boys, the banks of the Zambezi and the hippos and crocs."

The woman called Paula looked at her friend and gave a throaty, uncertain laugh. Then she looked at Ben, as if he had made himself part of their group and had a vote to cast too.

He smiled and tipped his head to her, as if to indicate "tough choice." He went back to his newspaper and the stark anonymity of those faces. Paula said something to her friend about next year, and to remember that the year before it had been the Australian outback and the year before that penguins on a glacier somewhere. When Ben looked back up, Paula was still smiling at him, and he was ready to believe that they'd known each other in the past, that she had made the connection before he had and was amused to see how long it took him to catch up.

Instead he turned to the woman beside him and said, "I couldn't help but overhear . . ."

She held out her hand, brightening at once. She was Leslie. He got a crunching handshake from her husband, Garret, and from Paula a grip with something of that amused and knowing warmth.

Gay and irrepressible again, Leslie said, "Would you come with me, Ben? I'm a good judge of character. You're peace-loving, you're gentle. Aren't all Bens gentle? You know your limits. You do know your limits, don't you? The animals would accept you at once."

"Do you also read palms?" Ben said.

She seized his hand and turned it over with a flourish. "What did I say? You've got a lifeline that goes off the charts. You may live as long as the elephants."

Her husband, Garret, intervened, "Let the man be, Les. You're pushing his luck. The zoo's the place for you, Ben."

Paula laughed and sat back. She wore glasses. Her lips looked chapped. In fact, she looked a little weathered. The fading blotched freckles contributed to the effect, as did the paling red hair.

Ben turned to Leslie. "That moment when you went from being terrified of the animals to feeling like you were in their safekeeping . . ."

"Yes," she breathed, "I listened to them, I finally heard what they were saying. . . ."

"Do you think it takes the animals?"

She cocked her head at him, puzzled, and he tried to clarify, "I mean—"

It was Paula who interrupted him. "He means does it have to look, smell and sound like a huge African animal. Can it be a 'masterful' being of some other sort?"

"As long as it looks, smells and sounds like something big enough to scare the holy bejesus out of you one minute and protect you like a babe in the woods the next. Is that it, Ben?"

It wasn't, not entirely. Once again Paula was looking at him, as if the two of them shared something, some element of common sense or deeper understanding, unavailable to this globe-trotting couple.

He tried and failed to return to his newspaper.

A face for what?

When he got up to leave he found himself apologizing. "Sorry," he said, more to Paula than the others, as if he were deserting her side. She gave him a grin at the corner of her mouth, as if to reply, Just one more of life's nasty little tricks. He joined the evening's promenaders down Castellana, left them and walked up Calle Alcala to the Puerta del Sol, where, with a motlier crowd, he circled the city's center.

It was back and forth, back and forth, but Ben stayed on. He did not go back to the Parque Santander, where his daughter had been killed. It occurred to him that it made no sense not to contact the police to see where the investigation into his daughter's death stood, in spite of what Madeline Pratt had said. His daughter's death would be considered incidental to the death of that murdered Civil Guard—he understood that. Still, he might inquire. Perhaps one of those ETA members being returned from Latin America had been indicted—one had even been extradited from the United States. If the trial hadn't yet been held, he could attend it. If an ETA member—*etarras*, they were called—had already been convicted he could figure out some way to visit the prison. Convicted *etarras* were imprisoned anywhere except in the Basque country—it was one of the Basque nationalists' bitterest grievances, that they didn't have their heroic sons and daughters nearby—so Ben would have to determine which prison and get on a train, get on a bus, get on a burro, and go there. All to see a face. To look into eyes so ancestrally committed to a cause there would be no way they could look back and see him. It would be like looking down a hall of mirrors, an endless generational regression.

The problem was that he was nothing like his dead daughter. Michelle knew why she was in Spain. She knew what she wanted and precisely by what stages she was going to get it. She knew where she was going when she got up to run that morning. She just didn't know what had taken her away. Or maybe she did. She would have known that was a Civil Guard headquarters she ran by. She would have known it was a potential ETA target, and a tempting one at that, and she would have calculated her chances, which she would have liked. They were good chances. A bomb went off, caught her in the back, blasted her on faster than her accustomed pace, and she would not have questioned her calculations. The chances had been good. But her calculations had not prepared her for this, just for the overwhelming chance that it would not happen and she could go on with her life. In that instant when a light blinded her before she blacked out, she would have understood. This is a bomb blast, this is ETA blowing up a Civil Guard headquarters, this is Europe cracking apart along its fault lines, this is a world as old as a fractured piece of porcelain being held together in a museum—I know all that. I studied it. I got informed. But what is this?

No, Ben was nothing like his older daughter. He was like his younger and surviving daughter, Annie. He too had a sort of quester's belief that at any given moment, as lost as he might be, there were always destinations to be had. Annie was impulsive in that way, it was the way she chose her classes, grabbed her friends seemingly on the fly. She was loyal and she was affectionate, and when she turned away from you it wasn't because she'd given you up. She was following her quester's intuition.

Have a plan, Dad, his dead daughter would advise him.

His surviving daughter would advise him to lighten up.

He tried to. At the Regina Hotel was a desk clerk named Juan, who spoke English and arranged day trips for him to outlying monuments and towns. Ben visited the great gloomy fortress-palace called El Escorial. Toledo, built up on its rock, was a fortress of some sort too. Stone, cold stone everywhere he looked—he was amazed at how quickly the temperature dropped when he entered one of its narrow winding streets, or stood on its cathedral floor, as if at the bottom of an enormous well. The El Grecos were white-limbed and cold. The castle in Segovia was even colder. Isabel, the Catholic queen, had held her court there and sent her warrior knights out the massive iron door to rid Spain of its last Moor, Jew or intruder of any sort. Down on the town plaza he stood beneath the aqueduct the Romans had built and marveled at how the unmortared stone had been cut and wedged into arches that still stood. It was hot down there. He stepped into one of the many bars, where hams and loops of sausages hung from the ceiling, and ordered not a beer or cool sherry or even a glass of sangria, but a brandy. But the cold was too far inside him for the brandy to reach.

He went back to the hotel and for three days talked himself into believing he was sick. Juan, the desk clerk, sympathized—those castles *were* cold; if he'd gone down in the dungeon he might have picked up *microbios* centuries old—and made himself responsible. Juan had broths and purees and omelets sent to the room, and herb teas. There was a heavy red wine that came from a *pueblo* in the Ribera del Duero region of Castile that he claimed could cure anything, and he sent up a glass of that. The *pueblo*, in fact, had been Juan's—its name was Medina del Rioseco—and it was from Juan that Ben first learned how bound each city-dweller was to his *pueblo*, and as sophisticated as he might become how unlikely he was to question the folk-truths he'd learned there.

Juan would remove the food tray and leave the day's newspapers. And when Ben got out of bed for good, it was because he thought he'd seen a face.

Actually, two faces. They belonged to a man and woman just arrested in France. They were identified as ETA veterans who had risen through the ranks and come to occupy leadership roles. In addition to being collaborators in terror, they were "sentimentally linked." Before they had established themselves in France they had had active roles in various *comandos* in Spain. The man, especially, had had a sanguinary career, with nine assassinations, among them a Supreme Court judge, held against his name. She, it appeared, was his helpmate. At a certain point they'd disappeared and reappeared in France, where they'd become first lieutenants to an ETA leader, nicknamed Txapote, who processed the information he received from Spain and then sent word back to the various *comandos:* these are the people you are to kill, x, y and z, for reasons we have deemed sufficient.

When Txapote was arrested, this couple took his place. They received the information, the "intelligence" from "on the ground." They made the final decisions. This month it's this x, this y and this z.

There's a Civil Guard headquarters fronting a park in Madrid. There'll be a young guard out patrolling. An American student will be running by. There may be others. X, y and z.

Ben couldn't be sure of the dates. More likely than not it had been Txapote who had issued the order to attack that Civil Guard headquarters. This couple had equally unpronounceable Basque last names. He studied the faces. The photograph of the man was clearer, better defined. He was in his midthirties now, and the face was fleshing out. The nose looked slightly swollen and out of line. There was a sinister look about the lower lip, a faint gleam that led to the darker gleam of the eyes, one of which, the right, was narrowed. Over the widened left eye the brow was raised. It was a look that said, I've seen you, I've pronounced your name, I've put you on my list.

The woman's face was slightly blurred. Her hair was disheveled, thick as a pelt. It half-covered her forehead in spiky black curls. Her eyes were opened wide and staring directly into the camera. Round eyes, straight nose, closed mouth, a chin softened in its line. She wore a necklace of some sort, with a large heart-shaped pendant, perhaps made of wood. She wasn't talking. She was pictured beside the man, who said all he needed to with his sinister, straight-ahead look.

The woman looked like a heedless girl who had been lured into following the man. Ben looked at her hard and said, "You and your man killed my daughter."

They hadn't killed his daughter. They probably hadn't even issued the order. Anyway, the French had them. They faced charges first in France, and only after serving their sentences there could they be extradited to Spain. Where they'd serve much longer sentences. If they were ever freed they'd be unrecognizable. This might be the last time anybody would see them side by side.

At least they had gotten him out of bed. Juan was pleased, off the hook, and offered to arrange more day trips, or to serve as a travel guide and make phone calls ahead to hotels in provincial cities. Ben declined. He walked to the Paseo del Castellana and took his seat in the outdoor café there. On his third time back to the Café Gijon he saw the woman named Paula again, sitting where she'd sat before. This time she was alone and reading a newspaper.

He sat down in front of her, with his back to that parallel street of two-lane traffic. If not at the same table, almost. But with that same angle of vision just off to his left.

He said, "Hello," and she looked up from her paper.

It became clear that unless they wanted to behave like children one of them was going to have to get up and sit directly across from the other.

Ben didn't give her the chance. He stood and sat at her table.

He said, "Your friends, Leslie and Garret?"

"They've gone back to Dublin. Unless I go there, I see them once a year. They stop by here on the way home after one of their exotic trips. Leslie and I were college roommates."

"I got that," he said. "When do *you* go back?"

"I live here," she said. "This is home."

She smiled at his surprise, that he wasn't faced with another tourist like himself. Her lips were still chapped, and a couple of bottom teeth were set at an odd angle. Just a hint of that angling and his daughters would have been at the orthodontist's, but the crooked teeth suited her. They were part of that weathering effect. Ground will freeze and thaw out and twist stones around like that. Gravestones.

She seemed to Ben eminently companionable, and in his experience not many women were. But then, he wasn't looking for a companion.

"I'm curious," he said. "How did that happen?"

"How did what happen?"

"That you made this your home."

"A life story already?"

"I withdraw the question."

They smiled at each other.

He said, "Do you come here often? I haven't seen you since that day."

"I have six or seven cafés I like to sit in. Depends on the circumstances, I guess, the weather, the day of the week." She paused, as if reviewing the week, or as if debating to what end she wanted to direct what remained of this day. "No, I probably haven't been back here since then."

He took her pause as a cue, vaguely, something of a test. He put his question to her again. "What *are* you doing here? It doesn't have to be the entire life story."

"It wouldn't be. I'm not done yet, Ben."

He smiled.

"And I'm guessing you're not just a tourist . . ."

"Toledo, Segovia, El Escorial." Ben recited his stops.

She sat back up, finished her coffee and nudged her newspaper aside. There was a moment when he could look behind her and watch the human traffic passing before that rushing backdrop of cars and trucks. Most of the motorbike riders wore helmets. The more daring ones didn't as they cut across lanes. He picked out a couple walking by, in this case two young women, both attractive, slender, dressed in some sheer Mediterranean fabric, in profile close enough to be sisters, their sunglasses worn back on their heads at this early-evening hour . . . but the motor traffic caught them and he couldn't follow them out.

Paula said, "I could make it sound more dramatic than it is. I am an innocent American woman, brought to a foreign country and abandoned by a Latin snake." She gave a mocking laugh, but with some reflection in it too, as if she were exaggerating only up to a point. "How's that, Ben?"

"I can't be sure," he said, "but I may have heard it before."

"The truth is I married a Spaniard who came to the States to get a master's in hotel management. Spaniards love to come to the States to get master's degrees. Among the wealthy it's a rite of passage. My Spaniard—his name is Jorge Ortiz—came and did it beautifully. He was straight-A from the start. I married him and he brought me back to his hometown, in this case a city, not a *pueblo*, Valladolid. I have a large Catholic family I was ready to take a break from, and I walked into another one. Castilian Catholic, not Irish Catholic. There's a difference."

Ben nodded. One had hosted the Inquisition, as he recalled, and the other stood each other to pints of Guinness, then took potshots at Protestants out on the streets.

"But there're links. There're even blood links. When the Spanish Armada was sunk, some sailors washed up on Irish shores. There're families with surnames like Martinez and Rodriquez that trace their ancestry back to those times. Did you know that?"

He shook his head.

"I didn't either. Jorge's father told me about the Spanish Armada. I think he wanted to make clear the ways in which the Irish and Spanish were bound. I didn't like him. I thought he was a tyrant. The family owned a large hotel in a wealthy part of the city. There were three brothers, two sisters and a saintly mother. Jorge was by far the best of the bunch. He was almost always good-humored and even-tempered, with a laugh that made you want to see the world his way. He had friends everywhere. When he asked me for a divorce, divorce wasn't that common here, and I had no idea it was about to come to that—really, no idea at all, isn't that strange? But it didn't take long before I realized that I wanted it too. I wanted to be Jorge's friend, not his wife. I wanted to be one of that admiring crowd. And since there were no children . . ."

She looked across the table at him, very levelly now, the frankness in her pale blue eyes—weathered, faded and warm, like everything else— about as much as he could take. He looked away. A waiter he recognized was finally approaching to take his order.

"I kept his name," she declared. "Ortiz. I had no desire to go back being an O'Malley."

Ben ordered his evening's beer. Then he called the waiter back and asked for a glass of red wine instead, *vino tinto,* from Ribera del Duero. Preferably something from a town called Medina del Rioseco?

The waiter changed the order on his pad. He said, *"Muy bien,"* then left.

Paula apologized. She wasn't used to talking at length about herself like this. As if to take a break, she said, "Did you know that the real Café Gijon," and she signaled to the wall of buildings beyond the traffic, "was the most famous literary café in Madrid. It's where the writers at the turn of the century held their *tertulias.*"

He didn't know the word. The café he could make out through the windows behind him had wood-paneled walls and painted iron columns around which tables were clustered. Tourists were crowding in and out.

"Conferences . . . colloquia," she translated for him. "The Spanish are great talkers. But you know that already."

Juan had talked to him about his hometown, but other than that the longest anyone had gone on in his presence had been Americans: Leslie in praise of her animals and Paula in praise of her ex-husband. He'd forced the words out of Madeline Pratt's mouth, and in the process had opened her wounds. Mostly he'd been looking at pictures, reading the Spanish papers word for word.

The waiter, his left arm folded behind him, served Ben his wine, which tasted something like the wine Juan had served him, but he couldn't be sure. It had a strong, dry, almost bitter clarity, and it passed down his throat offering no quarter. Ben asked the waiter to leave the bottle and to bring another glass for his . . . and the word he used was *"amiga."*

Paula said, "I won't bore you anymore—"

"No."

When Paula's glass came they drank to meeting again here sometime soon.

"That's enough of me for one day," she smiled. "The stage is yours if you want it."

He didn't. He wouldn't have known where to start. He and Paula Ortiz poured second glasses. There came a moment when he felt himself settle, the tension sloughing off him in low, shuddering waves. He thought of the sound of the hippos in the Zambezi River, their three-toned, chuffing descent of the scale.

"When I came down here this afternoon," Paula said, "I wondered if I'd see you again. I guess what I really wondered was how adventurous you were. On the strength of what Leslie said, had you already set off for Zimbabwe and the Zambezi River? I hoped not. And not because of the three mortal dangers. Because of the boredom. Leslie can find romance in mud and elephant dung. The rest of us would probably spend four or five sleepless nights and end up with a year's worth of aches and pains."

"I liked Leslie," he said.

"*I* like her," Paula insisted.

"I'm not sure I believed her, but I'm pretty sure I believed in what she said."

"I'll have to think about the difference."

"It's simple, actually."

"Maybe in *your* head, Ben," Paula replied. Then she added, "I'll have to think about you."

"Don't," he advised her.

"No?"

"Not worth your time."

"Don't be too humble, Ben. It's not your style."

He was curious. What was his "style"? He wasn't aware that he had one. Gail had accused him of being so stylistically outdated he could be said to be without, and he had believed her.

He stood. He said he hoped to run into her again down here, once she'd made her rounds. Her rounds? The six or seven cafés she sat in. Where she'd have six or seven sets of friends? He didn't ask. She'd made her ex-husband, Jorge, out to be such a friend to the world that maybe she didn't need any more.

She let him see her disappointment, and he showed her his exhaustion.

He took her hand, whose knowing grip was instantly familiar to him. He withdrew his hand.

The next afternoon he stood back at a distance, and she was there again. She was forcing him to find a new café to sit in if all he wanted was to watch the people parade by. Juan directed him to the Plaza Mayor, where he should have been sitting in the first place, an arcaded plaza so grand and spacious and symmetrically designed it was like an enormous theater in the round. Cafés with their clusters of tables were spotted on all sides. And another huge king on horseback presided over it all. If Puerta del Sol was where Spain circled a center, the Plaza Mayor was where Spain sat down. He tried it. But in the midst of the milling crowds he felt himself to be an isolated point. His mood turned somber, vaguely combative, and he thought of that ETA couple, "sentimentally linked," who might have ordered his daughter's death and whose divorce was now as permanent as prison could get. The man—his face—deserved all he got, but the woman—in her girl's round-eyed, blind, headlong rush—was about to begin a withering that would take her to the grave. Ben concluded she deserved it too, perhaps even more than the man, who had been sinister from the start.

The next day he went back to the Café Gijon on the Paseo del Castellana, where Paula Ortiz was waiting for him again and where he sat down.

H ere was a twist. Her mother, who had never worried about her ex-husband before because he had never given her cause, was beginning to worry, while Annie secretly hoped her father would stay at large longer than anyone had thought possible. She knew this seemed odd, and since she couldn't account for it herself, she didn't express it that way to her mother. It wasn't exactly a disappearing act her father had performed, since he had called. He'd actually called a second time and left a message that said basically what he'd told Patty—that they were not to worry, that he was taking a break, that one fine morning he'd surprise her and walk in the door. Then, since he assumed she was living in his house, he told her a trick to get the air conditioning to work. It amounted to a double click after a three-count pause. Annie loved the dailiness of that tip, and the intimacy, although she kept the windows open on the screens and the air conditioner off. The tall trees that surrounded the house brought the breeze. She played the message again and again. There was both a casualness and a firmness about his voice, and a curious sense of pacing, as if he were putting one foot down at a time.

She erased his message.

Week after week she stayed in his house, drove his car. She dealt with Patty and with other high school friends as they appeared. She listened as her mother's condescending amusement with her father turned to exasperation that masked a worry she didn't want to admit to. She said the man she had been married to for more than twenty years didn't have the resources to disappear and reappear like *that*. As illustration, she performed a crisp snap of the fingers. He had the money now—since his mother had died—and she didn't doubt he had the need to step out of his skin and be someone else for a while. But he didn't have the *inner* resources, and all this mysteriousness he was building up might come back to haunt him in a bad way.

"I'm saying your father can't take care of himself, Annie. He can't see what's in front of him long enough to do that."

"If you're worried, why don't you call the police?"

"Because I'm no longer his wife. You're his daughter. Why don't you?"

"Because I'm not worried," Annie said, without saying she was secretly thrilled.

Because she wasn't, not exactly. "Thrilled" wasn't exactly the word. She was in the town where she'd been born and brought up and she felt . . . dislocated. There were days when she felt she had never lived here. She'd step out onto the shaded streets and start to walk around the neighborhood, and the houses and the people who lived in them threw up a dull veil of strangeness. And this was a street she knew well; she'd had friends who'd lived in this neighborhood. No use to overdramatize it. She'd gone away, come home, and home had gone somewhere else. Happens all the time.

Then she got pissed. Since she wasn't answering his letters or calls, Jonathan had gotten in contact with her mother to express his concern, and her mother had taken his side. Annie did seem short-tempered and self-absorbed. And Jonathan had sounded so alert and winning, so "Bostonian," on the phone. If her mother didn't mind her asking, why was she treating him this way?

Annie minded enormously.

Jonathan, her mother had been told, had brought Annie halfway home and then been sent back while she took a bus. Why? If he'd come all the way Annie's mother might have had a chance to meet him. She wasn't being unreasonable. These were chances all mothers want. She didn't say these were chances all mothers were due. Nor did she say that with Michelle's death by how much her chances had been reduced, but Michelle's death was always there, it was the backdrop for everything, the climate in which they conversed. It meant that at every turn there was a loss to be made good.

On the other hand, Annie really didn't mind at all.

Jonathan had hinted that he was ready to give up Cape Cod or Mount Desert Island and complete the trip. Why didn't she let him?

No reason, it seemed. Jonathan could charm her mother, take her off Annie's hands. Probably no one could do it any better.

Her mother had him there the next day—it was as if he'd been waiting in the wings. It reminded Annie of the way Brian Paul had Patty convinced he was lurking behind every corner. And that really got her pissed.

Jonathan said to her, "Your mother is formidable, and she's very down home. It's exactly how I pictured her. She's a perfect match for the town, which is modern and growing fast but at heart is still a charming little place."

Annie replied, "Be careful. She'll sell you a house."

"It wouldn't take much," he confessed, letting his flattery spill over. He was saying a woman who could give birth to the creature standing before him could sell him soap.

It was strange to see him here, of course. He looked like JFK, except his chestnut-brown hair was straight, not wavy, and his eyes were large and open and eager while JFK's were set back in his skull and narrowed—not in a smile, as JFK would have had you believe, but in a cold assessing slit. JFK was stiff-backed and used women and sex as a way to get loose and limber so he could go out and deal in the nation's back rooms. But Jonathan really was lanky, loose and good-natured, whether he'd just gotten laid or not.

They had supper in her mother's condo, which overlooked a small lake.

Her mother served gin and tonics, zucchini squares and sauteed mushrooms. After checking to make sure Jonathan wasn't a vegetarian, she announced she had medallions of veal waiting on the stove. While she'd been preparing all this, she'd also sold a house that day, to a couple she'd gone up to weeks earlier while they'd been parked outside on the street, going over the listings in the paper with a look she knew well, that doggedly deliberate, one-listing-at-a-time look before panic sets in, and she'd said, "Come inside."

Nothing extraordinary—they'd settled for a modest Tudor-framed house on an untrafficked street, a house that needed some work. Everyone settled sooner or later. The agent's job is to take the dream house they have in their heads and deconstruct it until it resembles something they might actually find on the ground. The good agent is the house-buyer's guide back to reality. You bring them back too quickly and they'll decompress.

Annie had heard it all before—her mother's real estate agent philosophy, really her philosophy for life. Jonathan hadn't. He urged her to go on, and she didn't mind regaling him with a few stories. She was dressed in a lime-colored gown that Annie hadn't seen before, ample and elegant, whose neckline framed a necklace of silver dangles set with iridescent rhinestones. Her hair was teased and looked freshly frosted. Jonathan wore his tan blazer and one of those light-colored shirts with the long V collar that had been recycled from the '40s or '50s. Annie liked them. She liked the way they parted, as if they were inviting you to peel them off. They revealed a tuft of chest hair, not too hairy and not too dark.

She wore jeans and a blouse of no particular style and no particular date. She'd showered, and when the time had come to spray on perfume, she hadn't. She smelled her mother's perfume, essence of rose, and Jonathan's seafaring cologne; she smelled the toasted zucchini squares and the sauteed mushrooms, the gin and the effervescing tonic, the water below them, not too fresh and even fishy on a given breeze, the mud beneath the grassy banks, the metallic exhaust of air-conditioning units down on the ground.

She could break it all down—the peepers peeped, the frogs croaked and split-tailed swallows made strafing runs at the insects hovering just over the water, tipping the surface with their wings. Breaking it down was easy.

"My favorite sale of all time?"

Her mother launched into the tallest of her tales, the story of a man she delighted in calling Mr. Maverick, the orneriest hombre in town. Maverick had a house out in a forest, a house he'd built with his own hands, and when the time came to sell it so he could move to Arizona and build another house—of cactus, she supposed—he made a big deal of it: seller to buyer, straight stuff, no sticky-fingered middlemen. He put an ad in the paper that sounded like a citizen's revolt. Real estate agents were no better than government officials, tax collectors, parasites of the worst sort. Weeks passed, months, without a sale, and finally Maverick had to eat humble pie. He called her mother, who was instructed to come out under cover of night to hear what he had to say.

Her fearless mother. She pretty much was. Next came the geese.

"... enormous geese. I had never seen geese that big—big enough that when they stretched their necks they were looking at you eyeball to eyeball where you sat in the car—and they were fierce. Geese make great watchdogs. Did you know that, Jonathan? I didn't. They have this horrible hissing honk. Just like our man to have killer geese instead of killer dogs. I had to sit in the car and wait until he came out and ran them off. Geese went with the pond—they wouldn't make it in Arizona—pond with the house. Maverick had this proposition to make, and if I'd swear not to breathe a word he'd make it to me. If I didn't swear he'd call back his geese. Did I want some time to think it over?"

A strategic pause. Her mother would be right back after she'd checked on the veal.

Just for the record, Annie said, "You don't know how many times I've heard this story. Want me to tell you how it ends?"

"You do and I may never speak to you again."

"Promise?"

"Your mom's one of a kind."

"No one like her in Boston?"

"Not so far."

"Exotic?"

"Just a little bit larger than life."

"A little bit?"

"You know what I mean."

"How can you be 'a little bit' larger than life? Once you're larger, how can you even measure? Measuring is for people who are not quite larger than life. Extra, extra large and all the way down to petite."

"C'mon."

"Just find some other way to describe her."

"Bighearted."

"Sounds small."

"Hasn't she been a good mom to you . . . after all that's happened?"

This last Jonathan added hesitantly, and she knew if he could he would take it back. What did he know about all that had happened? Terrorists kill your sister half a world away for reasons that will never make sense to you, because you haven't been there, you haven't lived through it, and you're left with a loss, a subtraction of one, an abstracted life. Your parents' marriage enters that world of abstraction, and it's gone too. Then you enter it.

When the story resumed, real estate agent Gail Williamson accompanied the forbidding Mr. Maverick back into his house, and quite a house it was. There was a three-sided loft around the living room. There were built-in bookshelves, verandas and private decks off bedrooms. The dining area with its exposed columns and beams was charming. Maverick had taste. Flowers were on the table and prints and paintings on the walls. It quickly became clear to her: rough-hewn, fine-hewn, Mr. Maverick was more than one man. Prospective buyers couldn't get a fix on him and, smelling a rat and risking the geese, they fled. Whereas she stayed and staked her claim.

Her mother could size men up as fast as she could face them down. All true.

"He'd done some investigating, he said. Only a fool didn't know his enemy, and he'd discovered I was the worst—by which he meant, I don't mind saying, the best—of the lot. He proposed I sell his house for him strictly on the sly. I get the price he had to have, and the rest I could keep for myself. If I was as good as I was cracked up to be, I could get a lot—he wasn't interested. He was admitting without saying as much that he needed help and wasn't about to ask what it would cost. He gave me his figure. He demanded secrecy, and I set him a condition back. You know what it was?"

Jonathan leaned in toward her mother. By the expression on his face Annie knew that he could make a good guess. She'd seen that expression often enough in class when he'd anticipated the professor to the extent that he could have spoken the professor's next words.

"You told him," Jonathan said, "that when a buyer came out he couldn't be there. You told him you didn't even want him in the garage or barn or some toolshed."

"Off the property, entirely." Her mother beamed.

"It was as if," Jonathan went on, "he were deeding the property to you and then you sold it to someone else."

"Something like that."

"The geese?" Jonathan asked.

"The geese were the first to go. The geese didn't make it past that night. I stood there when he shot them both."

That Annie had not heard. She'd heard the impressive sum of money her mother had made on the sale, and she'd heard that Mr. Maverick had taken his money and beaten pride and gone to Arizona, where he'd written her a letter speaking out of both sides of his mouth, praising her and calling her a high-handed bitch. A love letter, perhaps. Perhaps even another proposal. But gunshots that night, and two dead geese, the whole undertaking baptized in blood from the start? She doubted it.

.   .   .

Later, back in her father's house, when Jonathan tried to claim his reward for the way he'd stroked her mother's ego, Annie didn't just say
she was tired. She wasn't tired. She was wide awake, with eyes in the back
of her head. She said, "Not tonight." Tonight she was keeping watch.
Tonight she had to keep her wits about her. She didn't tell him that. But this
was her father's house and she had to look out for her father's interests, and
her father was not interested in her sleeping with Jonathan in his house
tonight. Jonathan had run his hands down the small of her back to cup her
ass in a way that she liked. She stood there on alert. A clue was about to be
presented to her, a clue to where she could find her father. Not that she
intended to go out and find him. He would call on resources her mother
didn't believe he had and stay away as long as he liked, but a clue would be
nice. Where had he gone? She wasn't asking much. Where had that slightly
overweight, somewhat shambling, not quite mysterious but certainly peculiar father of hers gone? She realized the world was small. A day on a plane
could take you halfway around it.

In that moment Jonathan was pleading how far *he'd* traveled, only he'd
come in a car. She had her father's car, and for a teasing moment that clue
was near again. Patty, she thought. Jonathan was chuckling as he ran his
hand over her belly, up over her left breast. He had large hands and long ca-
ressing fingers. With hands like that he should have played the piano. He
could have covered the whole keyboard. Annie remembered her grandmother's hands, with their age splotches and swollen veins, and then her father's hands, as they turned the pages of the songbook. Her father and
grandmother seemed to sing through the whole book, but the song that
came to mind was "The Nearness of You." Annie smiled. She hummed the
tune to herself. She heard the lyrics and must have sung them too—to herself. Or maybe not. Maybe out loud. Jonathan had his whole long body
pressed against hers now, and the bulge of his erection fitted between her
legs. Did he think she was singing to him? Thrilling to his nearness? They

were in her father's bedroom, and he tried to move her toward his bed. But she pried his large hand loose from her body and led him into another room.

It was a joke, he understood. A game. Maybe even a fairy tale. She told him a little white lie. That bed had been hers when she'd been a girl growing up in her parents' house. If he wanted to reach her up through the years, he'd have to spend a night there. It was a task she imposed. He was to catch up with her. She didn't spell it out for him, but Jonathan with his resilient good humor would take to the game. She'd been little, midsized, and then full grown and far too big for this bed, but he'd follow her trail and find her before the night was out.

She tucked him in, but when she entered the room she shared with her father she locked the door and as insurance jammed a chair back under the knob. She hung every stitch she wore on the closet door, then brushed her teeth and washed her face and brushed her hair with long, practiced strokes and stared at herself in the bathroom mirror.

What if her father was dead? Only a voice on a machine, which she'd erased?

She didn't flinch. Her eyelashes stirred and her nostrils quivered, but barely, like the lacy side fins of fish.

That night Jonathan scratched and pawed at her door. That night Jonathan visited every room of the house but hers. He prowled through the house, dragging the sad animal weight of his rejected self behind him. Annie found him the next morning on a chaise on the sunporch, where his exhaustion had caught up with him. He was sound asleep. She moved him over and made love to him there, visible to the neighbors had they been awake at that early hour.

That afternoon she gratified another of his desires and took him to a horse farm. They watched the horses running around in green pastures, enclosed within long white fences, and then they visited them in their stalls, where their pedigrees were posted. There were separate stalls for the colts, who had enormous round eyes, almost wild. The stalls were kept clean—for horses' stalls—and the smells were invigorating, about as close to pure horse as they could get. Jonathan had the good luck to talk to a handler. They were standing outside the stall of Quiet Scion. Jonathan got the dope on his diet, training regimen, grooming practices and career possibilities. Nine-tenths of those horses he saw prancing around the pasture would never make it onto the track. Quiet Scion, though, was a thoroughbred's thoroughbred. Jonathan repeated the word as if he'd never heard it before. "Thoroughbred. Thoroughly bred. Bred through and through." The handler let Jonathan brush out the coat, and he ran the steel-bristled brush over the barrel of the body with long loving strokes, which Quiet Scion responded to with deeply pleased shudders. Annie had to laugh.

That night, curiously, Jonathan was subdued. Because of the horses or because she had allowed him into her father's bed? Or, since he had not been admitted on the preceding night, did he consider himself unworthy? She doubted it. The trip, her mother, the day at the horse farm and the night Annie had put him through had simply caught up with him. He took deep breaths—she thought of Quiet Scion, filling that barrel of a body— and he was asleep. She would have gone downstairs to read, but she didn't want to leave him alone in that bed. She was responsible for him. If he was there it was because she had put him there, and if her father walked in—as he might at any moment—she didn't want him to find that strange body ly- ing unclaimed in his bed.

So she claimed it. She lay like a dutiful wife at his side.

That clue to where her father had gone hovered near. For a period she concentrated on catching it, then she turned over, angry at being teased like this. Call Patty, she told herself again. Patty had had the conversation with her father she should have had. Patty knew more than she was saying. Promiscuous Patty. Patty the Pistol.

Annie never slept that night, not really. And around dawn she did it again. She woke Jonathan and fucked him hard, right there in her father's bed, as if she were the stallion, not he.

At breakfast they had bagels as they would have had up north. He asked what was it, what was going on. He asked if he could help.

He could. Annie confessed she should never have come back. She asked if he would take her away. To Boston and the Cape—wherever he chose. She'd lock up her father's house. He had his keys, just as she had hers.

Her mother was pleased. She'd had it both ways. She'd gotten to meet the young man and create a memorable impression. Now it was her daughter's turn to create one of her own. She'd want to hear all about it. They'd be in constant touch by phone.

Partway up I-75 to Cincinnati, Annie asked Jonathan to pull off into a rest area. In the spirit of getting back what was rightly hers, she made the call to Patty, standing out from the parked cars before a field of tall green corn. The corn gave off a prickly smell that was the smell of sex. She made that identification just as a man's voice answered the phone. Brian Paul. She asked for Patty.

When Patty took the phone, Annie said, "I don't hear glass shattering. I don't hear the furniture being knocked around. I don't even hear Lizzie crying."

Patty protested—on her ex-husband's behalf. "He's got a right to see his daughter, and Lizzie likes to see him. I'll never know why. Something between a daughter and father, I guess."

"He hasn't threatened you?"

"Nope." Patty tried to give a bright turn to her voice.

"Really?"

"No way."

"You're being honest?"

"Fuckin'-A."

"Tell me where my father is."

"Dunno, Legs."

"There was something he said that afternoon. Something *you* said. I told myself, that's a clue. It'll be there when I want it."

"What's the rush? I told you, your dad adores you. Let the man have some fun."

"I want to know."

"What, are you leaving town or something?"

There was the sound of semis at her back, the rushing sound of a world on the move. Traffic wind in the corn and that musky sex smell.

"For a while."

"Let me guess. That boyfriend in New York?"

"Boston."

"Wasn't there one in New York?"

"Maybe. There might have been."

"Don't be a slut, Legs."

Patty didn't give Annie a chance to say it. She added, "Don't be a slut like me. Look what I got for my loose living."

Patty paused so that the baby yelps of Lizzie and the mock growls of her father could get through.

"Patty, I want to know!"

Patty's voice went flat and factual. A badly tuned twang. "I told you everything he said. Everything he said to you was everything my father never said to me. I told you that. I don't wanna say it all again."

"Patty!" Annie waited.

Patty took her time. Her voice was cocky and cold. "People been screaming at me all my life. Not one of them is my friend."

In the noise of the world rushing by and the vigorous sex-scrape of the corn, Annie would abase herself if that was what it took. "Anything, Patty."

And she could hear Patty relent. For just an instant it was like the friendly outcome of any number of girlish games they might have played.

"I know what your clue is, Legs. It was nothing he said. I meant to tell you—you're living too much in your head. Crawl out here in the world with the rest of us and take a look in the glove compartment of your dad's car."

Instead Annie crawled back into her head, away from the world of traffic and corn and the boy waiting for her in his car, and there, of course, it was, her clue. She felt like a very dull-witted child. Her clue had not gone anywhere; she had. Patty could no longer be accused. "Sorry," Annie muttered, but the phone had gone dead or Patty had hung up. Either way, Annie was talking into the wind.

She asked Jonathan to take her back.

He smiled and shook his head and thought perhaps of trips his family had begun when his mother or one of his sisters had made a similar request. Typical. He asked what she had forgotten.

"Just take me back," she said.

Now she got his confounded look. His eyes clouded over with a strange sort of strain, and Annie escaped his understanding. He knew to keep her in sight, though, since she'd always come back before. But this time was different. This time he gave up on her. He did it by releasing a breath and by looking off to the side.

She wouldn't call it a sigh of resignation, nothing like that.

Finally he just looked away.

But gentleman that he was, he did her the courtesy of asking, "Are you sure?"

She couldn't match his courtesy, and didn't try.

He took her back to her father's house and carried her bags up onto the front porch. Since she made no move to open the door, he didn't offer to carry them inside. He said he'd see her at school in the fall, and he kissed her on the cheek, a last touch, very much like a dusting off of the hands. He left her standing there with her bags on the porch and drove down the street. When he'd disappeared, she walked around back and used one key to open the garage, another to open her father's car. There was no key to the glove compartment—it had been unlocked all along. Without pause she opened it and found the glossy white envelope from the travel agency on top of the maps, brochures, guarantee agreements, traffic tickets, bills. It was the sort of envelope travel agencies sent out with itineraries—more of a folder than an envelope. She paused then, weighing the consequences, and made her decision. She clicked the glove compartment shut. She knew where her father was. From that point on, he was in the glove compartment of his car.

Then he saw a face, which he realized he'd been seeing all along, and which he'd dismissed because it did not look Basque. And because the man's first name—Armando—sounded as if it belonged to some cruise-ship crooner.

The last name did sound Basque, and squint-eyed, pig-headed and crabbed.

Ordoki. Armando Ordoki.

The face was long and fleshy—vaguely egg-shaped. It bulged at the cheeks. The chin was heavy and the features—the eyes, nose and mouth—roughly modeled. There were deep fold lines from the wings of the nostrils to the corners of the mouth and small sagging folds under the eyes. By Spanish standards the eyes were not large; they seemed to crouch back in their sockets. Armando Ordoki wore his hair short and combed over his forehead in small leaf-like points, as though he had crowned himself with laurels. In almost all the pictures that had appeared in the newspapers he had on a black crewneck sweater or tee-shirt. In some photographs a small stud showed in the lobe of his left ear, and in one photograph his lower lip protruded in a childish pout, but this was basically a thuggish face, belonging to a man who seemed incapable of hosting an intelligent thought or carrying out an intelligent act, and Ben had dismissed it.

But it kept reappearing.

Having lunch one day, he saw Armando Ordoki on the three o'clock news and discovered that the hair was chestnut brown and the complexion faintly toasted. There was none of that stark contrast between the black hair and pale complexion of men who'd lived under the shadows of mountains all their lives. Basques could look as cold as their mountain streams and as steady-eyed as their peaks. This Ordoki looked like people Ben had known all his life. He was slouched back in his seat in some sort of assembly hall, and when he moved it was in a bearish roll. At any moment it appeared he would get up and leave, but he was held there by his disgust.

The camera remained on Armando Ordoki long enough for Ben to see what couldn't be seen in newspaper photographs: there was real drama in Ordoki's face. In its fleshiness and length, and in the puffy buildup in the neck, it was a face that appeared to be sliding off him like wax.

An ETA militant had walked into a restaurant at midday and shot a man in the back of the head, a town council member from a party unsympathetic to the ETA's nationalist aims. No innocent bystanders were killed. Everybody in that assembly hall raised his hand to condemn the killing except the members of Ordoki's party. Ordoki, it appeared, was its leader. That was the reason the camera held on him as long as it did. The speaker, a woman, was expressing the outrage the assembly felt that a democratically elected representative could be murdered for his views while other democratically elected representatives stood by and refused to condemn the act. Her voice trembled, but it did not break.

The trembling voice disgusted Ordoki, and Ordoki's disgust arrested that slide of flesh off his face. Ben saw it clearly. The jaw set, the mouth tightened; there was a curdling of flesh like lava cooling—going stone cold—on the spot.

The newscast turned to sports. Ben didn't catch the name of the party

Ordoki headed. He might have asked the waiter, or someone sitting at a nearby table, but this man Ordoki was someone he wanted to keep to himself.

He and Paula Ortiz talked about other matters. They had yet to talk about him—he had not kept his half of the bargain—and he almost believed she preferred it that way. She could make wry, educated guesses about the purpose of his trip, what he hoped to find here. He was leaving behind a busted marriage—she was right about that. His business or career had not gone belly-up, otherwise he wouldn't spend money the way he did; the Regina was overpriced for a three-star hotel—everybody knew that. She could show him hotels out of the way on charming plazas for a lot less money if he was planning to stay. But he liked the fact that the Regina was in the way, and he preferred to remain loyal to Juan. She laughed, and surmised: he was here because a midlife crisis had revived a boyhood dream of meeting a smoldering Spanish beauty before he got too old. One afternoon Paula showed up with one, a friend named Mercedes, perhaps ten years her junior and maybe fifteen years his, just to give him a look and to gauge his reaction. Mercedes was so stunning, so unapproachable, that she might have belonged to another species, and he must have let it show. So it was not Spanish beauty he'd come for. Spanish cuisine? and there was talk of a restaurant Paula would take him to. Spanish history? and there was talk of castles and palaces they could visit, trips they could take. Spanish art? and there was talk of museums.

They met almost every afternoon. It was like a game of Twenty Questions they played while the people passed by. They never met anywhere else. She said she'd make him a meal if he missed home cooking, and he shook his head.

One day she asked him if he planned to celebrate. Then she had to tell him the date: July 4. He gave her a smile that was mostly real and strangely ashamed. He muttered loudly enough for her to hear that he had to call home. Home? And that was how Paula learned he had a daughter named Annie, which was what he meant by "home."

Ben didn't mention Annie's sister, or her mother, or any of his other departed or dead. Yes, he had a twenty-one-year-old daughter, and since he didn't want to leave her placeless in such a vast land, he ended up telling Paula the name of the town where Annie lived. Then, with a bleak sort of honesty, he claimed that was really all there was to tell.

Paula excused him and he went back to the hotel to try his luck. He called first his home phone, where he got no answer and left no message. He tried his daughter's cell phone, which he couldn't even get to ring. He almost called his ex-wife but decided instead to call his own phone again and leave a message. Early afternoon there—at an hour more convenient to her he'd try again. He'd tell her so. Happy Fourth, he'd add, and imagine her happy, out picnicking with her friends. In the New World. On this the New World's day.

But she picked up on the first ring. She said, "That was you calling, just now, when I didn't answer."

Her voice sounded eager as a little girl's. Before Ben could respond she cut him off. "Dad, don't tell me where you are, okay? Not unless I ask."

He made her that strange promise. He could tell her he was fine. The word he thought of was "interlude." He was between one thing and another. He was taking some time for himself. More time than he'd thought. He didn't ask, Do you mind? He asked how she was.

"Me? I'm good. I'm simplifying. I make sure Mother's where she's supposed to be. I sent my boyfriend home. I'm taking care of your house and car."

"Don't be lonely," he told her. He knew she had friends in town. Annie had friends everywhere. He didn't want her to be lonely, and with a curious sort of conviction in his voice, he told her there was never any need for that.

She was touched. He heard a catch in her breath. Then he heard another kind of catch, a faint shudder, and he suspected she was thinking of Michelle. She warned him, "You better take care of yourself."

She *was* thinking of Michelle, and now he was. Simultaneously, Michelle had visited them both. They might have been walking in that park together, Parque Santander.

She had to rouse him. "Hey, Dad, 'Give me one reason to stay here and I'll turn right back around.' Remember?"

He didn't.

"'Don't wanna leave you lonely but you gotta make me change my mind.'"

Then he did. She was quoting him lines from a song. A love song.

Then she laughed, and that, Ben realized, was why he'd called, what he'd been waiting to hear. It was a laugh that cleared the decks, powerful, purgative, and in it he heard all the laughing she hadn't done for how long?

He wished her a happy Fourth. As her father, he advised her to go out and find something to celebrate.

In the next morning's papers he saw a picture of Armando Ordoki standing at an outdoor rally with two other men. They must have been up in the mountains, for Ordoki wore a light-colored windbreaker over his customary black shirt. His hands in his pants pockets, he was looking off to the side, with a pouting pursed mouth and dimple shadows under his bunched cheeks. He looked like a boy whose parents had dragged him off to a tiresome event and told him to stay put.

July fifth was an overcast day, drizzling rain. Ben ate in the hotel and watched the three o'clock news in his room. Nothing. Europe about to add more countries to the mix, shaking them up to see the shape that came out. The rain never let up, and by the time he walked down to the Café Gijon it was a mild downpour. Paula was not there. No one was. He walked until he came to a statue of a famous Spanish author—Ramon Valle-Inclan, the plaque read—who had been sculpted stepping off into the evening's *paseo* himself. He had a long bronze beard tucked into his vest, which over the years admiring or superstitious or just playful hands had rubbed yellow. In the rain, that beard shone. He too stroked it down its billowing length and just that quickly remembered there was a literary Café Gijon behind the outdoor one. He retraced his steps. Paula was seated at a table beside one of the wrought-iron columns. She said, "I wondered if you'd remember. It was like a little test. You passed."

Ben leaned over the table and kissed her on the cheek, both cheeks, as Spaniards did. She smelled of the rain, and the rain brought out the smell of her hair and skin. It was such a familiar smell, that smell of human nearness, that under other circumstances he might not have smelled it at all.

July sixth, and they entered a calendar of indistinguishable days. Paula told him more about her Spanish family. The father had died. The mother went to a mass a day and said a complete rosary too. She still dressed very, very well. One of the daughters was just as devout and was forcing her children to jump through all the Catholic hoops. The other daughter had been wild. She'd done a stint with the Communist Party, married civilly, gone to live in the Basque country, divorced, and refused to have her daughter baptized.

This maverick daughter, whose name was Pepa, Paula had remained close to. Jorge's two brothers she couldn't stand. As soon as the father died they had tried to squeeze Jorge out of the family's hotel business, and, unwilling to stoop to their mercenary tactics, Jorge had made them a deal. He would come to Madrid and take over a travel agency the family had started, and the brothers would stay in Valladolid and run the hotel. The brothers agreed—the hotel was worth five times as much. They ruined it, of course. Compared to their father, they were petty thieves. They ended up coming to Madrid and demanding that Jorge cut them in on the travel agency, which had prospered. Jorge never lost his temper, which aggravated his brothers because they were always losing theirs. He gave them his "look."

"It was the smile, just a grin on the right side of his mouth; it was the trusting way he leaned in close. It was the green eyes—the pleasure they took in everything and in nothing, next to nothing. Jorge has a rumpled face and a flattened nose, and when he looks at you that way it all gets transformed. You have this feeling there's no limit to how far he can see. It was the way he looked at me when he told me he wanted a divorce. Would you like to meet him?"

Ben didn't know what to say. He wanted to say, No, not yet, because as friendly as Jorge was touted to be, the man seemed to have an unnerving effect. But Ben was curious about that look.

Straining to see a face through her words, instead of Jorge Ortiz he saw Armando Ordoki. In none of the newspaper photos or television reports had Ordoki been smiling—the closest he'd come had been that distracted little pout—but it was a big broad jackal's smile Ben saw now, the fleshy nostrils flaring. The eyes were crinkled and the fellow feeling that came out of them smelled of rot.

He told Paula, "One day. Not yet. Soon, though."

And though she tried to toss it off, she couldn't help asking, "How many days you think you have left, Ben? Rough estimate."

"I don't have anywhere to go," he replied.

"It's funny. That first day I came back to find you, I was thinking you'd run off to Zimbabwe. I really was."

"You misread me."

"I don't think so. I still think you need to be accepted in some place like that. I wondered if you'd start with Leslie's mud."

He was a little defensive, a little abrupt. "And you don't?" he said.

"And I do."

"Need to be accepted in a place?"

She nodded. "I think it's what attracted me to you."

"So maybe Spain." He gave her a conciliatory smile and gestured around him, out to that stream of passersby you could never step into twice. He couldn't recall having seen the same person more than once. Except Paula. "Maybe I'll stay here."

She looked at him levelly across the table. "I worry about Annie," she said.

"I don't."

And he didn't. Perhaps he worried about a world suitable for his daughter to live in but, strangely, not about her.

B en went back to his hotel and tried to get Juan reminiscing about his hometown, Medina del Rioseco. But as willing as Juan might have been, he kept being called back to work and couldn't do justice to his client, who was no longer sick in bed. The next morning, though, when Ben came down to breakfast, Juan extended an invitation. The following day, a Sunday, he'd decided to drive back to his *pueblo*. Just to spend the day. His wife couldn't come with him. Would Ben like to?

Paula knew the town. It was close to Valladolid, perhaps no more than twenty-five or thirty kilometers. Its main street, the *calle mayor*, was arcaded from one end to the other, and the wooden columns were so old and stout they looked petrified. He should go. On Sundays these towns filled up with city-dwellers returning to their *pueblos*. It would be a Spanish moment.

A day with his friend Juan. She smiled.

In Bilbao two more *etarras* were killed by their own bomb, this time while they were transporting it to the target site. The police did not know what that site was to have been. The bomb had been in a backpack. It might have been left almost anywhere—not just a *guardia civil cuartel*, in a train station, an amusement park, a movie theater.

Police speculated that the dynamite had been in *mal estado*, of a poor composition, and that this had led to the premature explosion. There was further speculation about the "degradation" of ETA's explosives in general.

Ben scanned the article for the car's make. The charred remains, also pictured, told him nothing. But Japanese and Korean cars were being sold in Spain now; Hyundai, he'd read, had opened a plant here. ETA had a world of cars to steal from. Cars rolled off assembly lines, and generations of *etarras* replenished themselves. There was never a shortage of anything. There were always backpacks. That the dynamite would turn bad in their hands was just wishful thinking. The bishop of Bilbao was quoted as saying the two killed *etarras* were "victims of their own violence." But he could just as easily have said that they were progenitors of their own kind, that every explosion, for the damage and death it might cause, gave birth to stars. There was no end. In cosmological processes such as these, Michelle's death was no more than a speck of dust, which would eventually adhere to another speck and finally grow into something large enough for ETA to blow up again. He tried to see his way out of this, and failed. Then Juan picked him up and drove him to his hometown.

In an Opel—not a Seat Ibiza—they drove up the La Coruna expressway, past the turnoff for El Escorial, through the La Guadarrama mountain range guarding the northern rim of Madrid, and then on to a broken plain of granite boulders. The boulders soon gave way to small dusky oaks and sun-browned pastures. Then the trees disappeared, the last low hills leveled out, and they looked out on tableland, planted in wheat and spotted with towns clustered around their churches.

Tierra Campo, this area was called. Juan was providing a selective commentary.

He was dressed in pressed gray slacks and a white shirt. On the back seat lay a suit coat of gray, not quite a match to the slacks. He looked freshly groomed, his hair recently trimmed, and his cologne, that mix of lavender and lemon that was close to being a national smell, filled the car. He drove sitting straight up in his seat with both hands on the wheel. Was he taking extra care because he had a special passenger sitting beside him? Or was this the Sunday Juan, the Juan who on Sundays went back to his hometown? Or was he only stiff with worry that his hometown would not measure up to the boastful claims he'd made for it?

In all this space, rife with wheat and fluttered over by pigeons, there didn't seem to be a hometown worth going back to. Just a few shells of settlements with identical silhouettes.

Then they were in it, walking down its arcaded main street, its *calle mayor*. The wooden columns Paula had remembered as being so old and stout as to seem petrified were actually glassy to the touch, and Ben stood with his hand pressed against one as, again and again, Juan was greeted by friends and distant family members. Juan never forgot him, not once. Ben was introduced as an *"amigo,"* of course, but also as an *"amante de España,"* and the people whose hands he shook responded *"Encantado,"* or *"Mucho gusto,"* and once, by someone practicing his English, "Spain ess different, eh?" Ben smiled and defended himself as best he could. He saw people who looked like Juan, sallow-complexioned, with protruding bones and tired eyes that lit up only when they spoke. They were faces pinched at the nose and the corners of the mouth, and they did not look very healthy.

The *calle mayor* emptied out into the Plaza Mayor, with its own columns and arcades but with a sudden and welcome sense of space. Ben coaxed Juan out to its center so that he could take a look around and so that he could breathe. This was the space of the plain on which the town was built, and even though people continued to pour out of that noisy and smoky *calle mayor,* the plaza was large enough to absorb them all.

He asked Juan, "Is it always like this? So crowded?"

Juan gave him a bitter-wise smile and shook his head. "The town is actually dying. The young people all want to go to Madrid. But on Sundays everyone comes back—even the young people do. Even I did, as you see. Because the town is our soul."

Juan made a fist over his heart and thumped it twice. Then for a moment he closed his eyes.

They ate lunch with Juan's older sister at her house under the bell tower of one of the town's many churches. The bells when they sounded the quarter-hour had a thin and jangling tone, and Juan's sister had a fond, hectoring voice that jangled on the ear like the bells. Her name was Maria Rosa. Her husband was stooped, and looked up at Ben with bright, easily amused eyes. They had three daughters, two of whom were there with their husbands. There were three small children. Juan's mother and father came but remained in their chairs, the father, a trickster, trying to lure the children close so that he could trip them up with his cane. It seemed impossible that there would be a grandmother, although Juan had claimed that one still lived, and Ben heard Maria Rosa more than once speak the word *"abuela."* In addition, there was another sister, a widow, who seemed finicky and bitter but who had a daughter with an expansive laugh who waited on her and tried to humor her back into the fold. Juan had one brother they didn't talk about, except to say he was abroad, working in Germany, and another who had prospered in trucking and came with fine wine and champagne and a wife too loudly dressed and made up for such humble surroundings. The wife made perfunctory inquiries of everyone there, then sat off to the side and smoked.

The house was not small. It consisted of three stories, but they insisted on gathering on the third, in a small, low-ceilinged dining room that adjoined the kitchen and the pantry, where sausage and ham hung in the near-dark beside loops of garlic and swatches of vegetation that smelled like herbs. Onions and potatoes and turnips sat in earth-smelling baskets on the floor. The entire family welcomed Ben and asked him questions at the start, mainly about his country and how it matched with the movies they'd seen, and although he mostly understood and did his best to fashion an answer out of the Spanish he knew, they grew impatient and called in Juan to translate. Juan was busy with family members he wanted to talk to and grew impatient with their impatience. The children marveled at Ben for a while, then went back to their games. The daughter with the expansive laugh, when she wasn't busy pampering her mother, seemed anxious to include him, but her mother won out. The brother's wife assumed Ben was putting up a show but was as bored as she. "They do this every time one of them comes back to town. What do you think? Isn't it a *rollo?*" He could understand everything but the last word. He told her he didn't know what a *rollo* was, but family reunions like this seemed fine.

Ben didn't have family to reunite, but he didn't tell her that. She wasn't interested. She sat off on her sidelines, and finally, when the novelty of him wore off, he sat off on his. Juan kept in touch. And when time came to eat,

Ben got first servings of a stew called *cocido,* which seemed to have a bit of everything in it but tasted finally of turnips and sausage, and of the piles of bony lamb chops whose cooking smoke coated everything in the room. And wine and champagne. There were many toasts and competing conversations in the low-ceilinged room. The bells never ceased to ring. Finally it was all too much—although he didn't tell the brother's bored wife this. But with the *flan,* the coffee and cognac, and then the *puro,* which the brother insisted he take a puff of, he found himself dreaming back to the spacious Plaza Mayor and the way it absorbed all the humanity the *calle mayor* could pour into it. The closeness in Juan's ancestral home had gotten to him. Suddenly, for no reason at all, except the closeness, he remembered the two *etarras* blown up inside their own small car.

He thanked them all for having him, and just when he thought they were ready to step outside, Juan asked him to come say hello and good-bye to the *abuela.*

They found her in what must have been the smallest room in the house, so small it was hard to imagine what it could have been used for other than this: to contain Juan's grandmother. There was a round table, fitted with a fringed tablecloth, an overhead light. No window. On the walls hung a crucifix and devotional images of the Virgin. One of the children—one of her great-great-grandchildren, it would have been—left when he and Juan entered. The room was stifling, yet the old woman was swaddled in layers of gray and black cloth, and she was sitting with the tablecloth draped over her lap. On the table somebody had left a sprig of rosemary, but the dominant odor in the room was of rotted wood. All the time Juan spoke to her the old woman never ceased to whisper in the thinnest escape of air. Only when Ben was introduced and leaned over the table did he see the rosary wrapped in her hands, which were as earthen as roots. Her face was a small weathered knot of wood, and her hair was a thin fibrous yellow pulled back on her skull. The rosary with its silver cross and jet-black beads was the most alien object in the room. He didn't touch her. Juan kissed her, but Ben stood back by the door. His glamour had worn off completely by now. She wasn't interested in visitors from the United States of America. But to keep his word to Juan—and this visit to the family matriarch was like the very last course of a very long meal—he said, "*Adios,* Abuela."

As provisions until his next trip, Juan brought the town back with him—its cheese and bread, ham and sausage, wine and pastries made in a local convent. Back in Madrid, Juan's stand-in at the Regina gave Ben his key and a message from Paula. Thanks to a friend who owned a gallery, where Paula occasionally helped out, she had arranged a special pass to visit the Prado Museum on Monday, when it was closed to almost everybody else. There was a painting Paula wanted to show him. It was important. He was not to go to the Café Gijon. The hour had also changed. They would now meet at four o'clock.

Paula picked him up at his hotel, walked him down the Paseo del Castellana, past the Plaza del Neptuno and the Palace Hotel, where some time ago he had stayed, on down the stretch of Castellana that became the Paseo del Prado, past the museum itself and around to the Murillo door, where they were admitted. In room thirty-two she stood him before Goya's *Duelo a Garrotazos*. She asked him to give it some thought. Then she disappeared.

The painting—perhaps three meters long, a meter and a half high— was of two men standing off-center left, beating each other with clubs. These men were giants. One was dark-complexioned, and blood streamed down his face; the other was lighter, brown-haired, and showing no visible wounds, although his face was turned away from the viewer. Both men were mired in mud or sand to the knees. The valley they towered over was idyllic. A stream ran down its grassy fold. The sky was a watery blue with white clouds. Off to their right the sky was gray, and that half of the painting was occupied by the shadowed flank of a mountain and one rolling foothill. The men were proportioned to compete with the mountain, but the mountain would be there when the men had beaten each other to death. Mired in that mud, they couldn't escape.

The valley was a paradise and the men were a massive and monstrous violation. Cain and Abel, Ben supposed. The bloody, mustachioed man had his club raised over his head; the fairer-skinned one shielded his face with his left arm and with his right held his club out low as if he meant to swing it up under the other man's ribs. If the viewer followed the down-sloping line of those two clubs, he too ended up mired in the mud. Perhaps he was meant to look away from the line of those clubs up to the mountains, older than the men and closer to God. But Ben doubted it. The men took the attention and held it, and the mountains and everything else, including that peaceful valley and sky, became a trembling backdrop, about to disappear.

When Paula did not return, Ben proceeded to look at paintings in the adjoining rooms. There he discovered a different sort of strangeness. These were mostly very dark paintings. They frequently depicted groups or processions of people, even people who were airborne. He came quickly to see that these people were all clotted together and that it was impossible to delineate a body in its entirety. Perhaps with more light, but he didn't think so. A grotesque fusion was going on here, trunks joined, bodies that made use of the same leg, heads leaning in close and forever attached. Some of these figures were witches or satanic stand-ins—he understood that from the titles of the paintings—but the masses of people had lost their individual shapes and blended into one dark and diseased-looking amalgam. Ben returned to the painting of the two dueling men. Here the delineation was stark. The men stood out down to the hair, the buttons on their vests; in their violent individuality they dwarfed the natural world around them. The second they ceased to fight and fell on each other in a fraternal embrace, would they too darken over and fuse? That was the question. And where would the moral be in that? You were only yourself if you violently beat back all others of your kind? The greater danger was not the spilled blood but the breakdown of your lines?

When Paula stepped up beside him, she wanted to hear his impressions.

He told her he thought the men were monstrous, but compared to the other paintings close by, at least they were men. If they were searching for some tolerable view of the human condition, he didn't see a way out.

Paula said, "It's Spain, Ben. You were talking about staying and I couldn't feel honest with myself until I showed you this painting. Duels like this were actually legal during Goya's life. *Campesinos* went out in the countryside and fought to the death. You wouldn't have seen this in that lovely *plaza mayor* in Medina del Rioseco. Out in the *campo*, though, those promenading couples might have to step over pools of blood. It's a country of civil wars—that black-haired man on the left is probably Andalusian, and the other someone from the Celtic north. Napoleon's invasion started a civil war. There were the Carlist civil wars all during the nineteenth century. The civil war in this century was horrible. The communists took over the Republican cause and executed anybody who had anything to do with the church. Franco's forces executed anybody who had anything to do with the Popular Front. It's still going on, of course. The Basques might kill anybody anywhere until they get what they want. . . ."

Ben felt a jolt down his backbone and turned away from her. He didn't want her to see his face. He'd just seen a picture of Saturn eating his children and that was what flashed before his eye. The children had looked bloody-white and cartilaginous and Saturn had had to crunch hard.

"It's Goya despairing at the end of his life," Paula went on, "creating all those paintings on the walls of his house in the *campo*. It had a fascinating name, Quinta del Sordo—House of the Deaf Man, as if he just decided not to listen anymore to what was going on. History would prove him right."

"Yet you stay here," Ben reminded her.

She led him out of there, to a café on a tree-lined street between the Prado and Retiro Park. They sat outside, by the curb. The occasional car passed, but few pedestrians. It was not yet the hour.

Huddled over that table, Ben recalled yet another Goya painting, of two old people, so old that with their monkey faces and cave-dark dwelling they appeared to have evolved backward. They were huddled over a scrap of bread.

"I stay here," she said, "because I can count on the Spanish to be who they are. Most of the time I like them a lot. Honor is still important to them. But if their honor is violated, they'll find a way of getting their revenge. It can be wonderful theater. They can hold grudges for so long and in such devious ways that they become baroque. Baroque grudges! Like a good grade-B movie, where the passions run high."

She shot him an exclamatory look, as if she were about to break into applause. When he failed to respond, she continued in a more considered tone.

"They try to behave themselves. For a while they'll have you believing they can be as proper as some technocrat from Brussels. But that's not who they are. Their passions explode, and if you're smart that's when you'll stand back and give them room. Once their passions subside they go back to being the most attentive people I know. They have a word, *detalles*. It means 'details,' but they use it to describe little thoughtful acts and gifts suited to your needs and tastes alone. *Que detalle mas bonito*, they say. 'What a beautiful detail!' You're thinking: How am I being set up? When in fact it's more their pleasure than yours. Then the pendulum swings again, something happens, and they explode. It's a national rhythm."

The waiter, a boy, put their drinks down before them. Paula leaned in over the table, a scowling sort of fixity in her eyes. She was pressing him.

"So you see why I want to stay?"

"The theater?" he said.

"It's pretty much the whole human spectrum."

"You can't be a spectator forever."

"I'm not a spectator forever. I have things I do." Suddenly her expression changed. She was smiling, almost gaily. Her eyes had relaxed and beneath her wheat-reddened brows seemed to be dancing.

"Where does Jorge fall in that spectrum?"

She mimed a slump. In a playful, reproving voice, she moaned, "Oh, Ben."

But he couldn't help himself. "This Spaniard's Spaniard. Where does he fit in?"

"Nowhere," she admitted. "He's a mystery, someone to stand back from and study and shake your head."

"You're not still in love with him?"

She'd anticipated this. In an even-toned voice she replied, "I'm in love with the mystery."

She reached out over the table and covered his hand. Now her face was frank, so frank and cleansed of its expressions it reminded him of his wife's face when she was young and about to step off into the unknown. But Paula was not young. Her face was naked in a different way, and he felt an entirely different sort of urgency in the pressure of her hand.

"There's something missing, isn't there, Ben? There's some loss."

"You get to my age and there's always loss. That's like saying I'm no longer twenty years old."

"Some loss of a different sort. That won't go away. That won't stay still."

"If that makes it make sense to you," he said, and tested the pressure of her hand. She held him there.

"A loss like a hole you can't see to the bottom of so you don't know how deep it is."

"Don't keep this up, Paula. Goya was more cheerful."

"Okay."

His eyes strayed off, up the street where he could see the foliage of Retiro Park. Those couples, arm in arm. That pacing in praise of the life they'd lived. "Look at me, Ben." She didn't demand it; she pleaded with him quietly, and her hand went soft. "If you lie there in the mud with Leslie's animals you have only one thought, which is no thought at all. Will they let you survive? Either way you win. If they do and you get to spend the day among them, fine. If they eat you, they eat your painful thoughts."

She let go of his hand. She sat back and took a deep breath and her whole body trembled. He could feel it through the table. The glasses and the small plate of olives made a fine shivering sound. He thought of those pacing couples and pictured Paula and himself among them in that formal garden where no tumult was allowed. From the mud and Africa's animals to that garden, where you could actually hear a single spout of water pooling. He was about to propose they walk there when she said, "We could go back to the Gijon and continue the conversation. But we've left the Gijon, haven't we? I've got supper waiting for us at home. You see, I'm not just a spectator, Ben. There are some things I do very well."

She took his hand and he emptied his pockets of change. He had plenty left for a taxi to wherever Paula lived, but she insisted on the Metro since traffic was always terrible and there was a station near her house. They entered at the Retiro station, and when they emerged on a street of tall new apartment buildings he had no idea where they were. He might have worn a blindfold. They might have been traveling to the headquarters of some guerrilla leader whose need for secrecy had reached paranoid extremes.

She walked him through the house. The front balcony looked five stories down to the street. The back balcony looked down into a no-man's-land, a well. Paula liked big plants, palmetto-sized brooms and rhododendrons climbing the walls. In the living room she liked low-slung modern furniture, but in her bedroom she had a suite that was traditional, antiques, he supposed. There was a marble-topped dresser, a bed with a large scrolled headboard, and a wardrobe with a mirror so tall that when he stood in it none of him was missing. The kitchen was walled in *azulejos*, glazed tiles, some with a floral design, some depicting the process of making bread: the sowing of the seed, the reaping of the wheat, the pounding of the dough and the oven-fresh loaves. The figures were all happy *campesinos*, the men in their hemp sandals and peasants' vests and the women in aprons and billowing skirts. The photographs he saw were of her family back in the States, a world away. He saw a small photograph of Leslie and Garret dressed in parkas waving to her from the bow of a ship. There were no pictures of Paula's ex-husband, only spaces where they might have hung before she'd removed them. Jorge Ortiz made a good story, but who was to say he even existed?

They drank a Ribera del Duero from Valladolid. The *aperitivos* were chunks of squid in olive oil and cheese from La Mancha. For a first course she served him slices of Iberian ham and honey melon. For a second, flounder, which slid off the bone at the touch. These were simple dishes, delicately prepared. For dessert, a lemon mousse.

Coffee and a liqueur she'd discovered, anise steeped in seven sierra herbs.

She said, "I think you should call your daughter. You can go in the bedroom and close the door."

"Only if you put the pictures back," he said.

They studied each other then. They were going to have to settle for what they knew of each other, or thought they knew.

"I won't do that," she said.

"No, neither will I."

They embraced and kissed on those terms. She gave him her chapped lips and her two crooked teeth and her freckles that had faded and her red hair whose luster was dying out. Above all, he got her warmth. She pressed against him, and he didn't know how long he had gone without that. He ran his hands down her shoulders and over the flesh of her back, and, more than desire, what he felt in that moment was a vast relief. He sighed and she laughed.

They made their way to her bed. They laid their clothes across matching chairs from a bygone empire and found themselves standing naked in the wardrobe's mirror. They were not misshapen, not really. The lines were just beginning to break down. She spread a hand across his enlarged belly. He a hand riding the heaviness of her hip. They began to laugh at themselves like children and tumbled into bed, where, still laughing, they wrestled a bit. Then they went still and he felt that warmth rising off her like . . . certainly not like that bread after the wheat had been sowed and reaped, the dough pounded, and the loaf taken fresh from an oven. Like nothing he knew. Inside her, he thought he understood. It was one of those *detalles*, acts of kindness and consideration perfectly suited to your needs. Later the pendulum would swing back, dark passions would erupt and the world would explode, but they'd have had this interlude—because she'd read his needs so well. He smiled down at her and nodded in gratitude, and she smiled back. *Que detalle mas bonito.*

VIII

She hadn't slept. She'd given herself over to the thousands of night sounds, and they'd kept her awake in a thousand different ways. When a glimmer of gray appeared at the window, she got out of bed and put on the clothes she'd taken off. Then the glimmer went away. A false dawn. She'd heard the term, but thought it was only for poets. She stepped out to the front of her father's house. The streetlights at the corners were still lit, and there would always be distant traffic sounds—in the distance someone was always going somewhere with a sound of purpose—but there were dark, silent stretches she could walk through as the dawn came up.

She walked for a while. She ranged past her father's block, moving through an opening arc that might or might not bring her back to where she'd begun. Dogs were still asleep. Some front porches were lit, but few interior rooms were. No newspapers lay in their plastic sacks in the driveways. Only at the first birdsong did she realize she hadn't been hearing the birds.

Moving through this neighborhood, Annie felt the sort of fluidity a ballet dancer must long for. She stayed on the streets and sidewalks but might just as easily have slipped out into back yards, up onto porches, into cellars and garages. She felt disembodied. She could walk up to a wall and walk through it. She would stand inside and, one by one, identify the holdings of a house. One by one, they would be no different from her own. She would watch people sleep in their beds, and unless she wanted to take on their upset stomachs and aching heads, unless she wanted to take on the griefs they were hoping to sleep through, she would conclude they were bodies on a bed just as she'd been a body on a bed. At that early hour of the morning, everyone was the same. She could have stayed at home.

The bird call became raucous, and dawn did not break; it breathed its grayness out of each tree, window and wall. The sameness of things became all their trifling differences. In the light of day no one wanted to be mistaken for his neighbor, and she began to see how a gable differed from a gable, a chimney from a chimney, a front porch from a front porch, a rose garden from a rose garden. Then, after the strain to be different had become apparent, how each became a gable and a chimney and a front porch and a rose garden again. A dog barked, and so the one next door did. She heard the muted sounds of people waking up, water sounds, metallic sounds from a kitchen, a radio or television going on, someone letting out a cat. Finally a human voice, a man's, an expression of surprise and disappointment and a sort of grinding aggravation. Someone who'd awoken and found what he hadn't wanted to find but feared he might and ground out his displeasure to anyone who'd listen. Annie knew the sound. She'd made it herself. That was not the problem.

She was looking for a shelter that was not like a bus stop for an anonymous passenger to get out of the rain. She was looking for some place that was hers and bore the marks of her being from the start. A little nook on the face of the earth reserved for her. The earth was large enough for that many nooks, wasn't it? And what she wanted she must once have had, since she felt the existence of such a place in the very nature of her need. It was a yearning for the familiar; she'd been sheltered like that before. She wasn't talking about the womb. She was an educated and self-aware young woman—a place on the earth that in the grayness she couldn't remember the shape, sound or smell of, but whose shape, sound and smell would fit her perfectly. It had before.

She wandered her father's neighborhood until the first real light shone on the plastic-sheathed newspapers tossed in the driveways. When she found herself before her father's house, she admitted defeat and turned up the drive. She unlocked the side garage door and then the passenger door to his car. She lifted the travel folder from the glove compartment and took it out to the light of day. On May 14 her father had flown from Lexington, Kentucky, to Kennedy Airport. That same evening he'd flown to Madrid, Spain. There was no return flight itinerary, but she read down all the information on the sheet and tracked him to the Palace Hotel in Madrid for May 15 and thereafter. There was no departure date.

This was an advance itinerary—it said as much at the top of the sheet. Someone might be slated to fly to Madrid on May 14 and actually fly to Hong Kong. She quite understood. Beside the Palace Hotel booking her father—it was his handwriting—had scribbled "Hemingway." Of Hemingway in Spain Annie had read two books. *The Sun Also Rises* was about an impotent man chasing a promiscuous woman around half of Europe and finally, in his frustration, running with the bulls in Pamplona, none of which, even allowing for a radical personality shift, she could imagine her father doing. The other was *For Whom the Bell Tolls*, about an American going to Spain to fight the good fight, which she'd read in high school not for its political sentiments but to see if the earth moved. Her father was no soldier either.

It didn't matter. Her father had not gone to Spain following Ernest Hemingway. He'd gone to look for Michelle. But Michelle was right here, shaking her head, and remarking, There're just so many clear-minded, straight-thinking people in the world, and I had the bad luck to be born into a family without a single one. Annie lowered her head and let her arms fall. Grinding her jaw, she wept there in her father's back yard.

S he folded the itinerary into its folder and placed it on his bedside table as she got back into his bed. She closed her eyes and released a breath she must have been holding for hours, days, however long it had been, and sank out of sight. It was past noon when the phone woke her. Her father, she thought. But it was her mother and, strangely, in that moment it didn't matter. The voice pulled her up out of the hole into which she had fallen, and she agreed to have lunch within the hour.

Only after she'd hung up did she realize her mother had sounded upset, whether angry or worried or just perplexed she couldn't decide.

Some of all.

They had lunch in a converted mansion that had once been out in the country and now was pretty much downtown. And she kicked herself. With its white columns, wide-planked floors, quaint rooms and fireplaces on whose mantels memorabilia rested that would trace this house back to its antebellum owners, before she sent him home she could have made Jonathan's stay here even more memorable. Brick walkways wandered through magnolias outside. On the veranda stately rockers rocked. She didn't know about the food. Her mother ordered something with clams. Annie hadn't had breakfast yet, and asked, in the absence of bagels, for eggs, toast and coffee, which became Eggs Benedict.

Her mother said, "What are you doing with yourself that you begin the day at one . . ." she consulted her watch, "twenty-five in the afternoon?"

Her tone was disapproving, concerned and probing for the good stuff. Since Annie'd let Jonathan go off alone, her mother had insisted her daughter could swim for herself. She'd really meant "fish," with the clear implication that bigger and better fish than Jonathan would not be swimming by. Secretly her mother was intrigued that Annie could let such a prize catch swim back to Boston—it revealed a capacity that she at that age most certainly hadn't possessed. Even more secretly she might have been cheering her daughter on. Maybe her fondest and most unspoken ambition was for Annie to become a femme fatale.

"Let me ask you a question, Mother," Annie said, and because her mother prided herself on being a straight speaker ("I've made a list of every reason you shouldn't buy this house. Here it is.") and because she insisted on being spoken straight back to ("Save your moonlight on garden walls for your next wife."), Annie went ahead. "When you went to Spain to bring back Michelle's body, was it because Dad refused to go, or was it because you just wanted to do it yourself?"

Her mother pushed back from the table. With the years and extra weight her face had gotten more darkly toned and very broad. When she was young it had been a healthy squared oval, even tomboyish, but there were photographs of her mother at Annie's age when the large blue eyes had gone still and the full lips had parted and a woman of some strong and unsettling beauty had looked out at the camera. In a wedding photograph, her mother's mouth was open to take in a piece of cake, but her eyes were gleaming and feeding on the person holding it out to her, her husband of perhaps two hours. The woman who sat before Annie no longer had those large avid eyes or that adventurous squared oval of a face. For a moment Annie thought she was about to get up and leave.

But her mother had pushed back from the table only to push in closer, to retake her own position, as it were, and then advance it. "That's done," she declared, meeting her daughter head-on. "I've put that behind me now. That's been three years."

"No one ever told me."

"You knew your father. You knew me. Did it seem peculiar? Did friends of yours begin to talk?"

"Friends of . . . mine," and she lingered on the word, "never said a thing."

"Well, friends of . . . ours," and her mother gave the word a harsh emphasis, "knew your father and they knew me and they didn't talk either."

"So he didn't want to go? He couldn't face it?"

Once again her mother sat back. Then, pulling up close, she drew a breath through the congestion that had risen in her throat. "Sweetie, the State Department was going to send your sister's body in a government casket accompanied by a guard all the way to our door. Don't you see I couldn't let them do that? Through all the airports, through Customs? The State Department was cooperative, but they are very impersonal people. I just rode with her. I just stayed at her side, that was all."

"Didn't you have to identify the body in Madrid?"

Her mother drew another steadying breath. The room was small. Annie had noticed that all antebellum houses had small rooms. So they could be heated better, she assumed, but she knew that people had been smaller back then. Michelle would have been a little taller than normal and Annie a giant. In such close quarters her mother's control was admirable. "I didn't 'have to,' but I did. I asked everyone to leave the room and told her she wasn't alone, I just wanted her to know that." She paused. "That wasn't the reason your father didn't want to go."

"The reason?"

"That they would want him to identify the body."

"Oh."

"I don't think he was afraid of that."

"No."

"He didn't want to go because the minute they called to tell us what had happened he said good-bye to her. In some ways, whenever she walked out the door, when she went off to college, for instance, he said good-bye to her. It was how she was—it was how she was for *him*. A mother's different." And very briefly, a smile appeared on her mother's lips—a trembling, brief and intimate smile, too intimate for this public place. A smile of solidarity and of defeat. A mother's smile.

Her mother had never smiled at her quite like that before.

Nor had she ever, that Annie could remember, said anything quite that understanding about her father.

She touched her mother's hand on the table. In gratitude—no, really, in recognition of the moment—Annie took her side. "He might have said good-bye to her, but that didn't mean he couldn't go with you, just to help out, to offer his support."

"I know, sweetie."

"It doesn't seen fair."

"Not much is."

"I mean," and she kept it up, even as she wished she hadn't, "to carry the bags if that's all he could manage. If he wouldn't trip over himself."

She'd made him sound like the ex-husband and the father they knew, and Annie's mother was quick to accept this invitation back to familiar ground. "Your father was born tripping over himself," she said, and laughed.

They ate their lunch. Annie's eggs tasted of betrayal. Before she had finished, this small period room, with its little fireplace and token hearth, with its sepia-toned wallpaper and its high but narrow window onto the veranda that admitted a hazy column of antebellum light, had closed in on her and she felt the constriction in her throat. Her mother expanded to fill the confines of any room, and Annie hunkered down. Why was that? Antebellum, post-bellum, why was history always measured by its wars?

After lunch, over her mother's first cup of coffee and Annie's second, Annie let her thoughts hang inquiringly in the air. "And so you never really got to see the city. . . ."

"The city?"

"Madrid. You just sat with the body . . . where? in the morgue or the embassy, and never really got to see anything. That seems like a shame. If Dad'd been with you, you could have taken turns and at least had a chance to look around."

"Annie, stop it." Her mother affected a wearied tone.

"I'm serious. I want to know what it's like. A big city with a lot of noise, or does it have some special charm?"

Her mother lowered her head. They had the room to themselves. A young couple of good, solid, traditionalist stock rocked in the rockers on the veranda and, if she knew anything about the type, dreamed of finding an old mansion like this and restoring it themselves. Five years, they could even see ten, working on evenings and weekends with their careers in full stride, and they'd have it. All it took was the commitment, and they excelled at commitments. Responsibilities? It'd be a responsibility, a house like this, high on the historical register. They had responsibility leaking from every pore.

"I know it's a lot," her mother conceded, speaking into her coffee cup. "You lost a sister and then your parents split up. A bomb goes off in some foreign city and everything changes, overnight. Blame it on the terrorists if that's what it takes. But this is something you've got to get over and go on with your life." Her mother looked up, the eyes moist and heavy in their sockets. "I know that's easy to say."

Annie got up, walked around the table and embraced her seated mother around the heavily fleshed shoulders. Their eyes never met. She sat back down and, still looking to the side, reached out and squeezed her mother's hand.

"Tell me about Madrid."

"Do you know where he is, Annie?"

"He calls. He's taking a break. He calls it his 'interlude.'"

"How does he sound?"

"He sounds . . . he sounds like he's regaining his strength."

"Where is he?"

"I don't know."

"You're keeping him for yourself?"

"I don't know where he is."

"But not lost."

"Madrid, Mother."

"I got out of the embassy once. There was the inevitable bureaucratic delay, and they offered to take me someplace. To take my mind off it. Actually, the embassy people were nice. I said the Prado Museum."

"What did you see?"

"The Velazquez, of course."

"Did Dad like museums?"

"Not especially. He went once to the Museum of Modern Art in New York to see Picasso's *Guernica*."

"He liked Spanish art?"

"He went because everybody else did."

"And you didn't?"

"I took you and your sister to see the skaters in Central Park. Don't you remember?"

She didn't. Then she did. She remembered everything in a blazing clarity, in a cold so cold it stung. She remembered the heat in that cold, she remembered the way it shaped her face, and she remembered the fine stinging points of freedom in the air as she watched the skaters describe their effortless ovals around the ring. Then she remembered what had happened. Her mother had gone to rent skates for her sister and her. The man had handed Michelle's skates out first, and she'd raced to put them on. But he couldn't find Annie's size. Her sister had gotten the last pair anywhere near Annie's size, and Michelle, used to having her way, had been out on the ice before their mother could stop her. And Annie remembered what her mother had said. What all mothers said. She'd make it up to her. Let Michelle have her way, Annie's mother would make it up to her.

"I remember Michelle skating around and around and you and I sitting off on the sidelines watching her." And since her mother valued honesty above everything, Annie finished her thought. "I remember hoping that maybe she'd fall and break a leg and I'd have my turn."

"Neither one of you skated," her mother corrected her. "We all three sat and watched."

"No, Michelle did. We sat on a bench and you patted my leg and told me you'd make it up to me. Michelle wouldn't always be number one."

Her mother shook her head.

Annie said, "We froze."

Her mother prided herself on her tough skin because it wasn't tough skin, it was a resilient skin; it was a fresh and fearless growth and she would not be brought down. Not by the tragic violence of the times, not by her ex-husband's surrender to stagnation, and not by her daughter's—her surviving daughter's—headlong rushes when she trampled on her mother's tender feelings, which she still had in spite of her fierce survivor's code.

She rose and gathered her things. Annie had to follow her out of the restaurant and onto the brick walkways that wound among the magnolias. The heat had turned oppressive and the light harsh during the time they'd been inside. In the parking lot they stood in the additional heat of softening asphalt, and the clinging smell of tar, while her mother clicked open her car with the remote. When she finally did turn to her daughter, Annie saw how the corrosive light had left her overexposed—the scalp was visible through the hair, the crater of each pore—and how the heat made all that flesh hang on her like sacks of sand. There were those wedding photographs Annie had thrilled to. She had a premonition that what was coming was a form of good-bye.

It was a parting piece of advice.

"You have time before school starts. I'd spend it thinking about your feelings for your sister. I know how you feel about me. We have a nice little rivalry going, but that's all right because I love you, Annie, and at the end of the day I know you're going to love me back. You're sweet on your father, and that's nice too, that's the way it should be, and lucky for him—to have a beautiful, talented daughter who loves him the way you do. If anything goes badly wrong, he'll make it up to you. I will too. But Michelle can't. You either loved her or you didn't, but if you didn't there's nothing Michelle can do to change your feelings now. It seems unfair, but if anything's going to change you're going to have to do all the work. It won't be easy, but we're talking about the rest of your life. You understand that, don't you, sweetie? The rest of your life. You better begin to love your sister, or you'll end up hating yourself."

How was she supposed to do that? Give me an exercise, Mother, a tip on how to love an unapproachable sister and I'll do my best. Doubly unapproachable now, now that she was dead. Of course, being dead Michelle couldn't edit Annie's memories, but Annie's memories could present themselves so quickly that she wouldn't have time to edit them either. Michelle had grabbed that last pair of skates and raced out onto the ice and never looked back. Memories like that.

The question was—the question whose answer might have supplied her with some real tips—how had her mother found a daughter to love?

Annie stood beside the driver's door as her mother stepped up into her van. Down came the windows and on went the air. A moment later, she'd be able to lower her face into the jet of cooling air and take her relief. Similar relief awaited Annie in her father's car, but she stood loyally by until her mother had gotten hers. Would Michelle have done that? Annie might have asked her question then: the five most lovable qualities, Mother, your older daughter possessed? Or the five least unlovable, if that's the wording you prefer.

When her mother had sufficiently cooled off, she turned in the driver's seat before running the windows back up. "I have a colleague in the office. She's new, transferred from Chicago, and her son's here with her, visiting from the West Coast." She paused and gave her next words a playful, scheming weight. "San Francisco, if I heard her right." Annie didn't doubt she'd heard her right. Of the two most desirable cities in the country for her mother, Boston and San Francisco were a toss-up. "Providing you brought some presentable clothes with you back from school, I could arrange a small dinner. . . ."

"Have you seen a picture of this guy?"

"Not yet."

"Nothing on your colleague's desk? Family photos? When he was a baby, when he was a big-eared teenager with acne on his chin and when he was on his way to being a hunk?"

"I told you, she's new."

"We probably should wait."

"The pictures are bound to appear. They might be there when I get back."

"Sneak a look, okay?"

"Will do." Her mother gave a wink, which was like a mock salute. "In the meantime, see what you can do about finding a nice dress. If you want to we could do some shopping. It's been a while. It's been since," and she ran her mind down the clothes hanging in Annie's closet, wherever that might be, "that lavender dress I thought was too short for you. . . ."

"If the guy in the photo looks good enough to buy a new dress for, you call."

Her mother held her face up to the opened window. Annie leaned in for the kiss. She kissed with her eyes shut, as if she didn't want this last close-up look at what the heat had done to her mother and the air conditioning had failed to restore, or at what she, in the inconstancy of her own daughterhood, had done.

Her mother began to run the windows up.

Annie made a roll-down motion with her wrist.

"Did you really try to fix Dad up with one of your clients? Or is that just part of the legend?"

"I offered to introduce him to a woman who I thought suited him just fine. She also happened to be a woman I was hoping to sell a house to."

"Didn't work? A package deal, a house and a husband, and she wouldn't bite?"

But Annie's mother wouldn't bite either. Good for her. As always, there was a small boisterous part of Annie cheering her mother on.

"No, it didn't work. That doesn't mean I stop trying to sell houses to people who need a place to live. And that doesn't mean I should stop trying to make your father happy when it's within my means. Does it?"

Annie agreed that it didn't.

"Women love to see their ex-husbands happy and settled. It means they can turn the page." She paused a moment and added, as though passing along privileged information, "Some women do," then ran the window back up.

Alone in the parking lot, before she dealt with the heat in her father's car, Annie admitted to herself that her mother was more than one daughter could handle, and in that sense, she mourned the loss of her sister acutely. If Michelle had been alive, whom would her mother have tried to fix up with the eligible young man from San Francisco? Michelle, whose involvement with men, as far as her sister was aware, had ended with a high school sweetheart named Jimmy Spaulding? Or Annie, who was in and out of beds far more frequently than her mother knew? If, that is, there was anything in that respect her mother didn't know or hadn't imagined vividly enough that it could stand as knowledge. Michelle, who needed help, who needed supplementary experiences of almost every sort, and Annie who needed . . . what? Guidance? Call it guidance.

The truth was, she didn't want anything Michelle had had.

Her father's was the last car in the lot. She got in and closed the door and left the windows rolled up. She didn't turn on the air. Her mother was all over the place, but when she was right she was right. Annie had not come to terms with her sister because Annie was doing what she had always done, cutting her losses and letting Michelle go off and have her way. When Michelle was alive it had been a way for Annie to survive; now that Michelle was dead it was a way to pile up loses, that was all. The losses no longer redounded to her older sister's discredit. Annie was being deprived so that her sister could forge greedily out ahead? No longer. Her sister had been deprived once and for all. Now if Annie was being deprived, it was because deprivation was her middle name.

Who are you? I'm Annie Deprivation Williamson. Don't come too close or I'll deprive you of me, and me of you too.

She laughed, then she breathed down that stifling heat in her father's car. She took another quick breath—if need be she'd deprive herself of oxygen too. The logic was unassailable. If she was gasping for air now, it was because Michelle had just been here and gotten more than her share. Dead, Michelle was more hungry for air than when she'd been alive. Dead, Michelle had lured her father to Madrid, leaving Annie fatherless in a scorching parking lot in a car slow to cool down.

The air conditioner was blowing, but Annie could hear Michelle drawing those breaths. She was taking them right out of her sister's mouth. Which, of course, she wasn't.

Which, of course, she was.

A summer evening and he had been walking among the crowds around the Puerta del Sol. He'd felt some pressure from behind, a faint nudge, and then an even fainter nibbling in his hip pocket. The plaza was well lit, the crowd perhaps even more numerous than normal. Ben discovered he'd been able to whirl and, all in one motion, seize the wrist of the young man who had his fingers in his hip pocket. He'd moved so deftly that no one had seemed to notice anything out of the ordinary. The crowd flowed around them and he was left squeezing the thin wrist of a boy of no more than eighteen. When the boy tried to break and run, all Ben had to do to keep him there was squeeze some more. If he'd needed to, he felt sure he could have snapped the bones.

The boy had startled, extraordinarily alert eyes. In the streetlight's orange glow his face was jaundiced. It rose out of the shadows along the crest of the nose and the point of the chin. He had a predator's face. He looked like a fledgling hawk.

When Ben released the wrist he did so by stages, as if he were telling this would-be pickpocket, Wait, wait. Now, you can fly.

Armando Ordoki was no longer in Spain. He had gone to Brussels to plead the Basque case before the European Union. In the company of two other men he'd gone to Geneva to plead for self-determination before a United Nations commission. Afterward there'd been a press conference during which claims of torture at the hands of the Civil Guard had been made. Ordoki had been photographed there, wearing a dark windbreaker, a card of some sort attached to his lapel, his hands in his pockets, his legs spread. He fronted the camera while his two companions, also pictured, angled in, creating a triptych of which Ordoki was the centerpiece.

In one of the papers there'd been a short bio. Born in 1955. Armando Ordoki Urtain. Hometown of Eskuibar in the province of Guipuzcoa. Born into a socialist family. Member of the Eskuibar *comando* of ETA in his early youth. Fled to France when the *comando* was disbanded. Jailed in 1983 for assault and extortion. Released in 1990 after serving his sentence. Stepped out of the shadows and into the light of electoral politics. Elected representative in the Basque parliament. After rising through the ranks, assumed leadership of Borroka, a militant nationalist party, in 1997. Degree in philosophy and letters. Married, two children. Favorite pastimes: hiking, reading, walking through the town with his family.

Ben bought a Michelin road map that, unfolded, covered a good part of his bed. He found Eskuibar on a river called the Deba. It was in the mountains and looked to be roughly equidistant from the three largest Basque cities, Bilbao and San Sebastian, on the Atlantic coast, and Vitoria, the inland capital.

Armando Ordoki walked its streets with his wife and two kids. If he now lived somewhere else, as Juan, the Regina desk clerk, did, he came back on Sundays and brought his family. He'd wouldn't walk with that bear-like swagger on those streets; he'd have a different stride, and there were moments when he, Ben Williamson, on the streets of Madrid, thought he'd matched it. Lordly, at ease. A man on the way to his own coronation. *El hijo predilecto.* The town's favorite son.

Ben and Paula met at the Café Gijon at the evening hour, but they began to meet in other places too. She wanted to show him Madrid. He should think of Madrid as a hub with radiating spokes. Paula had a small car. He'd seen Toledo and Segovia. She'd show him Aranjuez and Avila and Alcala de Henares and Salamanca with its medieval university and its crown jewel, the Plaza Mayor. Follow the spokes out and she'd show him Seville and Granada and Valencia and Barcelona and Zaragoza and Pamplona . . . and he had to stop her. He didn't want to see Spain. He got in the Metro with her—as good as a blindfold—and went to her apartment, where she fed him and where, as a great consolation for whatever the first prize might have been, they made love. He didn't spend the night, but retraced their Metro route. Once they made love in the Regina, but that was neutral ground, not Paula's, and the warmth they generated between them seemed climate-controlled. Plus, Paula saw some of his clippings, the ones he'd left out on the desk. The clippings lay on the map.

He made another mistake with her. Out walking, they strayed into Retiro Park, with its wide sandy promenades full of performers and vendors and rowdy kids. Which was fine. But on the way out he let himself be tempted into that formal garden at precisely the hour when the couples took the evening's stroll, and he and Paula became one with them, up the park's main axis, around its geometrical subsidiary paths. The fountains, one in each quadrant, made their settling splash. He and Paula smelled the muted flower smells and the aging odor of the boxwood bushes. They promenaded in the timeless way the Spaniards did, and before they'd exited through that arched stone gate, it was as if he'd survived a fever during which he'd sweated out all his individuality. He remembered those processions of Goya's ghosts, massed in fungoid browns. Then those starkly drawn men, battling to the death.

He took her out to dinner, but mostly he wanted to go to her house and eat so that later they could undress in her wardrobe mirror, look at themselves and laugh, and then, united before all the breakdowns the flesh was heir to, tumble into her bed. He didn't mind that blindfolded Metro ride.

When he walked around the Puerta del Sol he kept his wallet prominently displayed and waited for a nibble in his hip pocket. He was prepared to test his reflexes against another petty street criminal.

Of the real criminals there was only one. Other ETA members would have their photographs in the paper occasionally, when they were caught, when their *comandos* were *"desarticulados."* One, a middle-aged man who'd been released from prison only to be charged again, captured Ben's attention for a few days. That man had an ashy line for a mouth and a face of such chalky pallor that he appeared to have risen from the dead. He was said to have been the most sanguinary leader of all that ETA had had. But he wasn't the criminal who counted.

Ben lost touch with himself. It was not as if he were drifting away with the crowds. He could collect himself, sit quietly apart, and still not be able to trace the thread of his life back to the man he'd been. The thread had either broken or been drawn too thin. He could remember a whole host of biographical facts, but it was as if they belonged to an acquaintance, not even a very close friend.

Paula caught it, of course. She said, "It's no use asking what's worrying you. Judging from the look on your face, I don't think you'd know."

She taught him a word, *ensimismado.* It meant to be withdrawn, turned in. Say it out loud and you could hear yourself spiraling out of sight.

"Hey, Ben," she hailed him, "when you're ready to go, just let me know, okay? We've had some good times, but this doesn't seem to be the place for you."

"I'm not ready to go, Paula." And he reached out and cupped the back of her head. Her hair was short, her head perfectly round. He might have been cupping the back of one of his daughters' heads—there was such a naturalness to the fit of his hand there.

"You're thinking about your family," she surmised.

"I haven't got a family."

"Your daughter."

"Annie'll be all right."

"You're sure?"

"You'd have to know her. She laughs a lot, but she'll never give in."

"Who's missing, Ben?"

"Her sister."

"Her sister?"

"She was killed."

There was a pause. The world went quiet around them.

"What was she like?" Paula said.

"I don't know. She was very private. She had a private vision."

"I can't imagine what it would be like to have a child and then lose her. Children should lose their parents, not the other way around. It seems like a violation of nature."

He nodded. They were talking about somebody else. Somebody he knew, not really a close friend. They watched the passing crowds. Four generations were represented, and their dogs.

She took his hand over the table. She searched him with eyes the glasses enlarged. Their blue was watery, but not the crystalline watery blue of Michelle's eyes. Not those mountain-lake eyes that could, as though through an act of intelligence, suddenly freeze over. Paula's eyes were in a constant state of thaw. The freckles were breaking down. The crooked bottom teeth were shifting. It was the secret to her warmth, this breakdown, this thaw.

"When it's over, it's over, Ben," she said. "You tell me. Like I said, I'll understand."

"No," he protested, even though he nodded.

"What is it?" Paula said.

"Why don't you have a child?" he asked.

Her expression turned wan, absent. Suddenly it was just two chapped lips. Now she'd turned away to look at the passersby.

"Is it too late? I mean biologically."

She shook her head. "Another question. Another topic, please."

"It's the only quantitative change that is truly qualitative. You're two, then you're three, and nothing will ever be the same."

She twisted back to him abruptly. He'd touched a nerve. "That's a clever way of putting it," she said, and for the first time he heard mockery, masking real temper, in her voice. "What *are* you doing here, Ben? I'm tired of these secrets. I know this: if I were down to one child I wouldn't let her out of my sight." She paused, as if she were about to apologize for such an indelicate way of putting it. Then she did it again. "If you're going by numbers, be careful when you get down to one."

He nodded.

"Don't do this to me," Paula warned him.

With his large hand he cupped the back of her head again, and she tensed against him. Her eyes sharpened and held, and for a moment they maintained this strenuous standoff.

As if on the count of three, they relented together. Her neck yielded and he lowered his hand. Any onlooker might have read it as the completion of just one more caress.

In a subdued and seemingly civil voice, she said, "You have no right to talk to me about the children I might have had. You can be as mysterious as you please and hint at some awful tragedy and make me feel a terrible pain—because I care for you, Ben. You were right. We do share something, this need for a place, I give you that. You told me I can't be a spectator forever and I told you I wasn't, but I'm enough of a spectator to know what you mean. Would a child make the difference? Maybe. A child might. But you can't come into my life dropping your hints like breadcrumbs about children of yours, touching and heart-wrenching stuff, and then tell me to get with it and have a child before the clock runs down. The only person I'm sleeping with is you. Are you proposing yourself as a father? You aren't exactly your own best recommendation, are you, Ben?"

"I'm loyal," he said.

"Are you?"

"I'm loyal to my children."

"What if I told you I'm pregnant already? Would you be loyal to a child of mine?"

The picture he saw in the wardrobe mirror was not of two people capable of making a baby. The picture he saw was of two people reaching back into their infancy to have a good time. Two baby-soft people. The little cupids that were always tumbling around Venus.

"You aren't," he said.

"If I were."

"Show me the child and I'm loyal," he heard himself say.

"Not to your daughter Annie. Does she even know where you are?"

"Not exactly."

"You mean as far as she's concerned, you *could* be on the banks of the Zambezi?"

Annie would know where he wasn't. He wasn't in a tent on the muddy banks of a river. Any river.

Still, he was loyal to Annie. He would never betray her. He was loyal to her survival. The world could come to an end, all except the cockroaches, and Annie would survive the cockroaches. He'd see to it.

"If you're not loyal to her, you're loyal to her dead sister," Paula kept it up, her reading of his mind, "which means you're loyal to a ghost. I can't talk about ghosts, Ben, it gives me the chills. What was her name?"

"Michelle."

"Michelle. It's Michelle's turn, for you to be loyal to her. Is that what you're saying?"

The names were familiar, intimately familiar—they *were* his daughters—but he no longer knew the man she was talking about. Loyal to Paula, to her freckles, round head, fading red hair, two twisted teeth, the thaw in her eyes, her warmth. "Loyal to you." He made it public, a public utterance, as he finished his wine and stood. As with all people watchers, there came a moment when he wanted to join the crowd. It was amazing, really, something in the nature of an instantaneous conversion. After being seated so long, all it took was one step and he became an object of other people's attention.

Who is that man?

He was loyal to her. She was loyal to him. The next afternoon he came back to the Café Gijon, and she was there. She was with a man. She introduced him as her ex-husband, Jorge. He had a rumpled face, a flattened nose, a disarming grin off on the right side of his mouth, and serene green eyes. When he stood it was with an effortless poise up on the balls of his feet. His shoulders were powerfully sloped. He might have been an athlete, used to pivoting this way and that.

She introduced Ben Williamson as her very good friend, and her ex-husband gripped him on the upper arm. He said, *"Hombre,"* as if he were addressing someone he hadn't seen in years, his pleasure palpable. His voice was deep; Ben heard good-natured laughter churning along its lower reaches.

This was the man who had good-naturedly divorced his wife and cut his scheming brothers off without a peseta.

This was the man who supposedly could gaze through you off into the future and see it all. According to Paula, he had the long look, an endless depth of field. She had described him as a friend's friend.

He hadn't been summoned. If Ben believed Paula, Jorge had just happened by, and this being a place where he and his wife had sometimes met, he had taken a moment to sit down with her. But while he was there he might as well provide a service. What kind of cloudy future was Ben Williamson about to step into? Jorge cleared up clouds.

He said, "What I like about America is the freedom you have to inquire into everything without feeling as if you're betraying your country. Spaniards can't do that. Americans can piece together the country they want, but a Spaniard has to swallow it all, from the Iberians and the Romans to the present day. You and Paula," and he swung his gaze over them both, "are very lucky."

It was like a blessing. He might have been placing her hand in his and sending them off.

"Everybody has their baggage," Paula reminded him. Since Jorge knew hers and she his, she must have been referring to Ben's. Ben's baggage.

"Baggage!" Jorge laughed baggage off. "We have big city dumps in Spain for baggage. We also dump a lot of baggage beside the road. We're not as clean as you are in the United States."

Jorge Ortiz had never stopped smiling at him. He appeared to be taking in at the eyes a sublime pleasure.

Jorge caught the waiter's attention and ordered a plate of mussels in paprika sauce and a cool bottle of wine. He sat a little off to the side, his chair pulled back at an angle.

Paula said, "It was the secret to Jorge's success as a hotel manager. Isn't that right, *querido?* Just how you relieve a guest of his baggage. They try to teach you that in school, but they can't."

Jorge smiled and nodded, rocking back in his chair as something, a private reference of some sort, seemed to pass between them.

"Relieve them in just the right way," Paula went on, "and you've got a guest for life."

Ben listened for sarcasm and didn't hear it. It was an admiring statement of fact.

Jorge turned his grin on his ex-wife. He wore a silky pale green shirt, open at the first button. He wore a gold chain around his neck. The neck was powerful and the visible chest hair darker than the hair on his head, which lay in thinning uncombed curls.

He said, "If you're going to leave home, you deserve the chance to step away clean. You just relieve them of their load, that's all." He turned to Ben with a sudden leap of interest in the eyes. "An author of yours, Henry David Thoreau. He watched people walking down the railroad tracks with all their possessions piled on their backs. He called it a big deformity. He said it was a metaphor for how people live their lives."

Ben had read *Walden* in high school. He remembered a man hoeing beans in rocky earth, and he remembered a man fishing in a very clear, very deep lake. Then, out of nowhere, he remembered the man's description for that lake: "God's eye."

The waiter came with the mussels and wine. Jorge took over, pouring the wine and dipping the mussel shells into the lemon and paprika sauce and holding out the first and plumpest mussel to Ben. Ben drank the sauce down, and with a tiny tug detached the mussel at the foot.

Jorge got Paula eating and drinking too. The treat was on him. He ate and drank nothing. It appeared he was about to get up and leave them to their pleasure.

Ben hurried to get the mussel shell out of his hands, the wine down his throat. "If Americans can take what they want from a country and piece together one of their own, what should I take from Spain?"

"You've found it already!" For an instant Ben thought he was referring to his ex-wife, but, motioning around him, Jorge meant this, the life on the streets. "The public," he insisted, churning that laugh up at the bottom of his voice, "Spaniards are at their best when they are on display. You can trust them then."

"And in private?"

He shook his head, clicking his tongue. That sage smile was there in a level line across the eyes. "Too much is going on."

"When are they weakest?"

"When they are strongest." Jorge paused, as though to emphasize the paradox. "They identify with their traditions, and in their traditions lies their strength. But when they are at one with their traditions they are most exposed."

Ben leaned closer.

"They are safe from themselves then, and defenseless before an outsider. Someone—"

Ben completed Jorge's thought. "—someone aware of the traditions but not commanded by them."

"Exactly."

For a moment Jorge Ortiz settled back in his chair. Ben and Paula were in no imminent danger of being deprived of his company. Jorge's eyes didn't narrow, but they took on some sort of intensity they hadn't had before, the green cleaner, less encumbered, more like a brightly faceted jewel than the iris of an eye. He looked a little oracular sitting there. But when he spoke it was more to confess a need than to prophesy.

"I'll tell you something else I like about the United States of America. You can be a renegade there. If you want to, you can escape it all. What do you leave behind—your machines and your beautiful land? But Thoreau's beautiful land was just a pond, do you see what I mean? You can find beautiful ponds everywhere. A Spaniard can't do that. We poor Spaniards are born captives. We are captives to the Iberians and the Romans and the Celts and the Moors and all the Christian soldiers. We have so much history and so many traditions it is like trying to walk through a forest of spiderwebs—you can never pick them all off. You Americans can. You can walk right up to the edge of it all and step free."

"And you don't think that can be terrifying?"

"Terrifying, yes, and maybe exhilarating too. Like a fresh start. No Spaniard can disown Spain. No Spaniard can be a renegade. Who are the most violent anti-Spaniards we have? ETA? No one is more bound to history and tradition than the Basques. All those bombs they set off? It's as if they are trying to blow themselves free. They can't—ever. They're like an exaggeration of all the rest of us. You can take that point of view, you know."

Ben nodded. You could take that point of view. He dipped another mussel in its shell into the sauce and poured himself more wine. When he met Jorge's eyes again, they had softened, that sharp, faceted green seemed shot through with sunlight. Jorge was smiling, laughing at his own bout of seriousness. He reached out to grip Ben again at the shoulder.

"*Hombre!*" he said in his rousing wealth of fellow feeling. "*Hombre.*" He modulated his tone, more an expression of compassion now, like the last knell of a bell.

After he left Ben and Paula sat a while in silence, then Ben got up and left too. Paula followed him. They walked up Alcala to the Gran Via, through thickening crowds to the Plaza de España. They continued along Calle Princesa, a narrower avenue, with more noise and exhaust. They passed three Metro stops. When they reached Moncloa, had they not veered right they would have entered a precinct of government buildings. They turned onto Calle Isaac Peral instead, where the heat caught up with them and the air-conditioned cafeterias became a temptation to stop. They kept on, Isaac Peral to San Francisco de Sales; there they turned away from the university and continued gradually uphill until they came to a park. They had been walking without pause for forty-five minutes. There was a children's playground just inside the park, with tables set out in the shade where they might have rested. They didn't. In the company of pedestrians of all sorts, including joggers, Ben led Paula along the broad walkway surrounding the park until they came to the far side, where a Civil Guard headquarters was located and, on a tight angle across from that, a carob tree whose blasted bark had had another three months to heal since he'd been here last.

"My daughter Michelle was killed here," he told her, "right across from this tree. It *was* a bomb blast from ETA. The target was that Civil Guard headquarters across the street. Michelle happened to be running by. Three years ago next month."

Paula stared at him, sweating freely, slowly nodding her head.

He added, "There've been so many ETA bombings. It'd be hard to resist making them into a comparison for anything you want. I understand." He had to catch his breath. He was winded. It was not his sadness rising up to block his throat. "But here is where the comparisons start." He chose his spot and went to stand over it on the sidewalk.

"I remember," Paula said in a stunned voice. Then she said it again: "I remember," in the awakened voice of someone recovering something buried in the past. "I thought then, 'What a horrible freak of chance.'"

"That was my daughter Michelle."

"I thought of you, Ben. I wondered who the parents of that poor girl were. You weren't just some anonymous people." She stepped up to him and placed her hand on his upper arm where Jorge had given him his parting grip. She insisted, "I thought of *you.*"

"I was in Lexington, Kentucky. I never left."

Her incredulity gave way to astonishment. She became almost fierce in her insistence. *"You!"* Suddenly she had him around the neck. She was wet all over. They stood over the spot where he'd determined his daughter had taken her last breath, and he could feel sobs rise up through Paula's back. He moved off the spot and into the shade of that tree the bomb blast had not killed.

The afternoon sun angled in over that tree and threw a glaring veil of light over the sidewalk and the line of cars and up to the door where the two boy soldiers stood in full sweltering uniform cradling their machine guns. Had Michelle not been there to take her part of the blast, this tree might not have survived. Ben broke a pod off the nearest limb, cracked it open and held it under his nose. It smelled of a rancid vanilla.

With the freckles swarming like shadows over the pallor of her face, Paula wanted him to understand. "I knew you long before you knew me. I saw you just like I'm seeing you now. I didn't see your wife, I don't know why. But you . . . This is very strange. When I thought of your grief I pictured *you.* That day you were sitting there and Leslie was talking about the animals, I knew I had seen you someplace before."

She shook her head. She seemed to feel some horrible complicity he didn't understand.

"You wanted an end to the secrets," he said. "It's the last one I have left."

She needed to sit down. The only place to sit was with her back to that tree. With his foot he tried to clear a space for her. Owners had failed to clean up after their dogs in the area, and lacking space for himself all he could do was squat beside her. Through an opening between cars he could see the two guards across the street, and they could see Paula and him. One had alerted the other, and together they regarded this middle-aged, clearly foreign couple as worthy of suspicion. One took the trouble to step up to the curb and peer threateningly into the sunlight. Of course, these boys were bored. It had been three years since one of their kind had been killed. There was a plaque there, which they had probably not bothered to read. The second you got your name written on a plaque you disappeared. Plaques just underlined the unreality of it all. What bomb blast?

Ben came out of his squat and, obeying an impulse of anger, stepped back out onto the sidewalk, then, when a young couple had passed, out onto the curb himself. He had the advantage of the sun. The guard wore a peaked cap, not the patent-leather tricorn hat the Civil Guard was famous for. He was round-faced. His eyes were narrowed in slits, his cheeks mounded into muscular balls. He had exposed nostrils and not much of a chin. For him, Ben might have been this massive, ill-defined shape stepping out of the sun. The guard raised his gun midway up his chest, and the man he threatened threw back his head and shoulders in a vaunting gesture he'd never made before. *"Que!"* Ben said in a barking growl, an equally new sound. He stepped off the curb and stood between the parked cars. With his right hand lowered flat against a car hood, which was burning, he demanded, *"Que vas a hacer, niño!"*

The guard tightened into a crouch and with the barrel of his gun motioned to his companion to join him. Then he appeared to make a similar motion to Ben. Was he taunting him into crossing the street? Instead of playing childish games, why wasn't he out shooting down ETA members and evening the score? No one had more right than Ben Williamson to cross that street and tell him so, which was what he was about to do, when Paula pulled him back. "Don't," she said, "that's not the way," and he said, "They're like children, no one remembers a thing," and she said, "I do."

As he'd led Paula to the spot, she now led him away. They took a taxi, and he knew enough of Madrid that if he'd been paying any attention at all he could have learned exactly how to reach Paula's house. But he failed to note the way. They rode the elevator up to her apartment and she sat him down on the couch. She was going to make them supper and he wondered why. He could still taste her ex-husband's mussels in lemon and paprika sauce on the back of his tongue. He was not hungry. He was not a man who could eat a meal, regard himself in a full-length mirror, then fall into bed and make love. He saw that boy with the machine gun again, dressed in a dense forest green. He had those round snorting nostrils in that pugnacious face. Not the way, Paula had said. But Paula had been sitting propped against a tree whose bark had been blasted bare. Incapacitated. Ben sank into her sofa. It had been that long walk. The sun. It was that word Paula had taught him, *ensimismado*. With a heavy displacement of weight—he was his own hillside caving in—he let himself go.

The television was on. The remote was in his hand. On the evening news Armando Ordoki was sitting at a table with two other men, the one on his left, student-aged and student-looking, with wire-rim glasses and an ascetic face, and the man on his right much older, the eyes pouched and the mouth fallen, and Ordoki, with his right index finger raised, was holding forth. Madrid's fascist government might hound the Basque patriots into hiding, but it would never destroy them, and the three generations sitting at that table offered proof. He named the man already in hiding, the man with the chalky pallor and the ashen mouth, who, in his contempt for the farce being conducted in Spain's courts, offered further proof. Ordoki leaned in over the table. Something about the Basque autonomous government collaborating with Madrid in this witch hunt. The consequences of that. His finger was raised high, and his mouth twisted in a loose-lipped snarl. His eyes shot from side to side, then stared defiantly at the camera. The flesh on his face had been brought to a boil.

Paula was sitting on the sofa with Ben. The remote was on the coffee table, the television was off, and he couldn't be sure it had ever been on. He didn't know what had happened to supper. Had they already eaten? Had she given up on it? Was she there to lead him off to bed? Paula kept her distance. She drew breaths as if she were about to speak, but when she did it was in a whisper. "I'm scared, Ben."

"You're scared."

"I don't scare easily. I've lived in this country for almost twenty years, and I'm scared."

He understood. They sat on the sofa waiting for something to happen to them. The next thing.

"I don't understand this afternoon." Her voice was like one of his daughters' when they were little girls. It was as clear as a trembling chime in a world of engulfing noise. "It was like I had to meet you. When Michelle was killed, it was like she was a daughter of mine I never had. It happened and I read about it—it was in all the news—and I said to myself, I'll never have a child if this is what happens to them. I think I decided then."

She paused. He heard her shiver. He could have moved closer, but it wouldn't have done any good.

"I don't believe in destiny," she continued. "I don't really believe in God. But something brought us together. Otherwise I wouldn't have seen you like that. You understand, don't you, Ben? I saw you! Not just any grieving father—I saw you! I saw the sadness in your eyes. I saw your shoulders. I saw the way you stood. Your empty hands."

She shuddered. She drew two breaths, but only the second got through. "That *guardia civil* could have shot you, you know. You don't know how nervous they are."

He couldn't remember how he'd come to be standing on the street, defying that boy and his machine gun. He could only remember Paula's hand on his arm, pulling him away.

"Please," she said, "call your daughter. Call Annie. I want to be here when you do. I want to hear the sound of her voice."

He owed her that. She was scared. There was death everywhere in this country she'd adopted. He did not get up, and neither did she, but her phone appeared in his hand. He pressed the numbers for Annie's phone, and nothing happened. He pressed the numbers for his own phone and heard it ring. Then he heard the sound of his own voice. "I'm not home now but I'll be happy to return your call." He let Paula hear it too. When the time came to leave a message he left that up to her. He saw that she was about to, she was about to speak, when a fine panic took control of her. If I leave my number now, what new forces am I exposing myself to? Call me back, and do I get God or Fate or some roaring animal or annihilating Chance? Ben read that in her face. She turned off the phone and hid it between them on the sofa. She kept her hand over it for a while, as if it were a shameful secret they shared. He didn't remember when she took her hand away and touched him on the cheek. By that time he must have been asleep.

X

When the phone rang she had already stepped out of the house and locked the door. Her father's car was loaded with her stuff and she was late in returning to college. What persuaded her to turn around, reopen the house, step back in and answer it? Afterward she'd tell herself there'd been a kind of desolate persistence in the ring. The kind of need that could only repeat itself. Please. Please. Please.

The woman said, "My name is Paula Ortiz. I live in Madrid. I'm a close friend of your father's. He's disappeared and I don't know where he's gone. I thought you should know." And before Annie could reply that disappearing was something her father was good at, the voice that belonged to Paula Ortiz added, "You're Annie. I know you. I know your father very well."

How well? Well enough for Annie to say, He's gone looking for Michelle. If Michelle isn't in Madrid, find out where she's gone.

She said instead, "He hasn't come back here."

"I've been waiting for this to happen," Paula Ortiz said.

Annie thought quickly. Her father and Paula Ortiz were having an affair. Her father had had enough of Paula Ortiz, as Annie had of Jonathan, and of all Jonathan's predecessors. Her father had split, but being kinder than Annie, he had made his disappearance seem mysterious, as if other forces were at work. Paula Ortiz was worried for Annie's father when she might have shown some consideration toward herself. She'd been left.

Annie said, "How was he? I mean the last time you saw him."

"The last time I saw him he was sitting on this sofa." There was such a quietness in the woman's voice that Annie had to listen closely. A quietness and something else. A stillness. A fright. "He had taken me to the park where your sister was killed. He was tired. We had walked a lot. It was hot, and . . . all the emotions. I thought something was about to happen to us all, and I asked him to call you. I wanted to make sure you were all right."

"Me?"

"I think about you a lot. Because I know he does. But to be honest, I wasn't sure you existed. I knew there was a need for you, I just wasn't sure you were there. Do you understand?"

The need for someone to exist? Did she understand that? "Where do you think he is?"

"I don't know. I can't think clearly now. He's checked out of his hotel. When he took me to that park and explained what had happened to Michelle, he told me that he didn't have any secrets left, but I don't believe him. He has a secret life, but I'm not sure he knows what it is himself. I believe he's gone off into another of his secrets. All I have left is your number because it was the last one we called on this phone."

Annie didn't know what to say. She wanted to say, If you'd called a minute later I too would have been gone, we would never have talked, and you would never know if I existed or not. Seconds, really. When lifetimes turn on seconds like that, what can you say?

Her quietness was like Paula Ortiz's quietness, and it lasted a long time. Finally Paula Ortiz said, "This is Annie Williamson, isn't it? Tell me the truth."

Annie admitted she was. It was as if she'd never truly had to identify herself before.

"And you had a sister Michelle who was killed by a bomb in Madrid."

Yes. She'd had a sister, largely unknown to her, who'd gone by that name and had been killed like that.

"I need help, Annie. I don't want anything to happen to you, but your father and I . . ."

Yes? She waited to hear more. My father and you . . . ?

"I just can't let him step off the edge of the world like this."

The edge of the world? The world is round. Wait long enough and he'll roll back around to you. It was what she'd been doing all summer.

"It's something my ex-husband said."

Is everybody somebody's ex?

"I'm sorry," Paula Ortiz confessed. "School must be about to start."

School had started. It had started five days ago. But Annie took down Paula Ortiz's phone number and address in Madrid, and then she got into her father's car and drove seven hundred miles north. Once more she'd gone off without any tapes, and once more she listened to Tracy Chapman repeating one reason, one reason, one reason. She drove interstates through Ohio, Pennsylvania, western New York, and with no man in the car to lure her off into a motel where a thankless trip could be offset with a fast fuck, she drove all day and most of the night and arrived at her apartment after two A.M. Valerie woke up and aired all her concerns—she'd doubted if Annie was ever going to come. Valerie's mother had also been worried—if Annie was not going to return to school, perhaps Valerie should begin to think about a new roommate since it was not good for her to be alone for long. And as Annie was well aware, Valerie's mother knew loneliness—she spoke and respoke, expounded and embroidered from experience. Valerie *was* lonely, but Annie arrived in a caffeine stupor that left her leaden-headed and of no use to anybody. She got only four hours of sleep.

The next day she attended three classes, for which she'd preregistered, but having missed two class days already she'd been bumped out of the two most interesting. In the third, a twentieth-century history of China, she couldn't understand the professor. He was the real thing, an exiled mainland Chinese man, who spoke with the strange clacking inflections of some exotic bird. Michelle would have sat in the first row and mastered ex-oticbirdese. Annie stepped outside and consulted the zigs and zags of their glacial-blue lake. A blue to clear your head, to bring you back to essentials. That same day—all in one day—she saw Jonathan and her Tennessee vol-unteer, Chad, across the Arts Quad. Both looked purposeful—neither was trailing along—and both looked as if they were biding their time until she appeared at their side. She went up to the bell tower that provided an overview of the university and the town, from which she could take her bearings. A spasm of self-disgust brought her down before she even reached the top. She didn't need an overview to make up her mind. She walked across the quad to the registrar's office, where she could square her-self with the university officials and save everybody time and money. Uni-versity officials had a code available for every student's trials and tribulations. It would be interesting to see which code they applied to her. She never entered the door. She walked back across the gorge to College-town, where two travel agencies had offices. She didn't enter those doors either.

Valerie stood in Annie's bedroom door and watched her recently arrived roommate pack one carry-on bag. Since Valerie never stopped asking ques-tions and mixing in dire forecasts about what was about to befall her friend, Annie really didn't have to say a thing, except "Don't tell your mother." Then she added, "Don't tell mine either." But she said nothing about where she might be going. Halfway down the stairs she remembered her passport, and even though she'd aborted every other activity she'd undertaken that day, she went back and got it. Valerie saw her do that. But Annie did not let Valerie take her to the airport. She drove there alone, left her father's car in long-term parking and paid a staggering over-the-counter sum to fly from their small town in upstate New York to Madrid. A half-hour later she was in the air, and although she had to switch planes at Kennedy, she would not turn back there. Once Annie was in the air she let them take her.

If she didn't count Canada, she'd never been out of the country. With her family she'd been to Hawaii, the island of Maui, during a Christmas break and had seen long waving sugarcane fields and tough bristly pineapple fields, and cavorting whales and iridescent schools of fish through her snorkling mask, and big glossy flowers and oiled and overweight natives performing their pageants. But in the end it was MTV in their rooms. She had gotten her passport when Michelle had gotten hers—her father had seen to that—but hers was still virgin. In Kennedy they made sure she still looked like her three-year-old picture, and then in Madrid a young man in a gray, tobacco-smelling booth pounded a blank page with a seal-affixing stamp, and she was officially abroad.

On the flight she'd sat beside a Spanish woman who had just been to St. Louis, where she'd visited her sister. This Spanish visitor to the American heartland had been on a riverboat, she'd gone to a baseball game, she'd stood beneath the arch to the golden West. She'd spoken to Annie in a mix of English and Spanish. In a test of her Spanish and nerve, Annie replied that she too was going to visit her sister, who was a student abroad, and together they would visit the great cathedral in Toledo, the even greater Moorish palace called the Alhambra, and the city of Seville, where orange trees grew along the city streets. The woman, who was from Valencia, said orange trees grew along Valencia's streets too, and even though it might not be a prime tourist attraction, Annie was not to omit Valencia from her travels. Then the woman went to sleep. When a Spanish boy across the aisle began to flirt with her, Annie risked trying out another story. She told the boy she was going to Valencia to meet her fiancé's family and was nervous about the impression she'd make. The boy taught her a line from a song: *"Valencia, es la tierra de las flores, de la luz y del amor."* In low festive voices they sang it together across the aisle until she got it right. With that line of song she'd make all the impression she needed.

At the Customs booths they all parted. The Spanish woman and the Spanish boy went off to collect their luggage, and Annie learned the first advantage of traveling light. If your travel companions were of the clinging sort, it was a surefire means of breaking free. If your ultimate objective was to be alone, you were alone.

She got into the first in a line of taxis and told the driver the Palace Hotel. She sank into the back seat and kept her eyes open long enough to see that Madrid was ring after concentric ring of high-rises growing out of an arid plain. There was almost no green, and the morning light was shattering. When she woke up they had just passed an enormous fountain, topped by a statue of some goddess riding in a chariot, and were headed up a side street that ran parallel to a six-lane avenue. Between the side street and the avenue she had all the green she wanted. Charming outdoor cafés were located there, and along a promenade people strolled. Café Recoletos was one name she remembered. Café Gijon was another. At the Palace Hotel a top-hatted doorman dressed in tails held the door for her. She had to pay the driver in dollars, which he didn't seem to mind since she was sure he'd jacked up the price. The doorman, used to informality in today's jet-setting elite, kept his composure when Annie told him, no, no luggage, just this carry-on bag. She was what he saw, wrinkled jeans and blouse, a wadded sweater she'd worn against the air-conditioned chill, uncombed, slept-on hair. She had a credit card good as gold. The Palace Hotel came at her in opulent waves, but she stood her ground and took a room overlooking another plaza, this one with a god, not a goddess, riding a chariot, standing as erect as the trident he held at his side. Gods and goddesses riding their chariots through recorded history, back into the mythic past. Europe. The Old World. The continent of the killer cornices.

When she woke it was dark—she hadn't reset her watch and had no idea of the time. Not even of the day. It didn't matter, though, because she wasn't through sleeping yet. In the interlude she did place a call to Paula Ortiz. The voice that answered sounded eager and anxious and exhausted in a way that might last for years. Or maybe that was just how Annie was hearing things these days. She told Paula where she was and the state she was in and asked her to set a time and place they could meet. Annie had been riding along on momentum she'd generated when she'd walked out of her father's front door, and it had finally run out. Paula told her the time, the day. She mentioned an outdoor café close to Annie's hotel, the Café Gijon, and Annie felt less lost, less cast adrift, since it was a place she'd identified on her own. She was to rest and regain her strength. She was to take care of herself as if she were an invaluable resource, and Paula would meet her there in the afternoon.

Her father? No, nothing.

There was a vacancy in her head, which seemed to extend around her wherever she went, but she was awake and clean and dressed in a fresh change of clothes. The second she stepped out of the Palace Hotel she entered a dailiness of life that caught her entirely by surprise. She'd known people shopping, people going off to lunch, people passing between offices, people killing time, but that had been at home and this was Madrid, Spain, where the ordinariness of things suddenly seemed extraordinary. A sweater in a shop window could possess a special luminosity. A bouquet of carnations could. Hardware—plumbing joints and drain pipes and lavatory fixtures—was no longer the stuff of the utilitarian world. In her jet-lagged vacancy, she let herself be carried along. She might find herself in a small plaza, with a fountain and a sycamore and a statue of some saint, where that ordinariness seemed enshrined, or she'd pass along arcaded walkways and emerge into much larger plazas, presided over by kings on horseback, where the sunlight flooded down on her like a hot, dry and very public bath.

She passed a large restaurant-deli of some sort called the Museum of Ham, where hams from all regions of Spain hung from hooks in the ceiling and dripped their last drops of fat into little paper cups. She fed the vacancy in her stomach there, ham from Extremadura and slices of cheese from La Mancha, little rounds of bread and a glass of red wine. She sat in a park that looked across an avenue to a palace. Older women walked their dogs, and younger people, people her age, dressed like her, some with nose and lip rings and some with tattoos, tattoos like hers, sat and sprawled on the benches or stretched out in the sparse grass or strolled in front of her with their fingers hooked into each other's hip pockets. As she had done. What was the difference?

She found a store and shopped for something to carry, just to see how it felt. She bought a small moleskin notebook and a pen. She paid with her credit card, a transaction so routine she felt a sudden kinship with the woman who carried it out for her. At a café close by she ordered an espresso and, in the space headed, "In case of loss, please return to," wrote her name in the notebook. Annie Williamson. The address she gave was not the Palace Hotel's but Paula Ortiz's. She wrote Paula Ortiz's name. Then she wrote her father's. Then, shaping the letters as deliberately as if she were incising them, she wrote her sister's name, Michelle Williamson.

Paula Ortiz was waiting for her when she found her way down to the Paseo del Castellana and the Café Gijon. Paula's face was freckled, and Annie had always had a special fondness for freckles. She'd never seen a mean-spirited person with freckles, except for one boy, whose hair was so red it flamed out at you. Paula's hair was red like the last glow of an ember, softened by a scattering of ash. She wore a gauzy blouse and skirt, of a pale gray-green, that trembled in the breeze. Her glasses magnified her eyes and gave their blue an aquarial glow. When Annie approached, Paula stood, and Annie saw the weight she carried, nothing like her mother's, which was an exercise in transportation every time she moved, but a ripeness of weight along the neck, in the bare freckled arms. She could imagine her father holding Paula Ortiz.

Still, this wasn't the only woman here. Others were sitting singly or in groups at the tables, and some of them were stunning, women of the fantasy sort a daughter might once in her life be willing to wish on a father.

"Are you Paula Ortiz?"

"Annie."

They sat. On one side traffic surged by. Annie had been in one of those taxis the day before, or perhaps days before that. On the other side the foot traffic of Madrid passed in a steady stream. Paula asked how she felt, if she was hungry or thirsty, and tried to determine the hours of her jet lag. If she were still home, on campus, she'd be between breakfast and lunch. Whether Annie, who'd almost never traveled, knew it or not, she was in two places at once.

Paula mothered her just a bit. She ordered a ration of *sepia a la plancha*, a dish the Spanish loved. But there came a moment when Paula couldn't help herself. She gave up small talk and mothering and gazed at the young woman in front of her. She searched over Annie's features. Had she been a doctor she might have peered into her nose, ears and throat. In that moment of fine, itemizing abandon, she actually reached out and stroked the ends of Annie's long brown hair, rolling the thickness of a strand between her fingertips.

Annie said, "Michelle looked like him. Michelle had that sunny openness in her face, although that's not how she was. I don't look like either one of them."

But I am Annie Williamson.

"I know you're his daughter, though," Paula said.

"How? How do you know?"

"Because of all the things he wouldn't say about you. I know it sounds strange, but you're just like the things he kept to himself."

It did sound strange, but she understood what her father's friend and lover meant, because he was just like the things she kept to herself. Knowing those things, she couldn't imagine him any other way.

"Whether I exist or not, his need for me does. That's what you said on the phone."

"Yes."

"What do you think he needs me for?" Annie asked.

Paula shook her head. When Annie's mother shook her head in that way it meant Annie had dumbed down or, for reasons of her own, was playing dumb, and her mother wasn't going along. Paula shook her head like that, and it meant there just weren't any words. "Life," she said. "A reason to go on."

It was a heavy burden to bear. "There've got to be other reasons."

Again Paula shook her head. "A woman knows," she said in a sad and considered tone that would have caused Annie's mother to cringe. If knowledge meant surrender it might be better to really be dumb or play dumb, just stay dumb at all costs. Paula met Annie's eyes across the table, then covered her hand with hers. "*You're* his reason to go on."

Paula applied a calming pressure to her hand. Annie knew boy-girl jealousy. She knew how a girl looked at you when you'd taken her boyfriend away, and on one occasion, at least, she knew with what powerless scorn she'd looked at a girl. Paula Ortiz could have been her father's reason to go on; instead, Annie was. What she felt in the warmth of the older woman's hand was not rivalry and not a questioning, nor was it the protectiveness a mother feels for a child; it was not a mother's defeated longing to live through a child, which could get very intense if you happened to be Valerie and Valerie's mother; it was not a clinging and it was not a sisterly act of seeing a friend through a bad stretch; it was not like any kind of closeness Annie had ever felt before. She reminded herself that she was tired, not fully recovered from her trip, not reassembled, as if she really were in two places at once. She was vulnerable and on foreign soil.

Annie said, "How do you know he's not coming back? It's only been . . . how many days?"

Again Paula shook her head. A woman knows.

"He called it 'an interlude,'" Paula said.

"That's how he described it to me too."

"He came to see the spot where your sister was killed, and then he went away. In between we had our moment. I won't call it a 'fling.' That's too stale a term, like some old dance routine. Like one of those old love songs. 'Interlude' probably is the best word."

"He liked those old songs, you know."

Paula shook her head again. Annie Williamson would have to have been there in Paula Ortiz's skin, age, say, forty-five, and she hadn't been. She'd been home, waiting for her far-ranging father to roll back around.

"Will you show me where Michelle was killed?"

They took a taxi to a park, where Paula told the driver precisely where they wanted to be let off. It was around this park that her sister had run before she went to class, so it had been early in the morning, when not as many people were out—Annie had to imagine it differently. Paula led Annie around a corner and down a side of the park with trees on one side—tall pointed cypresses and their opposites, squat, crooked-limbed trees with brown, arthritic-looking pods—and on the other a long brick-and-concrete building that reminded her of a prison since it had guard towers on the corners.

At the main entrance were two guards, young, perhaps no more than her age. They were squinting into the sun. A passing cloud cast them in a moment's shadow and Annie felt the urge to wave.

"They aren't the same as the other day," Paula said, sounding relieved. "I was afraid one of them might shoot your father."

"Why would he want to do that?"

Paula shook her head. "Your father wasn't himself."

Recalling the sound of Paula's voice on the phone that day when she'd been seconds away from walking out of her father's house, recalling the whispering stillness and the fright, Annie asked, "And you? Were you yourself?"

"I'm better now. There was a moment . . ."

A moment . . . when?

". . . when my imagination ran away with me."

Then Paula made a vow. "It won't happen again."

She pointed to a particularly disfigured tree; she plotted a line out to a spot on the sidewalk, then went there to stand while pedestrians passed by them. At a break in the foot traffic, Annie stepped out to join her.

She hated the spot at once. It smelled faintly of dog shit and exhaust and cheap cologne. Maybe something those boys were wearing under their heavy green uniforms. She knew her father had stood here thinking the same thing, and that only made it worse because the spot, closer to the park than the barracks but between the two worlds, had taken her father too.

"Here? Right here?"

Paula nodded. "According to your father. According to Ben."

They were standing there looking down at the sidewalk when one pedestrian didn't pass, but stood back from them, as if back from a mourner's front row, looking down at the sidewalk too. She was a tall woman, taller even than Annie, except she was slightly stooped, which gave her a hollowed-out appearance and the look of a woman who might nurse a worry over the years. Her eyes were large and seemed dulled with strain. She wore a sweater against a nonexistent chill.

"Are you Americans? By any chance do you know a man named Ben Williamson?"

The sound of her father's name, spoken in that polite inquiring tone, seemed intrusive to Annie in a way she couldn't account for, and she felt herself recoil. Perhaps she just didn't like the idea that there were now three women with Ben Williamson on their minds.

"I don't mean to interfere, it's just that you're standing here, where . . ." The woman paused, cast a troubled glance down at the sidewalk, then back up to Annie. She sighed and let her shoulders fall. With tiny shakes of the head she admitted defeat. But the head-shakes set off an even tinier clashing of the absurd bronze earrings she wore, a sound that roused Annie in a way she couldn't check.

"Here where his daughter was killed? By a bomb, three years ago?"

She didn't have to be mean. "Stingy" was the word. She could have been generous with her grief.

"Yes," the woman replied quietly.

"But *I'm* his daughter," Annie almost crowed. "He had two, you know. One a backup to the other."

It was then that Paula came to her relief. Perhaps Paula was just em-barrassed. She introduced herself and she introduced Annie. Annie was emotion-racked, exhausted after a long trip, and very young, but two middle-aged women could make allowances and restore an air of civility like that. Like that! Annie heard her mother's fingers break off a come-to-attention snap all the way across the Atlantic. She glanced over at the two boys guarding that barracks or prison, or whatever it was. They were slouched. She was tempted to cross that street and see if she could straighten them up. Put some iron up their johnsons.

Instead she listened to Paula Ortiz and the woman whose name was Madeline Pratt talk about her father. Madeline was director of the program Michelle had attended. It had been Madeline who had first brought her father to this park to show him the spot where Michelle had been killed. Since then, instead of trying to forget what had happened, she'd found herself coming back. She'd thought a lot about Ben Williamson, too, and won-dered what had happened to him. The truth was, she'd worried. That time she'd brought him here she'd left him in such a state . . .

"What kind of state?" Paula asked.

"He was very angry. He wanted to shout at me, but it was all bottled up inside and I could see he was shouting at himself."

"Yes," Paula murmured, "I've seen him like that."

Madeline turned to Annie. "I wanted to help him, but he wouldn't let me. I didn't even know where he was staying, or I would have called to see how he was." She added, with measured self-reproach, "I suppose I could have found out."

"When he decides to disappear," Annie had to offer some consolation, she wasn't an utter shit, "there's not much anybody can do."

Madeline smiled. Then she shivered—anybody could see that she was in a weakened state. "I'm so sorry about your sister," she told Annie. "Stu-dents have to have their independence. Your sister was very . . ."

"Responsible?"

Madeline nodded. "I just want you to know there was nothing anybody could have done."

She seemed about to cry, and Annie touched her arm. "It wouldn't have made any difference. Michelle would have demanded her rights and gotten them. If she came out here running, she had a right to, and she was right to exercise that right. That's how she saw it. Throw her out of your program and she'd petition to get back in, and she'd get back in. . . ."

"That never crossed my mind, believe me," Madeline protested. "She was an ideal student."

"I know she was," Annie quietly submitted. She actually made a little bow. "It's weird, isn't it, people walking by, like they live lives just like ours. That's just the sort of thing Michelle wouldn't wonder about, not for a second. That's what I mean. They have their lives and she had hers. Well, she *had* hers."

Again Paula stepped in to rescue her from her colliding emotions. She said, "Ben has gone away, Madeline. We think he's somewhere in Spain. But he could be anywhere. When you talked to him, was there anything he said . . . ?"

Madeline raised her head and looked off past the pointed tops of the cypresses. "He wanted to come here," she said. "He said if I brought him here and showed him the spot he'd leave me in peace. I got the idea no other place in the world was important to him then."

"And you didn't talk about anywhere else?"

"The Basque country because he asked about ETA."

"Where in the Basque country?"

"No particular place."

"What did he want to know?"

"What everybody wants to know. How the Basques could continue to let ETA kill in their name."

"What did you tell him?"

"That I didn't know." Madeline paused. She turned inward and drew a long breath. "I've never felt right about leaving him that day. I could see that I wasn't going to do him any good, but I thought it was my duty to stay . . . I don't mean 'duty.'"

"No, not 'duty.' I understand," Paula said.

"I come back to see if I can find him again. Mostly in the mornings."

"And you haven't?"

"No, but I think he's been here. Don't ask me why I think that."

"No."

"Those guards over there. Have you noticed, they're always boys."

"Yes."

"It was a boy who was killed. The waste . . . it's just sad, you know. . . ."

Madeline shook her head again, with more futile anger now. She turned to Annie. Annie wasn't used to seeing administrators break down, their emotions working up through that mask of efficiency they wore, and she wondered if it was her duty to lead this one back to her office and sit her behind her desk.

"Please forgive me," Madeline begged of Michelle Williamson's bereaved sister. "I shouldn't have intruded like this."

"It's all right," Annie said.

"It's something I have to work through alone."

Both Annie and Paula murmured their protests, but neither offered to take up her cause.

The three of them looked down again. Urban concrete. The swellings and tiltings, the cracks and stains of use. A lesson in the trampling ongoingness of life—and at least one death. With their heads still bowed to the spot, Madeline said, "Eventually he'll come back here."

W aiting for a taxi, Paula told Annie that she disagreed. She didn't think Ben would return to Parque Santander. Madeline Pratt's talk of ETA had recalled to her a time she'd been in his hotel room—where they'd gone to make love, Annie assumed. There Paula had seen newspaper clippings on ETA and on one leader in particular, a man named Armando Ordoki, a name that sounded as if it belonged to two different people, Annie thought. Armando was a Latin gallant from a bygone day and Ordoki a snub-nosed bully who smelled of a barnyard. These clippings had been lying on top of a map of Spain. In the cab driving back through the city, Annie shared with Paula what her father had said to her the last time they'd had dinner together. He had advised her or himself or the world around them "to dig in to face the day that was sure to come." That was not the kind of thing her father would normally say. But he'd said it with, as far as she could remember, no self-consciousness for the melodrama of the phrasing or the portentousness of the tone. She'd laughed at him, she confessed to his lover. He had provided her with a laugh.

Nonetheless, here was a day that had come, and Annie was nowhere close to being dug in.

She was tired. She had to rest. The next day they would decide what to do about her twice-missing father. But from the Palace Hotel, where Paula had let her off, she began to walk. In the plazas there was still some daylight, but in the narrower streets it was already dark. When she was a kid on her bike she'd played a game with her friends called "Coin Corner." At every corner they came to they'd flip a coin: heads they'd turn to the right, tails to the left; they weren't allowed to turn back or go straight ahead. Occasionally they'd end up in the country, where they wouldn't come to another corner for miles. Once, she remembered, the luck of the coin toss had had them circling home in a right-angled spiral. There'd been another time when they'd all gotten lost down by the river and she'd had to stop in a bait shop and call her father. But that had been all right. They hadn't disobeyed; they'd obeyed the toss of that coin. Michelle, of course, had never played. She wouldn't allow one minute of her life to be determined by a coin toss. The coin Annie and her friends had used was a quarter, and the head that directed them, big and shiny enough to see in the dark, belonged to George Washington, father of the country.

She decided she needed a guide, and the first she chose was a proud, up-right man with a pelt of black hair shining down his neck. She followed him until he came to a door where he growled, "Pedro," into an apartment intercom and was buzzed upstairs. Next a very thin girl, pale, un-Spanish, hair a phosphorescent blond, shivering in a minidress, led Annie on a quick-march into a bar where she pleaded with a burly man, who could have been her father, or a pimp, for money, which he finally gave her. The girl clattered back into the streets on elevator heels and disappeared. There was a young man Annie's age whom she followed because he had a re-signed, almost restful look on his face, until he met up with another whose resignation just seemed dull to her, more the result of sloth. They stood on the sidewalk talking—about computers, she believed. To get away from them she chose an elderly man dressed in a sort of jacket-shirt that looked vaguely tropical. His cologne was as sharp as smelling salts. She heard him muttering something to himself at set intervals that sounded like *"bueno . . . bueno,"* and she noticed that no one got in his way. Up a darker cross street with no stores and few bars, he stopped in front of a tall door, whose wood was so old it looked petrified. Above it she noticed the weather-corroded form of what might once have been an escutcheon. He opened a small door in that tall door, and the cool mustiness of a stone courtyard flowed out at her, mixed with his cologne. Once he'd stepped in-side, he turned to her. In the shadows, he had a narrow face of long hard lines, ridge lines, something shaped by the elements, and eyes giving back a sharp black light. "Lineage"—she thought of the word. The face of a conquistador; eyes as black and cutting-fine as obsidian. What you came to Spain for. *"Le puedo servir en algo, señorita?"* he said like a true *caballero*, but with a history of cruelty in his tone.

She backed away from him, not intending to offend. She was only looking for something else. Returning to a better-lit street, she thought she saw her father ahead, his shape at least, those familiar, slightly sagging but not yet broken-down lines. She didn't. It wasn't anybody she saw. She stepped into the near-dark of cross streets and came out at a Metro stop where a number of bars were located; the small plaza they fronted was covered with tables. Her father had been here, at this cozy little hot spot of Madrid night life. She'd bet on it. Doing what? Searching the faces of the boys and girls her age clustered around the bars and then going over each of the tables out on the plaza, lit by the streetlights' orange glow. A parchment-orange glow, just the right light for this Old World nook. Looking for? His daughter, Michelle, of course. Annie too found herself going over the tables. She saw groups of girls she identified as Americans because those were the shoes and socks and designer jeans, the name-brand tee-shirts and college-embossed sweatshirts, the ponytails and orthodontically straightened teeth they wore. She went to a bar open onto the street and ordered a gin and tonic from the bartender, although waiters were serving the tables. She took it with her and sat at a table where there were three girls and a vacant chair awaiting a fourth.

She introduced herself. No, she was not in an abroad program but did attend a quality university, which she named, and that was cool. She was here on a self-assigned sabbatical to scope out the scene. That was even cooler. That made her an object of envy. Maybe she'd do a survey of these abroad programs in all major European capitals. In that case, she'd want to know, Why Spain? That was not so cool, not if they had to defend their choice of country to her as they'd done in paragraph after bullshitting paragraph on all those application forms. But they'd try. At least one of them would. This was a girl named Susan, with glowing cheeks, a turned-up, glowing nose, a pink and glowing tongue tip. Spain was this and Spain was that. The old and the cutting edge side by side. Families who went by tradition and families who went by the latest fad. Boys who thought they were *toreros* and boys who were more technologically advanced than boys in the States. The classes at the university could be a bore, but there was this awesome life on the streets, which was a university in itself. That was the real reason to come to Spain. Susan swiveled around to take in this plaza, snuggled down in its rectangle of modest apartment buildings.

"And ETA?" Annie said. ETA? they wondered. "Yeah, you know, ETA, those guys that blow awesome places like this up and don't mind killing the odd American when they do it."

"ETA is a Basque problem," another of them said. "We don't go to the Basque country."

"Give them enough time," Annie told them, "and ETA will come to you."

They turned away from her then, even Susan, who gave her that drop-jawed look that asked, How could you bring up ETA after we've been so sweet to you?

"Armando Ordoki?" Annie overpronounced both halves of the name. "Armando" with a swoon. "Ordoki" with an oinking grunt. "Anybody heard of him?" Like a teacher tapping her chalk on the blackboard to get a wayward class's attention, she had to tap her glass on the metal table to get theirs.

"Armando Ordoki," the authority among them finally said, "is not ETA. He's the leader of Borroka," which, for Annie's information, meant "the struggle." "You should pay a little attention to current events."

"ETA, Borroka," Annie shrugged, "what's the difference?"

She entered the Metro and stood before its color-coded map of the city. There were ten subway lines, ten colors, and the longer she looked at the map, the more they came to resemble an elaborately designed swastika. She located herself on the lime-green line at the plaza of Chueca. From there she branched out. When she actually bought a ticket and stood waiting for a train, she had a detailed abstract of the city in her mind. The trains were more than half full, but she paid no attention to the people. The people were up on the streets. The lime-green to the fuchsia to the cobalt-blue to the yellow to the red to the battleship-gray. When she came up for air she was half a block from a park, which, as she approached, she thought she recognized. Had she meant to return here? She had not. She hadn't even known the park's name. It was large, perhaps the equivalent of three city blocks, and except for a handful of lonely lights, dark in its interior. Walking its perimeter you passed out of the shadow and into the light again and again. You did this until you came to the spot, which you could locate exactly if you could plot a line from that barracks door to the scarred tree. But she couldn't be sure of the tree; the one she picked out was so gnarly and rough there was no way to tell in the dark where its roughness was due to unnatural causes. If there had been guards in front of the barracks, she might have asked them. But the guards were gone. The city was teeming everywhere else, but here at the moment there were no passersby. That jet-lagged vacancy she'd started the day with was back on her. Love your sister or end up hating yourself, had been her mother's parting advice. As her exhaustion carried her closer and closer to Michelle's disembodied state, Annie could turn the tables and say, All right, Michelle, you've been a shade longer than I have. If you love me—if *you* love *me*—you'll come out of hiding and clue me in. They'd played hide-and-seek as girls, but sooner or later Michelle would just go off and not come back. A gamer, Annie would look for her and look for her before giving up in a loser's disgrace. Here they were again, in a foreign country, playing the same game. The only difference was that they were both twenty-one. Annie had caught up with her sister and had a right to demand that Michelle show her face. Hide-and-seek. She felt like a child, but she was so fucking far from home she had to find somebody. Being bitterly honest, though, she could admit that she didn't care if Michelle stayed dead another three years, as long as she could find their dad. But she didn't like being bitterly anything. It was not her style.

XI

He became a tourist, after all the years.
He was a tourist of train rides. In a light that was clear, equable and gray, he looked out his window and saw granite boulders encrusted with lichen, swaths of seasonal ferns, plots of sunflowers with their heads burned black; a perspective opened and he saw a plain, crossed in the middle distance by paths of an alkaline white. The train climbed, entered a tunnel, and when it emerged he looked out over an upland basin with yellowed poplars marking the course of streams. The basin was a natural pocket, before the age of tunnels an all but impregnable enclave, and as any tourist might, he thought of the fiefdoms of Old Castile, its history of high-mindedness and hard Christian steel.

The train crossed a river. It crossed the basin and entered a defile.

At close hand he saw a town rising out of the dirt and rock, a town the color of dirt and rock, except for the aged gold of the lichen-spotted tiles and the red tile of an anomalous new roof.

The defile deepened. More tunnels. Blackberry brambles when the train reentered the light. More blackened heads of sunflowers. More ferns, a cidery gold. Overlooking the tracks a low Romanesque church with a bell gable, within which he saw the bell and beyond which he saw the sky.

Ascending, another tunnel, another upland basin, already green with winter wheat.

Little stubs of towns, gathered around their churches.

A sheepherder and his flock of sheep, shaped by the darting feints of his dog.

Vineyards, gravid with grapes. Bunches being cut from the vine, heaped into woven baskets.

Truck yards, high-rises, building cranes, a lush green football field. They were entering a small city. A river flowed under the tracks with a steady, untroubled current. He saw the town's name. Arando de Duero. The river that watered half of Castile, gave its name to its wines.

Beyond, utter flatness, high and wide. To the west a vanishing horizon, to the east a barely perceptible wrinkling of the land.

He took advantage of the sameness and went to sleep. He awoke to the name "Burgos" being called over the train's speakers. Beyond some track-side warehouses, he saw twin cathedral spires, spiky with protrusions. But he didn't really wake up until the train came to a dead stop in the middle of the country and he looked out the windows to see workers repairing a parallel track. One of the rails had been ripped apart. Its ends curled up. He had never seen iron curled like that, as if the rail were as pliable as a paper clip. A tourist, and no physicist, he asked himself what force.

Night fell as the train was about to move up into the throat of a jagged pass. They entered the town of Pancorbo. In the last light he was able to make out on the crumbling station walls the spray-painted words *Puto Madrid*.

From that point until he arrived at his destination, he traveled with the reflection of his own peering face imposed on the rushing darkness.

He was a tourist of provincial cities.

Vitoria, capital of the autonomous Basque country. He was surprised by Vitoria's beauty. He must have been expecting something industrial and gray. The gray was there, the buildings on the city's main street, Calle

Dato, were faced with granite, but all of them had glittering bay windows, *miradores*, extending from the ground floor to the mansard roofs, whose sashes were freshly painted white. It was like walking down a canyon vertically veined with jewels. Men and women stood out before the *tapa* bars with their tumblers of red wine and their food. The canyon was a river of rich arousing smells.

The hotel he found rated only one star; the window in his room looked down into an interior well. Two framed prints hung on the wall. One was of a pretty street of white houses with charming iron balconies and red geraniums, somewhere in the south. The other was of a church façade, as imposing and austere as a cliff face, streaked by rain. Surely, the north.

He entered another street, Kalea Cuchilleria. *Kalea* must have been the Basque word for street, but the signs and banners he saw hung there, with all their X's and Z's, G's and T's, were unintelligible to him. This was a poorer, more dimly lit street, built on a gradual decline; it was lined with bars and inexpensive restaurants and one-room groceries. Most of the bars had a garish discotheque lighting. But there were others, bars that were plainly lit, hard-edged, and seemed to give off an uncompromising chill. Some had photographs in the windows, of young Basque men and women, under each of which a name was printed and a date in the past. He recognized these faces. They weren't the mug shots he'd seen in the newspapers, but they stared straight ahead out of eyes that might never have blinked. Whatever mercy they revealed was reserved for a future date.

Outside one of these bars, he stood reading a notice posted beside the door, written in both Spanish and Basque. The notice informed him that this was an establishment that valued free speech, and that lately police had been entering with the express purpose of denying patrons that privilege. In passing they ripped down posters and subjected customers and management to various kinds of abuse. He entered. Posters were still up—perhaps the police hadn't been here in a while. There was a large composite photograph on the wall to his right made up twenty-nine small photographs. He counted them. One was of a young woman with her head thrown back. She appeared to be laughing. A breeze appeared to be blowing her dark hair. Five of the twenty-nine had a black slash across them and the word *"Etxean"* written there. Dead, he assumed. Or maybe disgraced.

Two young women were sitting in back at the bar. They were speaking a language that seemed rough-hewn from the air. The only other patrons, a man and woman in a booth in the front room, looked as if they were keeping some sadness to themselves, perhaps a parting. The bartender, a young man, served Ben his glass of wine.

Ben alluded to the notice outside and asked the bartender what it was the police did, the abuses, what was the worst, and the young man nodded, as if this thoughtfully inquiring tourist, who might have been undercover police himself, had come to the right place. "They torture us for our beliefs," he said. "They don't want us to look like ourselves because we stand for everything they don't, and when they look at us they see their shame. So they do that," and he directed his patron's attention to the poster on the wall at his back.

It was another composite, but made up of only three photographs and all of the same man. The "before" was of a round-faced boy of perhaps twenty, with an alert and unwavering but undefiant gaze. He wore a striped collarless shirt, buttoned to the top. His neck was unmarked. There were two "after" photographs. In the first the boy wore a neck brace and a white shirt or gown of some sort. His face was badly swollen and, except for the area around the mouth, which had a nocturnal pallor, colored a raspberry red. At first glance he seemed to be wearing sunglasses; a closer look revealed that the area around his eyes had been beaten black and that the skin had a glossy sheen easy to mistake for glass. In the third photograph the back of this boy's head was pictured, and a sizable chunk of his hair had been ripped down to the white of the scalp. This boy had a name, Unai Romano. The Basque word for "torture" was a borrowing, as if the concept was meaningless until the Spaniards came along: *"torturak."* The text continued in Spanish: "100 prisoners were tortured this year alone. After seeing this, what are you going to do?"

A tourist of tortured Basque prisoners.

Ben asked, "This Unai Romano, what did he do? What did they accuse him of doing?"

The bartender shook his head. "Of belonging to a subversive organization," he said. *Una banda armada.* "They do that and think we won't recognize ourselves. One day they'll do that to me."

"The Civil Guard?"

The bartender nodded. "The Spanish national police too. The Basque police—our own police torture us. As soon as you cross the border, the French police. They all take turns. They're like occupying armies competing to see who can do the most harm."

"ETA?" Ben said.

The bartender smiled.

"ETA didn't protect him." Ben signaled over his back to Unai Romano, bruised beyond recognition.

The bartender smiled.

"How do you know I'm not police?" Ben asked.

"I watched you reading our notice beside the door. I saw you looking at the faces in the photographs, those of us who are in Spanish prisons. I saw the way you looked at them," the bartender gestured to the girls, "and I saw the way you looked at me. You're not police. You're someone else."

"Who?" Ben was keenly curious in that moment.

"Someone who wants to know the truth."

"A hundred prisoners tortured this last year is a very round number. What if it's a lie? What if it's only him, Unai Romano?"

"It's not."

"But what if it is?"

"If it is, it's as bad as a hundred. It's a hundred all in one."

"If it's just one," Ben said, "then it won't happen to you. That's what I mean."

"It will," the bartender said.

The bartender was no more than a boy.

A tourist of Basque boys counting the minutes until they become disfigured men?

He continued on a bus up winding valley roads. The valley rose in terraced steps. These were unrocked, grassy elevations; on the lower and broader ones cattle grazed, above them sheep. The grassed terraces formed pleasing patterns with the forests of pine and spruce. Where the trees had been lumbered, reforestation had taken place, and the young trees neatly planted in rows gave the whole hillside a combed look. There were no crags, no inaccessible peaks.

He might have been in Switzerland. On neutral ground.

The small river running down the valley was called the Duna. Built on its banks he saw the same town again and again. Narrow, long and tight, the highway on one side and train tracks on the other. Lumber mills and steel mills, a few still running, at the extremes. The nucleus, a small *plaza mayor*, a church, he assumed a town hall and frequently a two-walled court of some kind where a game like handball might have been played. Apartment buildings built tall and in close proximity to take advantage of the limited space. Housed at such close quarters, an apartment dweller might hear his neighbor's whispers. Only those people who lived in apartments whose balconies overlooked the river might be able to take a breath entirely their own. Except that the river gave off a whiff of sewage, its color a murky gray-green.

Wash hung from those balconies. It would have the river's smell.

Entering the towns he saw signs, erected by the Basque department of tourism, welcoming visitors. Of the four languages these signs were written in, all but the Basque language had been spray-painted out.

The name of the town of Mondragon was spray-painted out and only its Basque name, Arrasate, remained visible.

The bus reached the river Deba and followed it northwest to the small city of Eibar, no different from the towns he'd passed through except that two streets, not one, ran its length, and its length was long. The bus let him off and he found the city's only hotel, around the corner from its plaza and park. The desk clerk was a solemn-faced woman of surprising sweetness, who welcomed him to her city and offered to do whatever it took to make him feel at home.

He gave her his passport, and she gave him a room high enough to see beyond the tenement in front and the train tracks to the steep valley wall where buildings clung, one with a *mirador*. There was no luster left in those panes of glass and little paint left on the sash. He opened his suitcase and took out a tan windbreaker. He placed the suitcase on the luggage rack. Then, to take possession of the room, he inserted his bus ticket and yesterday's train ticket into the crack between the mirror and its frame.

He went back to the lobby and, since she was so eager to help, let the desk clerk find him the best transportation to a nearby town. A bus was available, but the best way, she informed him, was to take the train, which came through on the hour. In the direction of San Sebastian.

Close. *Al lado.*

He became a tourist of trains again, with local stops.

The town of Eskuibar had a small, wedge-shaped industrial park at the near end, a swelling before the midpoint where the church, Town Hall and main plaza were located, a long, tapering section where commerce took place and middle-class residents lived, and at the far point a squeezed-in area that was squat and monochromatic and hung with wash, which he assumed to be the workers' quarters.

Past that the valley narrowed and curved out of sight.

Ben stepped down from the train. With a town so narrowly built, he had to take only a few steps more before he stood in the Plaza Mayor. Of the mountain peaks, the tallest rose to the northwest. A radio or television antenna had been erected there on an outcropping of rock, the only rock he saw on the mountain rim. At every other point to the west the rim was forested. To the east, where the angle of ascent was gentler, those terraced pastures might reach all the way to the top. In the sunlight their green was lush.

The strollers among the athletic Basques would go to the east. The climbers to the west. He remembered: the Basques' need to ascend, to form manly clubs, climb their mountains and plot.

He took his bearings. One street, San Agustin, seem to run the length of the town, and another, San Blas, partway. He walked San Blas first, two banks, an elementary school, an insurance agency, a pharmacy, appliance stores, small shops. A plaza with arbors of wisteria growing at each end, fronted on one side by a modest but clean apartment building of four stories. When Blas fed into *Kalea* San Agustin, he walked that second street until the wall of buildings to his left gave way to a small park that bordered the river. The town market was on San Agustin, and a whole assortment of shops, the ones he'd expected, but specialty shops too, framing shops and health food stores and shops selling scented candles and soaps. The signs in front of these shops were written almost entirely in Basque. The bars were also on San Agustin, although none with those photographs displayed in the windows. At that small park he took his first close look at the river. He noted the smell and the graying of the green and the unclean way the water slipped over rocks, but the river was for later.

He walked San Agustin almost to its end, until he was sure that the sameness of dirty, cream-colored apartment blocks, broken up by the occasional bar and car repair shop, was all there was, then he came back to the Plaza Mayor and walked in the other direction. In the industrial park he saw warehouses housing businesses for car parts and machine tools and construction materials. There was an office-studio for industrial design. He stood beside a sculpture of a sewing machine, large and low-barreled, the size and shape of some African animal, a hippopotamus. Sewing machines must have given the town its light-industrial start. Past the industrial park he came to a large gothic-pointed gate, with statues of saints in its niches, beyond which lay the cemetery. He wasn't ready for the cemetery yet, but he walked down one row of wall crypts and back up another looking for a family name. The names he saw were all unpronounceable—he didn't even try.

Back in town, he ordered a coffee in a bar on the main plaza. Off to his right, hanging on the wall, were photos of two men. Both looked to be in their midthirties. They were square-faced with cleanly cut features beginning to flesh out. They looked enough alike to be brothers. Beneath the photos the names of two different Spanish cities were written, followed by numbers of five digits. Those would be the cities, he surmised, in which these men were imprisoned and the numbers their cell numbers. Between the photos was something, perhaps an insignia, made with a black ribbon.

He walked out into the plaza, where people had begun to gather, as they did, he assumed, at this afternoon hour in plazas all over the country. But this wasn't Spain, he had to remember. It was Pais Vasco. It wasn't even that. It was Euskal Herria. He'd seen the sign spray-painted in Vitoria and most of the towns they'd driven through that day. *¡Gora Euskal Herria!* was the way it was worded, and with no end to the bitterness of the irony, he knew that *gora* meant "long live."

There were two Basque names he'd taught himself to say. One was the name of this town—Eskuibar, Ace-coo-ee-bar—which he practiced until he could combine the vowels and out of four syllables make three. The other was the name of its favorite son.

He took the train back to the small city of Eibar, where for the indefinite future he would be spending the night.

But, like a tourist caught in a revolving door, the next day he was back in Eskuibar's Plaza Mayor, sitting under the pruned sycamores that grew in front of the church. Off to his left stood the Town Hall, a low gray stone building with arches, an arcade and a building-length balcony. Farther down and attached to the Town Hall was one of those two-walled handball courts he'd noticed in other towns. Across from it stood another building, where PNV, the nationalist party that ran the autonomous Basque government, had its local offices. Red and yellow paint had been splashed on the stone there, the colors of the Spanish flag, which he took to mean that some believed PNV was collaborating too closely with the government in Madrid. It was not his concern. Behind him rose the church and bell tower of San Blas, whose bells could sound jarringly off-key. Directly before him, just beyond that ball court, the plaza opened out to a bridge that crossed the river to become a street, then a narrow road leading up into the pastured hills to the east.

Days, and he saw nothing he might not have seen in other towns, in the town of Medina del Rioseco, for instance. Town functionaries, town petitioners, town officials parading in and out of the Town Hall. Women going up to the town market with their canvas-enclosed shopping carts, coming back with their carts full. Harried young men out on some urgent errand; young mothers, frequently in pairs, pushing their baby carriages. Children, in their school uniforms, with their overlarge satchels and book bags. Groups of retired men, in brightly colored running shoes, pacing up and down the town for their morning's exercise. Once they'd finished walking, these men would sometimes sit on benches close by and hold disputatious conversations with aggressive gestures. It seemed as if they might come to blows, but of course they never did.

He saw the young men too, in their groups of four or five. He saw the way they walked together, their odd rhythms meshing into some powerful locomotive force. As groups, they were angular, pent up, working off each other and leaving the air charged with a youthful tension as they passed. Judging from what he could hear, they spoke in Spanish, not Basque. It sounded like sex and money and cars. Never public controversies or current events.

The young women their age passed by too, frequently alone and mostly quiet. Their faces looked set, steeled to a life of self-denial.

Ben was waiting. He'd been given to understand that Spaniards returned to the towns they came from. Did Basques come back? He was betting that they did.

He spent the nights in Eibar and day by day returned to Eskuibar. Eventually certain men, harbinger-like, began to appear to him. These men all had long faces. They had heavy jaw lines and chins, or they had jaw lines and chins that had shelved away and allowed flesh in dewlapped folds onto their necks. If the cheeks were slack, the face could seem horsey, and in the pouched eyes he'd notice a pleading expression. But if the cheeks were strong and the face broader, the eyes took on a recalcitrant life. He saw all varieties. But the long fleshy nose, with the flaring nostrils, was a constant. The mouth was all in the lower lip. The upper lip was a ridge line, but the lower was loose, swollen, spilling off in the center with its own little landslide of flesh.

He saw young men of twenty with this face, and he saw at least one grandfather. Allowing for the discoloration of age, the complexion was always sandy and the hair color brown. He had not seen this face anywhere else in Spain or during his brief stay in the Basque country, and he wondered about inbreeding. He assumed there was a town type.

He walked the streets. He'd begun to be known. People greeted him with a nod. Or a *"Buenos dias."* Never in Basque. He hadn't thought he could remain unnoticed, and he nodded back. He found a restaurant to eat in, over which a *pension* was located. The restaurant featured a menu of the day, and he came to know the waitress who took his order, and the older woman who came from the kitchen with a tureen and ladled out his soup. He believed the two women were daughter and mother and the man manning the cash register the father and husband. A young man, who might have been a family member too, worked behind the bar, and he had the "before" face of that young man on the poster in Vitoria who'd been beaten into all the swollen colors of a storm cloud by the *guardia civil* or some other branch of the police.

Workers ate in that restaurant with him. On any given day, one of them was sure to make him do a double-take. He understood it might happen like this. They might simply be sitting one table away in a restaurant, eating soup ladled out of the same tureen. Their eyes might meet as they brought the soup spoons to their mouths.

Ben would leave that restaurant and walk the town to the end until there was no more working-class housing left. He didn't expect to find a plaque, and he certainly didn't want to ask anyone, but he asked himself: Where did Ordoki live? Where had he lived as a boy, when his father had made his living here? When he made his friends and found his group, his *cuadrilla*, and when that group became a *comando* that would be disbanded and its members dispersed to prisons in the four corners of Spain—where had he lived then? Somewhere in these blocks of apartments with wash hanging out and orange canisters of butane gas rolled onto the balconies, apartments smelling of gas and detergent and whatever had been left frying on the stove? And when Ordoki came back, a favorite son, a man with a college degree, two children and a wife, and when he set out to walk the town, where did he set out from?

There was a footbridge, a raised platform, crossing over the railroad tracks. One day Ben stood there as a train passed by under his feet. It passed the length of the town going west toward Bilbao and then, where the valley narrowed, leaned toward the south and curved out of sight. Almost certainly Ordoki had stood there as a schoolboy, before he'd gone to school and met up with his friends. What boy doesn't yearn to go away on a train? If only to play hooky for a day? Beyond Bilbao lay the ocean, and what boy doesn't dream of shipping out and seeing the world?

Ben looked for the sports fields. He knew boys left parts of themselves on fields of play that might be lost for the rest of their lives. But he couldn't find them. There was that two-walled handball court beside the Town Hall, but he meant fields of dirt and grass that a boy could stretch out in and exult when he'd just kicked a goal. He assumed they must be up one of those draws to the west. At certain hours of the afternoon, when the town went into a lull, he could hear the shouts of boys, all contained, sounding as one voice, like a tree full of warbling birds. But he didn't go looking for them.

Instead, he went to the river. Here, he was sure. He walked along its banks and saw the footprints in the muddy spaces between some of the rocks.

Boys came to the river alone, they came in groups. They came to mull over their thoughts or to plot among themselves. They came to race the current, to leap from rock to rock. Standing beside even such a small river as this, a man could remember what it was like to be a boy with an immediacy that was stunning. It didn't matter that the town was apparently trying to dredge out a deeper channel and had scattered a lot of gravel with heavy machinery, leaving tire and tread prints in the mud and ugly white gashes in the rock.

He walked the river's banks. He began at that small park on San Agustin, where a banner had been unfurled announcing in Basque an event of some sort, perhaps a demonstration, and walked the distance between the three town bridges. When he got to the third, the bridge that led into the Plaza Mayor, he crossed over and walked the bank back on the other side. The dirt was dry, crusted hard in spots, but he moved close enough to the water line to feel his feet sink into the mud. He could hear the squish his feet made, and added that to the sound of the running water. Very quietly, he filled his lungs with air.

He was about to pass under the second of the three bridges, one for pedestrians, when he looked up to discover a figure of some sort scrambling onto the bridge railing above him. The figure was winged; its hands were gripping a bar below the railing and its feet were pedaling air. Making use of a rock the dredgers had thrown up, Ben managed to scramble up the retaining wall. When he stepped out onto that bridge he felt a peculiar apprehension that had as its image those frantically pedaling feet, as the winged figure tried to tread the air. The wings, made of riveted aluminum plates, were of no help. It was a strange sculpture to be attached to the side of a bridge in a town like this. He walked out onto the bridge and stared directly down into the small upturned face. The aluminum nose came to a straining point. The mouth was opened in a rictus of fear. Cigarettes had been extinguished there in a small puddle from the last rain.

"*Curioso, no?*" a voice beside him said.

Ben looked to his side, toward the town. In the buildings facing the river, business was being done; in the apartments wash hung from kitchen and bathroom windows. He understood it would happen like this. It would not be on the Plaza Mayor as he studied the passersby. It would not be in a restaurant as he cast his eyes around at the other diners while sipping his soup. It would be when his attention was taken and no longer his.

"Icaro," the other man on the bridge said.

"Yes, Icarus, of course," Ben answered.

"Ah, English. You are English?"

The man was maybe five years too young. The pouches had yet to form under the eyes, the chin was less pronounced; those high and low water marks were missing from the neck. But beneath a green-and-white-checked shirt the tee-shirt was black.

"Yes, English," Ben said.

"I know some English. A little."

"Could you tell me what this sculpture is doing here? It is very strange. It makes no sense."

"The artist . . . how do you say? He make a gift to the town."

Suddenly the man was smiling. But the fleshy lower lip would not stay still, as if one smile were about to give way to a darker, more sinister one.

In a reflex action, Ben found himself clutching the rail, as the winged figure clutched it from below.

"Icarus," the man said, taking an almost juvenile relish in repeating the name in a tight-throated English pronunciation.

No, this was a much younger man, with a certain dissipation in his face Ben hadn't noticed until now.

He released the rail.

"Icarus falls to the earth," Ben said. "His wings burn up and he falls to the earth. He's just a wingless boy. But this Icarus has powerful wings. He's more like an evil angel crawling up from the underworld to enter the town. Wouldn't you say?"

The man cocked his head at a disapproving angle and backed off a step. "*Como?*" he said.

"What I want to know is what this angel is doing..." Then Ben stopped and tried it in Spanish, *"Lo que quiero saber es que hace este angel aqui . . . in your town?"*

The man shook his head, muttering, *"Yo que se?"* with something of a boy's petulant impatience in his tone.

Ben saw then that the man really was a boy, just a boy grown quickly old. The boy added something in Basque, something dismissive and brusque, full of consonants that left a hard hacking sound in the air.

This was the language spoken in Eden before the Fall?

Ben took a step toward his companion on the bridge. He wasn't sure why. Maybe he'd like to get him in his grip, and then, if the man cooperated, Ben thought he might like to throw him over the railing. Down by the river he could find other boys to play with, or take a walk along the river by himself. Ben closed his eyes in anticipation, and just as he'd expected, when he opened them the boy-man, whoever he was, was gone.

Ben went back to his hotel room in Eibar and stayed there for five days. He ate his meals not in the hotel but around the corner in a drafty restaurant on the plaza. Up in his room he'd catch himself staring across the way at that *mirador*, with all its cloudy panes, behind which no face had appeared in years. The hotel seemed mostly empty. The woman behind the desk was as solicitous as ever, but there was a limit to what she could do. In good conscience, she couldn't recommend a single tourist attraction in town. So he mostly sat in what passed as the hotel lobby and read a Basque newspaper called *Gara*. Half the articles were written in Basque. The half written in Spanish he could read, and piecing them together, he got the whole array of Basque grievances. There was always an article about torture and police abuse and an article about the imperiled state of the Basque language. There was an article about onerous decrees from Madrid regarding education and labor unions, an article about judicial high-handedness and the periodic prohibition of demonstrations, and an article about military exercises on Basque soil. There was an article about Basque soil, how it extended into Navarra and across the border into France. There was al-

ways more than one article about the hated *guardia civil,* how they battered
down doors in the pursuit of suspects, how they ransacked homes. How
they verbally abused. How they lashed out with their truncheons. How
they stole. How, it was all but stated, they deserved what they got.

A Civil Guard was killed during those days when he left his car to remove a sign reading, "*¡Gora* ETA! Death to all *guardia civil!*" behind
which a bomb had been hidden. He was thirty-two, the father of six-year-
old twins.

Ben kept reading. Above all, there were articles about Basque prisoners, how far they were imprisoned from the Basque homeland and how
many loved ones died in a given year traveling to reach them. How they
were interrogated and tortured with the sack over the head, the electrodes
to the testicles, the hose up the anus. How they were kept in solitary con-
finement, and when they finally got out, how they were prohibited from using the Basque language with anybody, fellow prisoners and visiting family
members alike, unless a prison translator was present. How one guard so
hated the sound of the language that every time a prisoner struck up a song
in that tongue he got beaten. A song, a beating. A song, a beating.

It was propaganda, Ben understood, of the most unabashed and trans-
parent sort. Nonetheless, he read on.

Eskuibar was also in the news. While he'd been away, a demonstration
had been staged in the Plaza Mayor in support of the two ETA members
from the town who were in prison, both of whom had finished serving
eighteen years. The authorities considered the demonstration "an apology
for terrorism" and broke it up. Seven citizens of the town had been arrested
and brought to the nearby city of Eibar to be interrogated.

He stopped reading there.

He spent a day walking up and down the city, but it was so narrow and
long he never reached the end. He passed a police *comisaria,* and he passed
a station for the *guardia civil.* He wondered where those seven men were
being interrogated. A civil guard stood before the station's door. This was

not a fresh recruit, not a boy. He had on his patent-leather tricorn hat, which was like the hats Napoleon wore and could make a man in this day and age smile. Ben had stopped before the guard; unaware, he might have been smiling. The guard had a ham-heavy face and eyes that moved in tiny reconnoitering lurches over every passerby. Here, in the heart of the Basque country, there were no innocent passersby. His hands were motionless on the machine gun they all carried strapped over their shoulders, but that reconnoitering motion of the eyes had speeded up, and the guard now gave off a bitter heat that the man before him could feel on his face. Ben turned and walked away. He got in among other passersby and tried to walk with their everyday pace. If he was ordered to stop or be shot, he didn't know which he would choose. He understood that those articles he'd been reading about the *guardia civil*'s brutal treatment of the Basques were too formulaic to be true, but he remembered them, nonetheless, the bag, the electrodes, the hose, and then he remembered the tortured boy's face on the poster in that bar in Vitoria, and the face of the young bartender, who awaited his turn.

A tourist of his own panic, which he confronted and overcame, Ben walked away.

The time had come to arm himself.

He returned to Eskuibar. The police had been here and gone and taken away seven of its citizens, but he saw no change on the streets. That banner, which he'd never managed to decipher, had been removed from the small park beside the river. That was all. He walked the streets of Eskuibar now, looking into stores, looking at what was displayed, because the signs hanging overhead didn't help him. He was looking for something he didn't yet know the shape or nature of. Not a gun. He'd once shot six bullets out of a revolver at a target twenty paces away and hadn't come close. The pistol had bucked in his hand with a willfulness that was astonishing; he assumed the shots had traveled straight up to the sky. Something else. Where San Blas and San Agustin rejoined before heading into the industrial park, he came to a hardware store and saw a small iron-shafted hatchet displayed in the window. He had a boyhood memory for that too, the time he and his friends had crossed the creek behind their suburb and cut down a number of tall poplars to make a log cabin. He remembered the hatchet biting into the soft wood, the chips flying, and he remembered the moment when the tree made that splintering crack and began its slow-motion descent to the ground.

The Basque were sportsmen. He doubled back on San Blas and found a hunting and fishing store, where sooner or later it had to be. A picture of a shotgun with its breech cracked open hung over the door. The Spanish word for shotgun, *escopeta*, appeared on the sign. In the window displaying fishing equipment, he saw a knife with a black, finger-grooved handle and a partially serrated blade of stainless steel, perhaps six inches long. Beside it was a sheath made of a translucent plastic. As objects, neither the knife nor the sheath evoked a moment from his boyhood. He entered the store and asked the salesman to remove it from the window so he could hold it in his hand.

The salesman was another young man, but of the round-faced type, with eyes so blue they shimmered. He was very friendly. The knife was for deep-sea fishing, he explained. It was for reaching under the water and cutting through particularly stubborn obstructions. That little serrated section allowed you to grate. The blade was flat on the top edge and curved like a cutlass on the bottom. It was as bright as the young man's eyes and shone like a mirror. To prove it, the clerk held the blade up to his customer's face, and it was so, his customer saw himself. The knife came with a sheath, also bright, of a deep-sea blue, which featured a safety latch. The young man demonstrated how you inserted the knife into the sheath with a locking click and how you released it by pushing a button. The knife made a little leap, then, into the hand, perfectly balanced; the grooves fit the fingers. He gave it to his customer to get the feel of, and all that the salesman had said of it was true. It was balanced, it fit, and it shone. Ben tested the blade against his thumb. It was sharp. He placed the blade's point against the tip of his index finger, and with the slightest pressure he would have drawn blood.

He paid 4,500 pesetas for the knife and walked down San Blas carrying it in a black plastic sack. At the Plaza Mayor he entered the second of the two bars and, while the bartender was preparing his coffee, stepped into the men's room, which he locked. He took off his windbreaker, slipped his belt through the opening on the sheath, then slid the knife around behind him, closer to his right hip than the small of his back. He tried reaching back for it once, and although his arm was muscle-bound his fingers managed to find the release button, which he didn't push. He turned before the lavatory mirror to make sure his windbreaker was long enough to reach past the sheath and that it billowed out enough to conceal the bulk. Then he washed his hands.

He sat for a good part of that afternoon at a table out on the plaza with the knife pressing into the flesh of his back. It was an insistent presence more than an irritation. If he sat at a certain angle in his chair he could make it disappear entirely. The sun turned tepid and a cool breeze blew down from the top of the hills. Later in the afternoon, the plaza took on a different kind of warmth as it began to fill up, mostly with mothers and their young children—school had let out—but he saw some fathers too. Two figures appeared on stilts, with heads disproportionately large for their elongated bodies, enormous flaxen-haired heads, round as a full moon, representing a boy and a girl. They were dressed in traditional outfits of some sort, full skirts and pants, aprons and cummerbund sashes and vests. The children flocked to them and scrambled for candies that appeared in their wake. For a period the ringing shouts of the children dominated the plaza, with the adults talking loudly enough to make themselves heard at the tables.

Then a traffic policeman began to allow select cars on to the plaza to park, a hearse drew up before the church door, and it was clear that a fu-

neral was about to take place. The children disappeared, their parents finished their *tapas* and glasses of wine, got up from the tables on the plaza
and became mourners. Ben got up with them. In the midst of the milling he
was able to move close enough to the hearse to be there when, after the
wreaths of flowers had been unloaded, six young men rolled the casket out.
There were no expressions of grief. Men and women put out their last cigarettes and followed the casket into the church. The air was heavy with perfume and cologne and, at the church door, incense. The dress ranged from
the somber to the gaudy to the plain to the incidental attire of someone like
himself, and he had to believe a cross-section of the town was in atten-
dance. He heard the amplified voice of the priest addressing the congregation, stepped inside and stood in back.

The service was in Basque. Two screens, placed to each side of the altar, instructed the congregation in electronic script how to respond to the
priest, and when a woman stood up to sing, presumably what she sang was
also printed there. It was a wall of foreign sound, as hard on the ear as
words gouged in stone.

He had no idea who had died, an old man, a young woman or a child.

He was a tourist of alien rites.

When the priest began to say mass, Ben slipped back outside. He stood
under a tree in the last light and, as the congregation filed out, inspected
them, one by one. His chances all depended on the circumstances. If the
deceased had been powerful enough, important enough to be worthy of a
favorite son's tribute. Or if the deceased had been an old friend, one of his
cuadrilla. Or if the deceased had been a teenaged love, a mentor, a protégé,
a wise old man of the mountains. Or if the deceased had been someone
he'd wronged, someone who carried a secret of his to the grave. Armando
Ordoki might have come, then, to make sure, to drive an additional nail
into the coffin, to throw an extra shovelful of dirt into the hole.

Except here, in their town, graves were holes in a wall.

To help seal that hole.

.   .   .

On a gray day, a day threatening rain from beginning to end, Ben climbed up the mountain. As a first leg, he walked up a draw to the chapel of San Antonio. He was not alone. Groups of women passed him coming down, and younger women, more purposeful striders than he, passed him on the way up. He was in no hurry. He was not out for exercise or to pay homage to a saint. He walked west on a paved one-lane road. A stream ran alongside the road, a clear stream, and he walked against the current. For a distance it was over-hung by oaks, and he crunched acorns underfoot. Along the shoulder of the road, dandelions and daisies and Queen Anne's lace grew, and beyond the stream, thick on the hillside, blackberry brambles. These were plants and flowers familiar to his childhood. Off to his right the narrow draw he'd started up broadened, and those grassy meadows and terraces appeared, muted by the grayness of the day. He saw milk cattle and flocks of sheep. Plots of vegetables, pole beans and squash. There was almost no wind. The sound of the stream was always there, as though on one frequency, and on an-other, from out in that valley-wide draw, he might hear a dog bark or the scat-tered notes of a sheep bell as the bellwether moved among the flock. For a while a chain saw ruined it for him, but when the sound of the saw ceased the sounds of water and of animals came back to him pure.

He walked toward the forested rim. He wore a black sweatshirt he'd bought for the occasion. Between his right hip and the small of his back he wore his knife, designed for underwater fishing. He wore no cap; his thin-ning fair hair was exposed. On his feet, running shoes, which he'd bought where the retired men who walked up and down their town-long street bought theirs. The shoes were white.

He came to the chapel of San Antonio, nicely kept up, but with nothing venerable about it. Here the women, out for their pilgrimage and exercise ses-sion, turned back. The chapel was locked. Through a small barred window he looked inside, but all he could see was the austere and shadowy outline of an altar. An off-center bell gable was attached to a small tower. Adjoining the chapel he saw what, on first glance, because of the chicken wire stretched across an exposed wall, he took to be a henhouse. But he soon realized it was another of those ball courts, with a balcony built at one end for spectators.

Behind the chapel was a small park with picnic tables beside the stream. For those who wanted to stop.

The road narrowed, and he continued uphill.

The road and the stream had parted ways. The road ran through open pastureland, long clumped grass the sheep and cattle had yet to graze on, while the stream flowed down the valley crease. He heard the distant rush of its water. When he came alongside a group of cattle, they regarded him with sullen indifference. He heard them uproot the grass and grind it heavily between their jaws.

The road wound higher and higher, increasing its angle of ascent as it neared the tree line. He took his first rest sitting on the side of a terrace. He'd brought no food and nothing to drink. When he turned to take his first look back, there was no town. Even the chapel of San Antonio had been obscured from sight.

He had ceased to be a tourist of that sort.

When the road reached the forest, it continued on along its flank until, he believed, it ended at a farmhouse some fifty yards above. Off to his right he saw a broad grassy path that might have once been a logging road. He cut off there, moving up between two spurs as the valley narrowed to a draw again and the draw drew to a point. He had to step over a small stream, a tributary, but the main stream was directly below him now, a more turbulent flow than down on the pastureland.

Emerging from a tunnel of pines, he came to a zone of the hillside where reforestation had taken place, and these young pines, set out in rows to his left, smelled strongly of their resin. Off to his right the drop to the stream was precipitous. The freshening and rank odor of stream water and leaf mold and mud rose straight to his nose.

On an outcrop of granite, he shifted his knife farther up his hip and took his second rest. He heard the water and a low soughing sound that must have been wind, although he felt no wind on his face and the pine needles were still.

What remained of the logging road ended there. The path continued, in an arduous, switchbacked ascent, up the mountainside. There at the path's mouth, just where he'd begun to need it, he found a walking stick. It was of a stout green wood he couldn't identify—certainly not pine—cleanly cut at both ends with an axe. Planted in the ground like a staff, it rose a good foot above his waist, and there was a spot near the upper end, between nubs where the side branches had been cut off, that fit his grip as naturally as a baseball bat. It was stout and straight enough to be used as a club if he needed to fight off animals, stout and straight enough to support his weight as he worked his way up the mountain. He'd found it propped in open view against a rock, left, clearly, for the next hiker who came this way.

He was that next hiker.

He climbed the mountain in a three-legged ascent. The air was cool and damp the higher he went, and the rock in the path was slick. Water sluicing down the path had taken most of the dirt, and human and animal traffic had done the rest. The path was very old. In stretches, the rock was worn smooth, and even with his rubber-soled shoes the footing was treacherous. Without the stick he wouldn't have had much chance. He wedged it in between rocks or in spots of earth off to the side and pushed himself farther up. In the parts of the path where some earth remained and the going was not so steep, he used the stick like a cane, to test the footing a step farther on. If a wild boar had come charging down the path he would have used it as a club. But he saw no boar, he saw no animals of any sort, not even a rabbit or a squirrel. He heard the isolated cheeps of birds, and occasionally he'd see small birds flitting among the branches, but the tree cover was thick and his vision was mostly reduced to what lay up the path. A brief clearing might give him a glimpse of the sky, but the sky was a uniform gray and close overhead, like a lid. Once he saw a hawk rocking back and forth on wind currents he didn't feel a trace of.

He stopped to rest, but almost at once started up again. That uphill motion was in his heartbeat, the surge of his blood. The walking stick would not lie quietly at his side.

At a turn of the path higher up, a cairn of rocks had been erected. He sat there for a moment and settled his breath. He found a stone and placed it, not on top of the cairn but safely to the side. Then he continued on.

Eyes on the path, leaning on his stick, Ben Williamson paced his panting breaths to his step and climbed this Basque mountain. With no change in the light, he lost track of time. There was a moment, an interlude, when a break in the foliage gave him a view of a distant house, a house set out on its own private spur, a front lawn, a second-story deck stained a cedar red. He saw a dog out front, standing statue-still, as if on point. He didn't stop, the moment passed, and it was as if he hadn't seen this improbable house and dog at all. He felt pains in his lower back, spasms in his stomach and an ache in his lungs that demanded more air, but all at a certain remove, as if he'd reached a stage in his climb when the body became a machine whose travails were its own affair, something all bodies went through.

He climbed not until his body gave out but until he'd distanced himself sufficiently from it to see himself whole. He saw a pale man dressed in a familiar black sweatshirt leaning into the next step. He saw a man leaning earthward, propped on a stick, his flesh hanging heavy on his bones. He saw that same man standing naked in a full-length mirror, a woman with a thatch of red hair, freckles and a heaviness in her hip standing at his side. He saw another woman who could fill a mirror by herself but who, in her quick humor and massive ease, revealed to him the young woman she'd been: hungry, fit, athletic, golden. He saw, in profile, an older woman seated at a piano, and as that older woman began to sing—songs of love, longing and loss—he saw two young women, who at the same time were two children and two girls.

Once they'd started he couldn't stop these pictures from forming. As all tourists finally must, he had become a tourist of himself.

Legs trembling, he sat on the rock of the path with his knife printed into his hip and the walking stick laid across his lap. With the rock so slippery and his legs so weak, he'd need that stick even more going down. Whether he'd gone high enough up the mountain or not, he couldn't say. No one had sprinted past to put him to shame. No one had passed him coming down. There'd been that cairn of stones, a record, perhaps a mortuary record, of those who'd used this path. And there'd been that house, which, in the glimpse he'd had of it, seemed like a shrine to those who'd given up and put themselves at a distant remove. His choices were to crawl under those stones or to try to reach that house. His other choice was to climb back down the mountain and reenter the town.

W hile they were deciding what to do, Paula Ortiz insisted that Ben's daughter leave the hotel and come stay with her, and then she insisted that Annie take the master bedroom, which was absurd, since there was a perfectly comfortable guest bedroom. But Annie slept in the bed where she was sure her father and Paula had made love. It had a high, scrolled, ornately carved headboard; there was a wardrobe with carving and a marble-topped dresser to match. Perhaps Paula wanted to give her a taste of Spanish history. She began to bring Annie gifts. She brought a hand-painted fan with a lacy fringe, and she brought an embroidered shawl, of a bone-colored white that looked as if it had lain at the bottom of a noblewoman's chest for centuries. She mothered Annie. She wanted her there where she could keep an eye on her. While Ben was missing, the least she could do was keep his daughter from harm. Annie might have been kept from harm back at that college she attended, but that was not what Paula meant. She meant here, where danger was rife, where young women out jogging could suddenly be deprived of their youth, their old age, everything, she wanted to make sure Annie Williamson was safe. To be made safe, there had to be a threat, and the greater the threat, the safer

Paula would make her. Annie understood the logic, but she already had a mother. If Paula confined Annie to the bed where she and Ben Williamson made love, would that same logic allow her to consider Annie the fruit of that union just by virtue of her having slept there?

Was that how Paula Ortiz conceived of it? Was that how Paula Ortiz conceived?

She brought Annie earrings with silver filigree and teardrop pearls, to go with the tasseled shawl, and had her stand in front of the wardrobe mirror to get the full effect. Paula stood off to the side. With her eyes, cheekbones and hair, with those statuesque legs and that aristocratic poise, Annie could be Spanish, she said. Annie stood there looking at herself and at the zealous, gift-giving woman at her side, and asked herself how much longer this could go on. She assumed her father had stood before this mirror, and she could imagine him asking himself the same question. One minute he was standing there, his volition, his self-regard, the whole history of who he was, in a state of suspension, and the next minute he was gone. The last he had seen of himself was, in a manner of speaking, what Annie saw of herself now. Her image superimposed on his. This was an old wardrobe, and perhaps mirrors like photographic plates retained their images. She looked past her own and found his and said, All right, Dad, tell me. It'll be our secret. Where have you gone?

Annie got Paula to bring her a map of Spain, and then, beginning with the heavily touristed Andalusia, she moved her finger over it asking her father's lover if she could imagine her father there? Or there? What would he be doing among those Moorish towns of the south? What would he be doing among the orange groves of Valencia? La Mancha, following the footsteps of Quixote? Barcelona, to see the Gaudi? She swung her finger north; across the north stretched the old pilgrim's trail to Santiago de Compostela, in the westernmost province of Galicia. Maybe that was where her father had gone, Paula suggested, to perform a penance on the road to Compostela. A penance for what? Paula did not know.

Annie coaxed Paula's hand to where her own had been. From Santiago de Compostela she moved Paula's index finger back east and left it squarely in the Basque country, by chance over a tiny dot of a town, beside a hair-thin river she could not see.

"I think he's gone there," Annie said.

Paula did not answer.

"And if he's gone there," Annie continued, "it's to look for Armando Ordoki. Why else would he cut out all those pictures?"

Paula shook her head.

"There were a lot of them, you said."

Paula admitted there had been.

"If he cut out all those pictures, he's gone looking for the man."

"Revenge?" Paula asked

Annie nodded. "For what happened to Michelle."

Obstinately, Paula shook her head again. "That's not the man your father is."

"Maybe that's the man my Spanish father is. The man my father is in Spain. Isn't revenge, defense of honor and all that, part of the Spanish code?"

Paula uttered, "I'm so sorry, Annie." But whether she was apologizing for herself or the country, Annie was unable to tell.

"We should find out where Armando Ordoki is. If we don't find my father there, we can look for him on some pilgrim's trail to Santiago de Compostela, I don't care."

Paula wanted to talk to her ex-husband. She had an ex-sister-in-law in whom she confided, and she wanted to talk to her. Or the American Embassy. What were embassies for if not to locate missing citizens abroad? But Annie's father wasn't missing. Her father knew exactly where he was. And Annie believed that because of that corny thing he'd said to her, about digging in to face the day that was sure to come, and because, in spite of her mother's heckling from the sideline, she believed her father had it in him to perform an extraordinary act. Her mother might have her local successes against such opponents as Mr. Maverick, but beyond that, was her mother capable of anything extraordinary? Annie admitted she didn't know. She'd been a Daddy's girl from the start.

She had that Metro map still in her mind. The red to the cobalt-blue line and she was within a block of the main office of the public library. On the Internet, she scrolled through dozens of verbose pronouncements Ordoki had made about the victimization of the Basques before she came to an article with a short bio. She learned where he worked—when the Basque legislature was in session, in the capital of Vitoria—and she learned the name of his hometown. Family, education, hobbies and pastimes. His activities as a member of ETA. Time served. She saw a photograph. He had the face that suited him, if he was the bullying man-of-one-idea he seemed. She printed out this information and the picture and took them back to Paula's apartment, where a man was visiting, whose rumpled, slow-to-respond face couldn't mask what was going on in the eyes. He was all over her at once. Then, on a blink, he was suddenly quiet, seemingly serene.

It turned out Paula had not told her ex-husband, Jorge, anything. She'd shown the consideration of waiting for Annie to arrive before she did that. But Jorge Ortiz knew Spain, he knew the various Spanish peoples, he knew how the people in Cantabria differed from the people in Andalusia, the *gallegos* from the *catalans*. More than anyone Paula knew, he would be in a position to make the best-educated guess. Ben Williamson was at large in the country. Where had he gone?

In a cultivated drawl, Jorge said, "I believe your father is an idealist. Would you agree? The last thing we talked about was how Americans could create an ideal country for themselves. Your father wanted to know what part of Spain he should include in his ideal country."

He paused to see if Annie too was an idealist and would want the same advice he had given her father toward the realization of his ideal. She distrusted this man, with that easy grin off to the side of his mouth, as if he'd never had a conniving thought in his life, and that smile drawn on a line through the eyes, like a horizon one might gaze on and gaze on, not an enemy in sight. He had glossy chest hairs, and even they seemed to be curled in a friendly smile.

She finally gave in. "So what did you tell him?"

"That Spain was its life on the streets," he replied. "In Spain we have many streets."

"That's good," she said, "because I know the one he's on."

Jorge nodded—he was encouraged, she was to continue. Annie glanced over at his ex-wife and was amazed. A woman of intelligence and tact, Paula appeared to be in complete accord with her ex-husband, with no sense of how insufferably patronizing he could be.

"I mean," Annie lashed out, in her own restrained and winning way, "I know exactly where he is. I know what he's doing. We've communicated and I'll be joining him soon."

"Ah," Jorge sighed through this new turn of events.

"We'll be walking down the same street. Walkin' the talk, we say in the States. An expression from the black community. Which means, if you do the walking you don't need to do the talking. There's no reason left to say a word."

She couldn't knock him loose from that grin, but a scowl passed through his eyes and he shifted his weight, as if he'd just taken a blow to his self-esteem and intended to deliver one of his own.

But he surprised her. A true *caballero*, if she preferred walking to talking he would defer to her wishes and not say another word. He broadened his grin. When he got up to leave, he performed a sexy ambling strut on his way to the door.

Paula said, "You haven't talked with Ben, have you?"

"We've talked."

"Not really."

"We have a hotline."

"Annie, you don't know how this country is. You think there's no end to the charm, then one day you wake up and they're hitting each other over the head. There's a painting by Goya—"

Annie cut her off. "Then it's a good thing you divorced Jorge before his charm ran out and he began to hit *you* over the head. Take me where I want to go and we'll find a man who'd never do that to you. I promise."

Jorge's sister Pepa knew the Basque country, she'd lived there for years. Her first husband had been Basque. She'd told stories about the brainwashing that went on, the cold and self-righteous way people got killed. One day you're having a *vino* with a friend, and the next day he's ETA with a gun to the back of your head. Her ex-husband, a small-time entrepreneur who sold frozen food, had made good on back payments of his revolutionary tax, and they'd taken the gun away. For a while he'd had a bodyguard, who'd been such a loudmouthed macho she was sure the bodyguard alone was enough to get her husband killed. But then, they were all loudmouthed in the Basque country—the only way to drown out the guilt. So maybe the bodyguard was just trying to make himself heard. They all wanted to be devout Catholics, and they wanted to be ruthless revolutionaries. Pepa divorced her husband, took her daughter and got out. The daughter was Annie's age. They should talk to Pepa before they went up there.

Pepa showed up later that afternoon, without her daughter. Annie pleaded a headache and went back to lie on her bed. Then she got up and packed her small bag. Pepa had a barely mastered wildness about her. She was small and nervy and intense, with indomitable black curls. She gave the impression of having saved her energy to settle a score. If someone as gutsy as Pepa had had to get out of the Basque country, it must be pretty bad up there. Annie spread the shawl Paula had given her out on the bed, the fan open, the earrings placed to each side. Then she walked back out into the living room.

She didn't mean to be an ungrateful shit, she really didn't, but she was leaving in fifteen minutes and if Paula wanted to come along here was her chance.

She didn't like giving ultimatums either. Paula deserved better. Fifteen minutes was the same as saying, Cancel all your other priorities and turn yourself over to me. Paula went to pack a small bag of her own. While she was gone, Pepa gave Annie a parting piece of advice.

"Never push a Basque to the limit. They'll kill you before they'll admit to the truth."

They drove out of Madrid on national highway 104. The surrounding countryside was high, flat and dry, with boulders giving way to scrub oak and scrub oak to patchy farms. Farms to towns. There'd be a church and the remains of a castle and a clustering of houses, set like the planes in a Cubist painting. In the distance there'd be a shadowy wall of mountain, which they'd eventually pass through, only to emerge onto a higher plain, surrounded by similar mountain walls. They rose in this way, plateau by plateau, as they traveled toward Burgos and the north. The car they rode in was a little plum-colored Renault. Paula drove as if at any moment the highway might end, and when night fell and her deliberateness made the darkness of the plain seem interminable, Annie took over. She drove them over the river at Aranda del Duero. On a roundabout they passed Burgos and its cathedral spires. The night became immense then, moonless and mountainless as far as they could see, the car and truck traffic thinning out until they were a tiny cockpit of a car speeding toward a point that might have existed only in a mapmaker's dream.

Only then, when they were alone and perhaps the last living things on earth, did Paula ask her where they were going. Annie said the city of Vitoria, which the Basques called Gasteiz.

Things called by such wildly dissimilar names might belong to different orders of nature entirely.

Paula said, "I'm not going to let you go crazy, Annie. This has nothing to do with Ben."

Annie nodded. "Vitoria," she said.

She knew at once that her father wasn't there. She was looking for an arena of some sort, and the city was too given over to commerce and the parading of fashion to stage the sort of showdown her father must have had in mind. They spent the night at a hotel on the main highway and drove in the next morning to find the Basque parliament out of session. The day was gray and the temperature dropping by the hour. They walked down an elegant main street whose tall bay windows made the grayness glitter. Then they walked into the old part of the city and eventually down a street hung with banners in an incomprehensible language and spotted with bars with photographs of young men in the windows. It began to rain, and Annie wanted to duck into one of these bars for a coffee, but Paula wouldn't let her. She got them into a *cafeteria* on a neutral street. Then she explained about ETA streets and ETA bars and how they did not take kindly to tourists. Not even to tourists ducking out of the rain for a coffee.

They sat at a front table in the *cafeteria*. Through the window they watched the rain fall and the wind blow and the people pass by under their umbrellas. Paula carried a small collapsible umbrella in her bag. Annie asked to borrow it, and then, as a personal favor, asked Paula not to move. Annie walked back down that street hung with banners and ducked into the first bar she came to with photographs in the window, where she ordered another coffee. The bar at midday was desolate and cold, with six more photographs hung inside, just where she could study them as she sipped her coffee. The difference between the young men in these photographs and photographs of young men, say, back in the States was the Basques' un-smiling un-self-consciousness. As far as she could tell, these young men weren't posing or aping some idol. She turned her attention to the bar-tender and placed her father at her side. When she paid for her coffee, she paid as her father. She lingered over the face of the bartender as her father might have, but the bartender was tired and jowly and far past his prime. His face told her nothing. She returned to the *cafeteria* where she'd left Paula.

Paula watched her approach as if she were monitoring every motion Annie made.

Annie gave her a kiss and told her it was okay.

The rain was steady and the wind cold. They huddled under the umbrella together, arm in arm, on their way back to the car.

There Annie said, "He's been here and gone."

"What makes you so sure?"

"You can see it on the map. You come from Madrid to the Basque country and you start here. It's the capital. It's the point where it all fans out."

"If you believe Pepa," Paula nodded, "it's the capital only because the Basques couldn't decide between San Sebastian and Bilbao. She claims it's the least Basque of all the cities."

"That's not the real reason I know he was here."

She still had possession of the keys and she took possession of the car, letting Paula in the passenger door, inserting the key into the ignition, buckling her belt. She checked the side and rearview mirrors and readjusted the seat to accommodate her long legs. She started the motor and let the defroster blow. Then she turned the defroster off so they could talk. "The real reason," she said, "is because I can feel him here the same way I could feel him back home when he came to visit me at school. Sometimes he'd come without telling me, but I knew he was around, and when friends said they'd seen him I was never surprised. How did I know?"

"Yes, how did you know?"

"Because I was the only person he had left in the world. Now he has you. Maybe that's why I can't feel it as strongly now. Or maybe it's being in a foreign country. It's like the waves are on another frequency over here. I don't know. But there're traces. Down on that street with the bars and the photographs in the windows there were traces. He's been here and gone."

Paula drew back in her seat.

Annie said, "There's a warmth. A kind of cooling warmth. When it gets cold, that's how I know he's gone."

"Annie," Paula cautioned, "not too crazy."

They left the city and drove out onto the plain. They skirted a lake, a reservoir, with chalets and summer homes built up on the hills. Beyond the dam they picked up the river and followed it to the east. Soon they were in a steep mountain valley, and the hillsides were terraced in grassy elevations to the forest line. Through the misting rain the green of the grass took on a lushness that made the gray towns, strung out along their narrow river, seem even more drab. The forests that rose to the mountain rim were of a dense, dark and more sculpted green, and anyone could see in an instant why a Basque with any poetry in his soul would want to get out of town and up into the mountains.

They began to see the spray-painted signs. *"¡Gora Euskal Herria!"*

The smell off the river was not always clean. It was the sweetness of detergent overlaying the sweetness of shit.

Clothes hung out in the rain, their colors half-gone.

The people in these towns had a steamed look—in the paleness of their faces and the dullness of their hair—as if they had stood too long in the rain.

They passed through a town called by its Spanish name, Mondragon, and its Basque name, Arrasate. Annie parked the car off the town plaza, close to the river. In addition to the grayness of the air and the rushing grayness of the river, in Mondragon-Arrasate part of the hillside had been sliced away so there was a scarred grayness of stone. She sensed that her father had been here and gone, and she took from the town a hard foretaste of what was to come.

Before they left, she and Paula entered a small restaurant on the town square and had a meal. The food tasted of that steamed grayness—it was there in the beef, in the beans and the greens in the soup. Like the taste of iron, but more bitterly plain. She engaged the waiter in conversation, determined to take from him one word that went beyond the menu of the day. It was like prying back the jaws of a trap, opening a rift in a wall of stone. What was it like living here, in this town, beside this river, between these valley walls? Winter, spring, summer and fall? Paula signaled her to be quiet, but she was determined.

In the end Annie struck from the waiter the thinnest of smiles. "It's always the same," he said.

"No way out? What if the politics change?"

And the smile went back to stone.

"Don't do that," Paula reprimanded her once they were outside. "You don't talk politics up here."

"I'll talk any way I goddamn please!" Annie voiced her defiance in the uniform grayness of the day. "They murdered my sister!"

"There're things you don't say," Paula responded under her breath.

Annie apologized. This was not who she was. Paula happened to have caught her in a string of bad days. But then, so had her mother, and so had Jonathan and Valerie and Patty and how many others.

Annie kissed her newfound friend, her father's lover. For an instant they stood on a street in Mondragon-Arrasate pressed cheek to cheek.

They drove up the valley in the near-dark and must have crested a hill because when Annie looked again the direction of the river had changed. From here on out, Basque streams flowed north to the Atlantic. They drove until the stream they were driving along, whose name she had not caught, joined another whose name she knew. The Deba. There, at a confluence of rivers and valleys and a darkness that settled like some foul sediment out of the sky, she had a decision to make. The town she'd determined as their destination lay to the east, but it was not a town she wanted to enter in the dark. To the west was a small city, which she thought of as neutral ground. As a gesture of goodwill, she might have consulted Paula.

But instead, Annie drove them west, to a city with all the unattractiveness of the towns, multiplied by ten.

Eibar.

It was a city built in a chute. There was a moment's widening where a terraced park was located, and she tried to stop there, but a policeman moved them on. The area around the park was reserved for pedestrians, and in spite of the chilling fine rain, the side streets were full. A fiesta day? Paula didn't know. They parked farther along and walked back. Families, teenagers, the middle-aged and the elderly—a promenade was moving sluggishly down the center of these streets, and in front of every *tapa* bar groups had gathered to drink tumblers of red wine and eat *serrano* ham on small buns.

Paula led her into a bar and insisted she eat. Annie ate her ham and drank her wine, and in the thick of it, in their perfume and cologne and smoke, in the wetness and warmth of their collective odors, in what they dumped into their rivers and built damply on their banks, she felt as if she were swilling down the entire Basque nation.

They had to buck the pedestrian current to get back up to the park, where Paula learned from the policeman the location of the nearest hotel. The second they entered it, before the desk clerk could attend to them, Annie detected traces of her father everywhere. He'd stood at that counter, sat on those sofas of cracked vinyl and waited before the elevator door. He'd come and gone any number of times.

The desk clerk, a woman like most of the women she'd seen in the Basque country, but whose large, still and stoical eyes belonged somewhere else, took a personal pleasure in being able to serve Annie and her companion. She put herself at their disposal. Annie handed over her passport, and whether it was the name, the address or the photograph, something caused the desk clerk to start and glance back up at the young woman before her.

Annie said, "What?" and the woman smiled and shook her head. Nothing, it was nothing, she had a lovely room for them.

Something. No, nothing. Breakfast was served from seven-thirty 'til ten.

"Something," Annie insisted, and her tone of voice caused Paula to shift uneasily at her side. "What was it?"

"It was nothing. A mistake."

"I reminded you of somebody, didn't I?"

"Not really."

"There's another American here."

The desk clerk shook her head.

"Pretty strange," Annie muttered under her breath.

Paula said, "Leave it alone."

Annie smiled and turned to face the desk clerk. "You have a guest here whose right to privacy you're trying to protect. I think that's admirable. You have an American guest here who has the same last name and the same hometown, and who looks a little like me. That's even more admirable because the coincidences are piling up. You have a guest here who for some reason wants to be left alone, and you're doing what any true professional would do, you're protecting your guest with seniority, who also happens to be a pretty sweet guy, much sweeter than me."

The desk clerk shook her head. She didn't understand. Annie didn't doubt her. Her Spanish and English were crashing around her, and it was as if she were running to get out of a burning house.

Annie shook Paula off. "I am truly sorry," she confessed. "I am looking for my father. I thought he might have come through here, that's all."

The desk clerk had begun fighting her emotions. Her eyes were moist. Here was another chance for Annie to make amends.

"What's your name, if you don't mind my asking?"

"Pilar," the desk clerk said.

"I'm Annie, or Ana. I guess Annie would be Anita. That's Spanish. I don't know how to say it in Basque." On a sisterly impulse, entirely unpremeditated, she reached over and squeezed the desk clerk's hand.

Pilar said, "I can't tell you his name. I'm sorry."

"Could you put us in a room beside his?"

The desk clerk hesitated and then, with an unfurtive but very quiet motion, exchanged the key she'd originally chosen for another, and passed it over the counter. Meticulously, she noted the change on the card she included with the key and on the guest register she kept behind the counter. The number on the card and key was 361, and Annie got the impression that the desk clerk was waiting for her to ask on which side of 361 she would find her father's room, a question that might provoke another seizure of conscience. Of course, 361 might have been a corner room. Even though Annie knew it wasn't.

It was located between 360 and 362, neither of which responded to her knock. She stood before both doors, and neither yielded a trace of her father. There was no connecting balcony outside the windows, as there would have been in a movie, and any maid who might have been persuaded to open the two doors would not be on the job until the following morning. She couldn't wait that long. Paula counseled patience, but at one o'clock in the morning, after hearing nothing all evening on either side of them, Annie returned to the lobby and ten minutes later came back with the two keys. How had she gotten them? Did Paula really want to know?

Since they had the keys, wouldn't Paula agree it made no sense to talk of breaking and entering?

Not too crazy.

They tried 360 first. The room was empty and smelled disinfected. With their expectation aroused, it was like walking into a room-sized tomb. Room 362 was the one they wanted. Her father's clothes hung in the closet and were folded on a chair; a pair of shoes was half under the bed. His shaving kit lay on a bathroom shelf, and his toothbrush and toothpaste were set out beside the lavatory. Newspaper clippings were scattered on the desk, photographs not just of Armando Ordoki but of various ETA members as well. It was all there, especially her father's smell, something nutty, warm and benign. Stuck into a crack between the mirror and its frame were three tickets—the train and bus ticket that had brought him from Madrid and a little cardboard stub that had once taken him to a nearby town.

She motioned Paula back out into the hall and shut the door. Annie's first reaction was that somebody who knew what they were doing wanted them to believe that that was her father's room. Somebody who knew him as well as she did. "That *is* Ben's room," Paula responded. "Those are his things. I recognize every one of them." Annie shook her head. Those tickets were too obvious a plant. Those shoes looked exactly like his. Run down at the heel the same way his were run down. "He's here, Annie. I don't know how we found him, but we did." Annie wasn't buying it. When he came back, Paula would see. He'd look like her father and the man Paula had had her "interlude" with. But he wouldn't be the same.

She waited until Paula fell asleep, then went to lie in the imposter's bed. When he returned and didn't find his key, he'd either flee into the night or summon his courage and come see who'd invaded his room. She really didn't believe the man was her father. It was too easy. Paula might be deceived by appearances into believing otherwise, but there was a difference, all the difference in the world. Annie waited in a half-sleep until dawn. When she went under, she dreamed of a train she couldn't get out of clattering along toward a gorge no longer spanned by a bridge. She woke to a feeling of such displacement, such utter arbitrariness, that she was filled with a cold impersonal fear. She knew where she was but, in that instant, saw no way to make where she was real. She returned to her own room and got into bed with Paula, whispering into her ear, "No, don't wake up, don't wake up. Just lie there and I'll lie here."

XIII

Ben Williamson lay in yet another bed in a room that looked out on that narrow park beside the river, where banners announcing protest meetings sometimes hung. Below his window *Kalea* San Agustin intersected a street that, if followed into the hills, would lead to the chapel of San Antonio, where he'd already been. Two stories directly below his head was the restaurant where he often ate. They knew him there. The night before, he'd been about to board the train that would have taken him back to his room in Eibar when he'd sensed to a certainty that he belonged here. With the train before him and his ticket in hand, he'd felt the base of his being shift. He'd told himself he would return to Eibar and get his things, but in the end he hadn't even done that. He'd backed away and walked down a flight of stairs to the street. He knew what day it was and that on the following day, a Sunday, native sons frequently appeared, but in that moment he was not calculating his chances. His tour as a tourist had suddenly ended, and here was where he'd found himself. He was reminded of a game his daughter Annie had played with her friends on their bikes. They'd toss a coin at each corner they came to and allow chance to take them to the most improbable spots. Ben had chosen his spot, he'd located it on a map and come here with a purpose. Still, seen from a moment, say, five years earlier, with his family around him, all healthy and reasonably content, this spot where he stood would have seemed so absurdly random as to go beyond the element of chance and argue a willful design. Something had led him on a five-year journey and brought him here, and somebody had pulled him back from that train. He didn't believe it, not for a second, but it was as if somebody had. He'd presented himself in the *pension* with a passport he wasn't even asked for. Other than the passport, he was the clothes on his back. And his knife, which was also on his back.

Everything else, changes of clothes and shoes, objects to shave and clean and brush his teeth with, newspaper clippings he no longer needed to remind himself what the man looked like or what the man had said, mementos of his journey, along with traces of himself, fingernails, skin flakes, fallen hairs, his lingering odors, with all of that around her Annie no longer entertained the illusion that this wasn't her father's room. She awoke in her father's bed, not in Paula's, which forced her to conclude that her early-morning move to lie at Paula's side had been a dream she and her father had shared. She hung out a do-not-disturb sign—*No moleste, por favor*—and lay listening to the trains, those going to the east with their destination in San Sebastian and those to the west and Bilbao. The trains made local stops, and she didn't need her map to tell her what the stops were. She had a way with maps. She could lie in this bed her father had slept in and project a map of the Basque country across the cracks in the ceiling. San Sebastian was called Donostia, Bilbao shortened to Bilbo. To the east was a string of Z towns: Zestoa, Zumaia, Zarautz. To the west the G towns: Galdakao, Getxo and Gernika, which Franco and Picasso had made famous. In her immediate vicinity was a clustering of E towns. Eibar, where she lay. Just to the south, Elorrio. And not many stops away on the train line east, Eskuibar. If Vitoria was the southernmost point of a triangle that opened equilaterally to include Bilbao to the west and San Sebastian to the east, she lay in a crescent between the two major Basque cities, and that crescent had a cradling effect. She wanted to get up and leave, to continue the search, but surrounded by her father's belongings and caught in the lulling rock of that cartographer's cradle, she stayed put.

Her father had staged it all with uncharacteristic cunning. She might have been a bloodhound and these belongings such powerful possessors of his scent that nothing could persuade her to leave. It would take an unbreakable leash and five strong men tugging to get her out the door. Or it would take bringing in another bloodhound, a backup bloodhound. That shirt, for instance, hanging on the chair. It was tan with green checks, made of some combination of wool and polyester thick enough for this mountain cool. Its collar was buttoned down and its arms hung straight to the cuffs, which were also buttoned. Over the pocket, over the heart, was a small stain. Had he spilled some soup? A drop or two of wine? She wasn't sure she'd ever seen that shirt before, but just the way it hung on the chair back was enough to keep her there. The chair was narrow-shouldered and her father wasn't. Nonetheless, he might have been sitting there. The expression he might once have worn—his characteristic expression—of a fond and powerful longing for nothing he could name had been replaced by some judicious balance of approval and disapproval, directed at her.

She got out of bed and went to the chair. She sniffed at the collar of her father's shirt. It smelled of his hair and of his warm, slightly nutty flesh, and it smelled of her childhood, of cars they'd traveled in together, of easy chairs big enough for two and of good-night stories, of what he'd left of himself on her pillow, the scent she would go to sleep to, and the traces of him she awoke to in her child's room. She could always tell by the scent if he'd been to check on her during the night. Her nose was uncanny in that way. And he almost always came. Those nights he didn't, the air she awoke to was dull and undistinguished in the most depressing way.

Paula entered the room. She'd had the good sense to return the key to room 360. She'd asked about breakfast and, in passing, had bent down and pretended to find the key on the floor beside the counter. The Sunday desk clerk, the sort of man who wanted things in their place and didn't care how they got there, formally expressed his thanks and pointed her to the dining room, where she'd hurriedly had her *café con leche* and brought up another, plus a croissant, for Annie. Annie had to eat and she had to face the possibility that her father might not be coming back soon. He had taken an impromptu side trip. He'd gone over the mountains and reached the high seas, where he'd shipped out. They were back where they had started, waiting for him to return. In some ways, it made better sense to wait for him in Madrid, where he might have already circled back.

"I know where he is," Annie said.

"You do?"

"In Ordoki's town. It's called Eskuibar. It can't be more than two or three stops on the train line going east. It's close. If you had to, you could walk there."

"Then what's this?" Paula motioned around her.

"His base of operations." Annie shrugged.

Paula looked at the closet and the chair, where Ben's clothes hung. She looked at his shoes on the floor. She stepped to the mirror, took out the ticket stub and read the name of the town. Experienced, resourceful, cultured, well traveled, a veteran of the wars, she appeared to be reviewing all she knew of the man, how needfully he'd come to her, how long he'd stayed, how suddenly he'd disappeared.

"And you propose we search for him there?" she said. She was looking out the window, across the way, where dilapidated buildings clung to the valley wall. One building had a *mirador,* where at that moment the sun, streaming into the valley, glanced off its many panes.

"Yes, but we have to wait." Annie got back into bed and checked an urge to bury her head under the covers. "But not long," she assured Paula. "*Can* we wait?"

. . .

After days of cold drizzle and rain, the sunshine brought a dizzying surge to his blood, and Ben stood for a moment outside the *pension*, his grip firm on a lamppost of wrought iron, until his dizziness subsided and his sight cleared. The hills to the east were as he'd first seen them, a glistening green, on which black-and-white cattle and wool-heavy sheep grazed and cast their shadows down toward the town. The pine forests looked as cleanly delineated as if their curving flanks had been drawn by a draftsman's pen. Along fence rows and before farmhouse doors, late-season flowers had come back to life, sprinklings of white and orange. The sky he saw as a shell of pristine blue. He walked to the river, its grayness shaded entirely to green now, a clouded jade-green that in the right flash of sunlight could turn emerald.

There had been mornings when he'd stepped into the street before his house in Kentucky and something as tiny as a corpuscle of his blood and something as vast as the dome of the sky had struck a single universal chime, and he'd known the world was his. He'd been a boy then. Sometimes his mother had played a chord on the piano that was an echo of that chime. The melody that grew out of that chord was like a luring promise that it might all be true. He'd experienced that chiming again when he'd married and beauty had come to rest in the body of his wife, in the life they'd lived together, in the day-to-day. In certain days of the day-to-day. The chiming struck deep, to the very biological origin of it all, the days his daughters were born. He had not been present at Michelle's birth, his wife's labor having been so prolonged he'd come to think of himself as an impediment; he'd left the scene so that Gail's suffering could end and his daughter could be delivered. But for Annie's birth, he'd been there from start to finish. He'd gone through the Lamaze training and tirelessly practiced with his wife her breathing exercises and the tricks they'd taught her to relax. It had all worked; at least her labor had been much easier, even though there had come a moment when, he understood, her pain was next to unbearable and like nothing he'd ever be asked to endure. It was then that one of the nurses summoned him down between his wife's upraised legs and told him to look up the birth canal, where he'd see a shiny spot of black, the size of a quarter. That was the top of his daughter's head. He didn't return to his wife's side but remained looking over the doctor's shoulder as Gail made a last heroic shove and his second daughter squirmed out of a bloody darkness and into the doctor's hands. In that moment the chiming struck a chord so deep it no longer sounded as sound. It was seismic. He felt it in his knees and in the aroused blossoming of his own flesh, and when they placed his daughter on the tray to be weighed, there came a moment when she twisted her head around and somehow managed to look behind her, directly at him. Annie had been born with her eyes open. He saw a boldness in her look, and he saw a wildness of fright, as if she'd just changed from one species to another and woken to a world of infinite peril. He had never imagined such boldness and such fright could coexist, but that had been the message she'd sent him.

Once more Ben walked the town. From his *pension* all the way to the cemetery at the far end of town. He passed along six walls of crypts he had not passed before. "Here lies" in Spanish was *"Aqui yace"* and in Basque, it seemed, *"Hemes dago."* A number of the deceased had Spanish names. He found one Benjamin. Many of the graves carried black-and-white photographs embossed in glass ovals onto the marble slabs, photographs taken from years past when men didn't appear without their berets and women wore grays and blacks. He studied these pictures, which, in their sternness, seemed to have been taken expressly to appear here.

He turned and walked back. When he finally got off his feet it was to take a table in the Plaza Mayor while one was still available. Crowds of people were entering the plaza from *Kaleas* San Agustin and San Blas. They were stepping down from the train station and coming across the river on the bridge. When mass was over they filed out of the church door. If he'd been stationed on the highest of the hills overlooking the town, up on that lone outcropping of rock where the television antenna had been erected, he would have seen people moving through their town as blood circulates through a body, thinner at the extremities but dense and rich there at the heart.

He ordered a *café con leche,* nothing to eat.

Actively now, face by face, Ben was looking for Armando Ordoki. In the thickening crowds he saw a couple of men who caused him to look again, but he was no longer given an adrenaline start by everyone who came close. He knew the type. Face long, chin heavy, mouth full, nose fleshy and flared, eyes pouched and protuberant when opened wide, hair brown and cut short and combed forward into those Caesar-like points, complexion sandy or meal-colored, neck puffed and beginning to wrinkle, something bearish in the slope of the shoulders and the sway of the gait; the clothing of choice, black: a tee-shirt, sweatshirt or turtleneck sweater.

He fully expected Armando Ordoki to come back. If Spaniards returned to their towns on Sundays to renew their spirits, it stood even more to reason that Basques would. Here were their roots. Here they had formed their *cuadrillas.* Their whole sense of who they were was determined by the remoteness of these mountain valleys. The Moors had never been here. No Jews had. The Romans, it was said, had tried to conquer the region and failed.

Of course, he might have sought Ordoki out in the Basque parliament in Vitoria. He might have followed him on one of his well-publicized trips abroad. Or marched with him in a protest he'd called or agreed to take part in. He might have met up with him anywhere. On a city street. At a corner when he stopped his car. The shower room in a gym. In a barber shop, when he was having his hair cut and combed into those points.

It didn't have to be in his hometown.

Ben got up. The crowds had cut off his sight. He left the plaza and walked San Blas until it intersected with San Agustin, where the bakeries were doing a brisk business selling traditional Sunday cakes. Then he followed San Agustin back to the plaza. He established a vantage point under one of the sycamores in front of the church, from which he could survey the entire plaza. The crowd, he soon saw, was made up predominantly of couples, ranging from the elderly to newlyweds. The teenagers and the children were somewhere else. He saw some single men, as he and Juan had been single men in Medina del Rioseco, but these men soon found couples to attach themselves to. Couples themselves met other couples and began to fuse. He was watching extended families form. An elderly man, a father of families, and his wife might spend an hour touring the plaza and town, and before they left to go off to their Sunday meal they'd be joined by as many as ten. There was something ceremonial about it all. Had children been there, darting in and out, the effect would have been ruined, but without them it was like watching a dance whose steps had been determined long ago. There was no evidence of political divisions. He saw no banners, no signs in the windows, no raised fists or other inflammatory insignia on tee-shirts. Those streaks of red and yellow paint splashed between the windows of the offices of the governing Basque party were a barely distinguishable part of the backdrop scenery, flaking and dulled.

There was an office for the local police within the Town Hall, and occasionally he would see one of them directing traffic or walking the streets. Except for their billy clubs, they went unarmed. It occurred to him that in this town he'd never seen the hated *guardia civil*.

He waited for Armando Ordoki to appear. He wanted to see Armando Ordoki take his part in that generational dance.

At one-thirty, as the crowd began to thin, he was still waiting.

Then, off toward the far left corner of the plaza, he noticed an obstruction to the flow of pedestrian traffic, and the steady undercurrent of voices he heard took on an edge of expectancy. A number of people had left the tables or stepped out of the promenade to form a crowd around the ball court. Someone eager to address the crowd and turn it to his political purposes might do so from there, at the point where the court's two high walls intersected. In the time it took him to walk from his spot under the sycamore to the outskirts of that crowd, he was convinced that Armando

Ordoki was among them, that the excitement he heard in the crowd's collective voice could be explained only by the appearance of a local celebrity, some man of the town with a following. Then he heard a sharp report, a clap, almost wooden, succeeded by another, which in the instant he mistook for gunfire and stopped in his tracks, waiting for the crowd's panic. He heard the sound again and this time identified it as the sound of a ball with a wooden core wrapped in leather striking a concrete wall.

A game of *pelota* was about to begin. These ball courts were everywhere in the Basque country. They played some role in Basque life he did not understand.

Taking advantage of his height, Ben stood at the rear and watched the game unfold. Two players, whose white karate-style jackets were belted in red, were going to play another team belted in blue. One of the red-belted players was particularly powerful and could stand behind the back line and fire the ball into the corner, where the ricochets were trickiest. He had blond hair, not brown, but the face was long and the jaw pronounced and there was a heaviness in the swing of his shoulders and the thrust of his legs. The other players were more agile and better scurriers over the court. They ran down balls seemingly out of reach, and the crowd rewarded them with applause. But when the blond-haired man struck long and hard from the baseline there were expressions of deep admiration, verging on something else.

As the game progressed Ben was able to move up, and before it ended he was standing in the front row.

A young man with a portable scoreboard was chalking up the score. It stood 13 to 10 in favor of the red team when a man beside him said in Spanish, "You understand, don't you?"

Ben was guessing the score went to either 15 or 21 and the first team there won. You scored a point by ricocheting a shot off both of those walls that your opponent couldn't reach. It couldn't be simpler. Really, the only peculiarity was that the game was played on a court of two walls, rather than three or four. But that allowed the spectators to stand as close as he was standing now, just as the blond-haired player retreated to within five feet of him to play a long hard shot.

He heard a grunt he might have made himself. The ball made a stinging splat against the palm, which was bare.

"*Creo que si,*" Ben said to the man beside him. He believed that he did. The man was a generation older than he and stood a head shorter. His gray hair was cut and combed into those Ordoki-style points. As a foreigner, Ben pleaded ignorance. "What don't I know? What should I know?"

"They must be careful not to hit the ball over the wall," the old man replied with dramatic foreboding, which was absurd since the walls were extremely high and no one had even come close. Then he added, "There is always a lot at stake, even in a match such as this."

The red team scored two quick points, and that was the game. And that was the sequence of events. First the old man had spoken to him, the red-belted, blond-haired player had retreated to the baseline to hit a powerful shot, his team had scored two quick points and the old man had said something absurd, followed by something mysterious, to put him on alert. So Ben wasn't taken entirely by surprise when, with a clear view from where he stood, he saw Armando Ordoki himself walking in over the bridge. He was accompanied by a small black-haired woman Ben took to be his wife. With the game over, a number in the crowd hurried out to the entrance of the bridge to welcome Ordoki into town. The old man made a comment in Basque, in a tone mixing exasperation and relief, and hurried off himself.

Ordoki's arrival was the final event in a sequence that had begun not with the old man but as far back into the past as Ben cared to trace it. He traced it to his marriage vows, which grew out of the vows he and his mother made every time they sat down to sing. There he stopped.

Annie lay drifting, unsequenced, and every time she got out of bed she tumbled back in. She slept and awoke, and only when she felt an empty ache in her head, as empty as a room with no windows, rugs, furniture or bed, did she know she'd woken up for good. She was alone. She heard trains coming and going, and there was street noise now, a welter of voices, as if a flea market had been set up in front of the hotel. She went to the bathroom and searched her father's overnight case for aspirin. She went next door, where the door was closed but unlocked and the room was empty, and searched there. Then she decided that what she really wanted to do was stand under a shower until the hot water ran out and the ache went away. But the water was tepid from the start. She stood under its spray until it turned cold, then, dressed in jeans and a school sweatshirt, she stepped to the window and looked down on the street. Tables and stands covered the narrow strip between the street and the rock wall buttressing the train tracks. She saw Paula standing in front of a table on which a mound of tousled scarves lay. In the midday sunlight Paula's red hair looked even more faded; she wore a patterned poncho of some sort with black tassels. Annie watched Paula sift through the scarves and then hold two up to the light. She sent her a message not to buy the first, a Madonna blue. If she had to buy something, it should be the second, a pale yellow or gold that gave off a sparkle of champagne. A scarf to toast her father's return? Annie asked herself: When she took her father home, would that be the end of Paula Ortiz? Her father had left Paula once, would he leave her again? If he did leave her, where would he find another woman willing to go to her lengths? Overcoming her apprehension, Paula had driven into the Basque country looking for her lover, and until she found him she was doing what she did instinctively. She was buying gifts. She bought both scarves. She crossed back over the street and, just before she disappeared from sight, appeared as a foreshortened dot of red hair with a poncho skirt. This was the woman Annie's father stood to lose.

Annie returned to her father's room and made the bed. When Paula knocked, Annie was there to lead her inside and take the scarves from their plastic bag to spread over the double-length pillow. They stood for a moment looking down at the diaphanous blue and the pale gold. Faced with such colors, they were no longer compelled to look at her father's clothes or shoes or tickets or his newspaper clippings of Armando Ordoki's long bulbous face.

Women—maidens—gave their champions scarves to carry into battle. Annie denied herself the scarf she wanted, took the blue, and rolled it into a ball she could fit into her hip pocket.

"We both have one to give him," she explained. "So he'll be carrying our colors. You're gold."

"I bought the scarves for you, Annie," Paula said.

"I know you did."

Paula placed the gold scarf over Annie's head, then slipped it around her shoulders. As deliberately as if she were sorting her desires and misgivings one by one, she looped the ends of the scarf through each other. She did not tie a knot.

"The color suits you," Paula said.

"We have to split up, you know that, don't you?" Annie said. "Someone has to stay here in case he comes back and someone has to look for him in . . . Eskuibar."

Paula corrected Annie's pronunciation, then shook her head. If Annie couldn't even say the name of the town, how did she expect to go there and accomplish anything?

"Two or three stops east. Trains have been going that way all day."

And if it wasn't two or three stops away? What if the train didn't even stop there and Annie got off in some anonymous town no one had ever heard of before? Paula said, "You don't know your father is there, Annie. Tell me. Convince me. How do you know?"

Annie wanted to say because her father had been circling a spot for as long as she could remember. She never knew at what point on the circle she'd find him, only that wherever he appeared he'd be off-center, beyond the bounds of home. In Kentucky she'd slept in his bed and had never felt more . . . untethered. Here in the Basque country she'd slept in another. She could tell Paula she and her father shared a sixth sense for . . . untetheredness. Michelle, of course, carried her center with her. She'd never been more tightly tethered than when she'd been running around that park in Madrid and had gotten blown up. Centers could be dangerous places.

"I just know," Annie insisted.

"How? Do you 'feel' it? We're sitting in this hotel and you can 'feel' his presence two or three stops down the line?"

"Don't mock me, Paula."

"And don't *you* go crazy on me!" Paula's tone was stern. "What if I told you I promised your father that if I ever got the chance I wouldn't let you out of my sight?"

"Did you?"

"Not all promises are spoken out loud."

Paula gripped Annie by the upper arm, and the grip was her mother's back when Annie was a misbehaving child and her mother wanted to warn her there was no limit to how hard she could squeeze.

Just as quickly, Paula dropped her hand—the strength seemed to go out of her. Her eyes looked as brittle as fractured glass. "Why didn't Ben come back last night? Is it because he discovered we're here? Do you think he doesn't want to see us?"

"I don't know."

"Annie, is he all right?"

Annie stepped to the desk and took one more look at the man her father had come to find. Yes, Armando Ordoki's face might belong to a thug, but past the newspaper's smudged print was a gleaming well of darkness in the eyes, the dark, self-replenishing fire of a zealot.

She summoned her conviction. "Yes," she assured Paula, "he's all right."

"Why shouldn't I go look for him? Why shouldn't you stay here?"

"Because I didn't come this far to spend the day in a hotel room."

"And I did?"

"No, you didn't. But you should stay here to welcome him back. You're his reward."

"And what are you?"

"A pest, a nuisance. Just a backup," Annie added and kissed Paula on the cheek. "Wait," she said. "Don't move. Count to a hundred."

Annie went downstairs to the dining room, where the midday meal was not quite ready to be served. She brought up a bottle of mineral water, an omelet *bocadillo,* a jar of olives and some grapes. Moving aside the newspaper clippings, she placed the tray on the desk. "You've got to eat," she told Paula. "You shouldn't even leave the room. Dad looks slow, but he's not. He can come and go like that." She tried one of her mother's finger snaps, but managed only a thin scrape. She laughed at the poor attempt.

"I'll call," Annie promised. "I'll get the hotel's number and call you in this room. You're doing this for me, Paula. It will be the best thing anybody's ever done for me in my life."

"Letting you go, after what happened to your sister?"

"Michelle was a solo act. You and I, we aren't like that. We're a team."

Paula wasn't buying it. She gave her young friend an almost fierce measuring stare. "I'll come find you, Annie! Don't think you can just disappear!"

Accompanied by a core of friends and admirers and that old man, Armando Ordoki and his wife left the plaza and took the long walk down *Kalea* San Agustin. It was not always possible to keep him in view. He was shorter than Ben had expected him to be, and his shambling gait was more like a sailor's roll. Then Ben realized it was the result of a limp. Ordoki favored his right leg, and every time he came down on it he seemed to perform a curtseying little dip. His wife walked at his side, but in her expression she might have been miles away. It became clear: this was not her town. Her husband was animated. Politically, he'd always been animated, richly venting his indignation and wrath. Now he was festive, directing his pleasantries to the men around him, members, perhaps, of his original *cuadrilla,* and to those who crowded in on the edges and hung on his words.

The old man, who was old enough and like-featured enough to be his father, brought up the rear and had not been addressed or embraced individ-
ually, but perhaps Ordoki was waiting until they were home and the core's
core became a matter of blood. That downward flow in Ordoki's face,
which had always been stanched with the fury of his politics, was now
caught up in little eddying pockets and puckers of his pleasure to be back,
so that he looked like a chubby and good-humored boy. His cheeks shone,
his full bottom lip.

Ben had no doubt it was Armando Ordoki. He had only to look at the
people they passed on the street. He was not everyone's favorite son.
When townspeople saw who was walking toward them, they averted their
glance—some of them did—and gave Ordoki and his group a wide berth.
Others, seeing it all in advance, stepped off into doorways until they had
passed. Seconds later, when Ben passed these people, he couldn't fail to de-
tect their expressions of disapproval. He heard the powerlessness of their
long-standing opposition under their breath.

This was fear. There was no mistaking this.

Once, when the group unaccountably stopped in the street, Ben got too
close. The old man might have turned around and seen him and motioned
to him to catch up. He'd turned and motioned to somebody, as if he were
enlisting recruits.

Just down from that little park beside the river the group turned off
into a bar that had never caught Ben's attention since it had no photographs
in the window or posters on the door. Ben sat in the park and waited. In the
time he sat there, the people who came out of the bar seemed to move with
more decisiveness than usual; there was something purposeful and ringing-
clear about their voices, even about their jokes, and he got the impression
that they had been in the presence of an inspirational force. He waited until the street was empty and the two bakeries nearby had closed their doors.
The bakery scents had been replaced by the odors of steamed vegetables
and broiled beef. Finally, convinced that Ordoki and his friends had left

and he'd somehow missed them, Ben got up to stroll past the window in an effort to see inside; then he entered. Ordoki was sitting with the others at a table in the rear, where the light from the street didn't reach. Once again the old man, stationed on the outskirts of the group, made an intemperate old man's gesture for him to come join them, and Ben had no choice but to wave back, no, he'd sit at the bar, where he ordered his *vino* and *pincho de jamon.*

He had just been served when Ordoki and his followers left. They brushed his windbreaker, and one of them brushed hard enough that he felt the location of his knife shift. From the man himself, at the actual moment of his passing, Ben was no farther than three feet. He was even closer to his wife, who had a cleaving sort of face, as clean-featured as a hawk. Along with the festivity on Ordoki's face was a slyness now, as if he'd just heard a joke whose meaning only he and a few others got. Someone said in Spanish, *"No solamente parece un cerdo, es lo que es"*—"He not only looks like a hog, that's what he is"—which got a laugh, but the response came in Basque. When the old man passed, he grinned at Ben, the foreigner, and shook his head.

Ben ate one bite of his *pincho,* took one swallow of wine and was on the street in time to see the group break up at the bridge beside the park. Ordoki and his wife crossed the bridge in the company of three others. The old man was not one of them. The majority of the group entered the neighborhood of working-class apartment buildings just beyond the *pension.* The old man remained at the entrance to the bridge, glancing into the cars that passed, but primarily, Ben suspected, waiting for him.

He walked instead back down San Agustin toward the plaza. A passageway beside the market led him to the river and that pedestrian bridge with the statue of Icarus. Ordoki and his wife walked along the river on the other side, in the company not of three men now but two. At the bridge they lost another, but not before they had stepped out and taken a look down into the upturned face of the boy whose powerful aluminum wings no longer served him. The men seemed to be agreeing on plans for a future date, perhaps that evening. They nodded to each other, taking their cues from Ordoki. His wife spent all her time inspecting the workmanship of the statue, leaning over the railing as though to study the engineering involved.

One of the men added his cigarette to those already in Icarus's mouth. It was just possible that Ben heard, thinner and keener than the water's rush, the hiss of the extinguishing ash. That man then crossed the bridge and passed within five feet. Their eyes never met. Ben had seen him before, middle-aged and overweight, small eyes and a long fleshy slab of a face.

Ben let him pass, then continued down San Agustin to the plaza, stepping out onto the bridge Ordoki had entered town by.

Across the river, and about to turn up into a hillside street of modest chalets, Ordoki and his wife were down to themselves.

She was dressed in a stylish high-belted jacket, the sort women who show horses wear, and tan slacks that even flared a bit at the thighs like jodhpurs. She wore midsized platform heels.

Ordoki wore a white windbreaker, a black sweatshirt over which a rim of white tee-shirt showed and khaki pants, the clothes of his photographs. Essentially, he and Ben were dressed the same, only Ben had no tee-shirt showing and his windbreaker was a darker shade. Ordoki had lost his limp—perhaps the uphill gradient gave his right leg more support. Without his followers and solely in the company of his wife, he had regained his height.

By the time Ben got to the mouth of that hillside street they had turned into, he had lost them. The street curved around the base of a spur, but by his calculation they would only have had time to enter one of the first four or five chalets. The houses were all small, of white stucco and red tile, and set so closely together that it might have been possible to jump from one roof to another down the length of the street. Back when sewing machines were manufactured here, Ben could easily have imagined these homes belonging to employees of submanagerial rank. If Ordoki's father had worked his way up to such a position, he might have escaped those blocks of working-class apartments and come here. His son might have bought the chalet for him with a bitterly satisfying laugh, since, in its smallness, with room in its garden for only a few plots of flowers and a single tree, it had survived while the factory had not.

Ben had not forgotten that the man he was calling Ordoki's father was down on that bridge. He was willing to entertain the possibility that Ordoki had more than one father, fathers of various sorts. That Ordoki and his wife had arrived so late in town that they'd missed both the promenade and the game of *pelota* was puzzling, but that could be explained by whatever the afternoon's activities were likely to be. If a meeting, for instance, had been planned.

He walked around the bottom of the spur to make sure there was no hidden stairway coming off the hill by which a man might slip away. He saw a concrete niche partway up, glassed over and lit with a flickering tier of votive candles. A shrine to a local saint, he assumed. Another day he would have climbed up to investigate, but today he returned to the mouth of that street of chalets.

Since breakfast he'd had nothing to eat but that bite of a *pincho de jamon*. There were at least two hours on a Sunday afternoon when no one would appear on the streets—as far as he knew, that was an absolute in Spain. Ben had time to go back to his *pension* and eat. Just up the road was a small bar that was open, and he certainly had time to go there. But he stood his ground. Eventually he hoisted himself up on a retaining wall and sat. There were bushes just behind him and three or four small pines, and when he began to feel conspicuous he backed into those. He sat not on rocks but, he soon realized, on the hard, deep-sea plastic sheath of his knife. For a moment he accepted the discomfort, then, as he shifted the sheath's position, his fingers found the release button and he gave in to temptation. He heard the click and felt the finger-grooved handle slip into his hand. He didn't hold its stainless-steel blade up to the light, but he held it beside him, out of sight along his leg. He might have been holding some wildness of life at his side, until its breathing and pulse beat were one with his own. Then he put the knife back into its sheath. Michelle would laugh at him, but Michelle was no longer alive. Annie had been born with some of that wildness and some of that boldness in her eyes. She'd been frightened too, frightened to the very root of her being. But Ben reminded himself that Annie was alive. He reminded himself so often that it became a mantra, entirely unconscious, the words in and out with his breath.

Annie is still alive. Annie is still alive.

But sitting there behind bushes and pines, he missed her when she arrived in town, walked down from the station, and he missed her again as she took her first look at the Plaza Mayor. It was empty. Tables were still set out, but even the two bars were closed.

Annie could have gone into the church, and by one means or another she might have found her way into the office of the local police, where a missing-persons report could have been filed. But she didn't consider her father missing. She stepped over to the bridge. Weekday wash hung from some of the windows fronting the river, even though it was Sunday. She noted what at another time she might have regarded as the beauty of the hills. Attached to the next bridge upstream she saw a winged aluminum figure whose feet were pedaling air, but she wasn't in the mood for local artwork, either. Nothing about the town pleased her; she'd seen several like it driving up in Paula's car, just in a different weather. She returned to the plaza and sat on a stone bench beside a brutally pruned sycamore. The clock on the church tower behind her read three-forty. If everybody in town was out of sight, it stood to reason her father was too. The smart thing to do would be to sit there until the townspeople began to reappear, and then begin her search. Almost at once a middle-aged woman passed at a quick pace, late to get somewhere, angry, but seemingly blaming herself. An isolated case. Then two men, strolling, conversing in quiet but aroused voices. Annie picked up stray words and phrases: *mal asunto, mala gente,* bad business, bad people, *un gilipollas,* which she couldn't translate, and *Vaya que lio mas gordo,* a big fat mess. One of these men looked like every Spaniard she'd seen, so she didn't look twice, but the other, doing the talking, voicing his complaints, bore a certain resemblance to Armando Ordoki, so she followed them out of sight.

She was on the town's main street—the market, clothing stores, a pharmacy, two bakeries, a bank, a number of bars, an opening to the river, a thin wedge of a park—and then she was standing in front of the only hotel, *pension* or *hostal* she had seen. She entered and sat down in the dining room behind the bar, where she was told that the menu of the day was no longer being served. All that was left was some potato soup and grilled sardines. When she said she'd take them, the woman noting the order gave her the same sort of double-take the desk clerk in Eibar had, and that was when Annie knew. It was not something in the passport, it was something in the looks, or the voice. It was something she and her father did, a gesture or mannerism they had. It was a need they gave off, a hunger—or a special sort of willingness to be served. She waited. When the woman came with the soup, Annie didn't ask her if she knew her father, but she commented on how much she liked the soup and the town and the beautiful valley—she threw it all in—and waited for the woman to ask her. The woman did. Are you an American? There's an American here. I don't know what it is, but you remind me of him. Your voices—of course, he's an older man. Also an admirer of our town. But there's something else. You don't know him?

No.

Vaya, que curiosidad.

She could wait for him here in the *pension,* just as Paula waited for him in the hotel in Eibar. Eventually he'd have to sleep. But, too impatient to sit still, Annie stepped out of the *pension.* There was more activity now on the streets, mostly children after the large Sunday meal; while their parents took their *siesta* the streets belonged to them. They ran in packs of four or five. She saw them in the park, eating sunflower seeds and spewing out the husks; she heard them throwing rocks down by the river. Up to her left a street ran beneath the railroad tracks and climbed into the hills. Anyone oppressed by the long narrowness of the town could follow that street and in fifteen minutes be out of it all.

She began to walk the town; the geometry now lay in her favor. If she patrolled the axis in a town so narrow, there was a good chance that when he crossed it they'd intersect. Or she could search out those pockets of warmth. She'd get hot and hotter, then come up behind him and slip her hands over his eyes. Except she suspected that those pockets of warmth originated more with her than with him. She might project a warmth that she could walk through just so she could say, If only I could be that warm again. Her mother had given birth to her, but her father had always tucked her in.

Annie walked the town looking for evidence of ETA activity, but there was nothing to compare to what she'd seen on that street in Vitoria. This was Armando Ordoki's hometown, and there was always the chance that the man himself would come swaggering down the street. He'd have a bully's bulging eyes and a bona fide fascist's jaw. But he'd know his Marx, and his Bakunin and Frantz Fanon and Adorno. He'd have them down chapter and verse. You wouldn't want to argue in the abstract with the man. Men never lost those arguments anyway. They ended up abstracting themselves and left you stuck in the mud.

Back in the main plaza, she sat at a table, and told the waitress to bring her anything, anything she wanted. The waitress brought her a bottle of mineral water, compliments of the house, saying she, the waitress—a girl approximately Annie's own age with a round face, and cute, cute as a Basque button—hoped that improved her day. Annie drank the water with a real thirst, the day still warm, her walk long and her search fruitless. Every person she saw returning to the plaza after the midday meal looked so satisfied with his lot and fundamentally fulfilled by his Basque being that she couldn't imagine how any more Basqueness could be appealed to in the name of whatever separatist cause. She tried to visualize her father among them, and, such was the foulness of her mood, she couldn't see him at all. She tried picturing him where she'd seen him last, on the campus of her school, and managed only a familiar and heavyset blur. For a moment she gave in to a rage at these Basque families who had taken her father away from her. In a small lucid part of her mind, of course, she blamed only herself. She breathed deeply and let that lucid part expand. In the margin of the light she cast, her father reappeared to her, and she saw him as clearly then as she had when, in the candlelight of a restaurant, he'd told her to dig in for the day that was sure to come. He'd had a naked and obstinate sort of honesty in his eyes that she'd missed at the time but caught in retrospect. Back home, she'd laughed and shaken her head at this lover of old ballads. Now, she set her jaw and faced him with all the frankness she could muster. She committed her missing father to memory.

H e might have slept. He'd been warm in his spot in the brush and the pines, and although people had passed below him along the road he hadn't stirred. Perhaps no one had passed—he couldn't be sure. But he was awake when the person he waited for came by; he was cold and sore, and it was nearly dark. The man he'd identified as Armando Ordoki was alone. Ben crawled out of his hiding spot, lowered himself from the retaining wall, and followed at a distance. Maybe sixty feet. Pitcher to catcher. The man was dressed as he had been, except that he now wore a beret. In no photograph Ben had seen of Ordoki had he worn a beret, but he'd seen no photographs of Ordoki in his hometown. Unlike the berets the old men wore, which could seem sculpted to the tops of their heads, this one was large and floppy and fell off to the side. It had something at the top, a little clipped-off pig's tail. It reminded Ben of a nightcap, or something a jester might wear. Its immediate effect was to make the man who wore it into a problematical figure, perhaps a figure of fun.

Ben followed the man down to the river, where he turned left and re-traced the route he had taken earlier. During the walk along the river he was greeted by only one other person, a very young man. The older man placed his arm around this subordinate's shoulder and talked close to his ear. They never broke stride. At the Icarus bridge the young man stepped away, per-haps to carry out a mission. The man in the beret continued on alone. There was no trace of that limp. His gait resembled neither a bear's nor a sailor's; Ben couldn't even call it a swagger. It was straight up and straight ahead.

At the bridge beside the park the two of them crossed the river. Ben ex-pected to see the old man he'd spoken to at the *pelota* court lurking some-where nearby, but he did not. The last couples with young children were lingering in the park. The bars on San Agustin had begun their *tapa* hour. The man in the beret turned left, away from the bars and smell of food, and into that neighborhood of working-class housing. The door he entered led to a staircase and an upstairs apartment. Ben was sure of the apartment be-cause he'd seen the old man standing out on the balcony watching the man Ben would continue to think of as his son approach.

He sat across the street on two cinder blocks and waited.

D usk fell. The temperature dropped. A breeze sluicing down the val-ley made itself felt. Ben sat in the shadowy zone between streetlights, while his daughter sat at a table in the more generously lit Plaza Mayor, two empty espresso coffee cups before her now. Finally she took the chance. The waitress in her irrepressible spirits had proved loyal. Had she seen a foreigner, a tall blond and balding man anytime lately in the town? He would be a friendly man, well behaved, a little heavyset, who kept to him-self, moved slowly, but somehow made you want to match your step to his. The waitress had seen such a man. She'd waited on him. He'd have his *café con leche*, watch the people, then get up and do more or less what Annie had been doing. Yes, he moved slowly, but he sometimes seemed like the most restless person on the planet. The waitress wasn't sure when she had seen him last. There were so many people.

Judging by the look on his face, would the waitress call him happy or sad, lost or found, or what? The word the waitress used was *añoranza*, which was an elusive word, so she and Annie tried to pin it down, until it was something deeper than homesickness but not so clearly defined. A longing? A longing for something missing? A longing for something you can taste but have never had in your mouth? Something like a guarantee?

Well, the waitress wouldn't go that far. *Añoranza*. You want to be where you're not.

Annie walked the main street again until she was back at the *pension*, where from the pay phone she called Paula. She wasn't surprised that Paula didn't answer. At the *pension* bar she had yet another coffee. A few last *tapistas* stood to either side, with their little forks eating cuts of ham or *chorizo*, sepia or shrimp off little oval plates, washing it down with little tumblers of red wine, but *tapa* hour had all but passed. She hadn't eaten since breakfast, but she was not hungry. Empty the body out altogether and she might achieve the sort of clarity that would allow her to entertain a presentiment.

She stood at the door to the *pension* and, in her mind's eye, watched Paula in her little plum-colored car drive across the bridge into town. Annie crossed to the park that fronted the river, and there, in the shadows, put her faith in her powers to the test. Five minutes, no more. As other cars were leaving town to return to the cities after a day in the *pueblo*, Paula drove in. She parked in a spot Annie had all but picked out for her in front of the *pension* and went inside. With her flawless Spanish and her canny reading of the Spanish scene, Paula would have no problem. Had anyone seen such and such a man and such and such a girl? Yes, such a man and such a girl had been seen. Five minutes, no more, but when Paula reappeared at the *pension* door, dusk had given way to night.

It was as if Annie had summoned her. Pale Paula, with her fading freckles and ash-red hair. Annie should have gone up to her. Instead, she waited until Paula, following the directions she'd almost certainly been given in the *pension*, walked off down *Kalea* San Agustin toward the Plaza Mayor. Annie crossed the bridge and walked a parallel route, between the highway and river. Two cruising Basque assholes blew their horn at her, which, curiously, allowed her to feel closer to home. At the pedestrian bridge, she stopped to see just what it was hanging off its railing. Like her father, she failed to recognize the figure as Icarus. But she didn't see it as a fallen angel either. Dim light came off the metal of the figure, the ghostly aqueous sheen of a fish glimpsed at the limit of sight. She thought of it as something risen from the river, its face designed to cleave the water like that, the round of its mouth gasping in this alien air. A winged human figure emerging from the realm of fish, it was caught between three orders of nature and belonged in none. She felt a strange affinity with this creature and took the time to lean over the railing and pick the shredded cigarette butts out of the mouth. What sort of town would bolt this statue onto the side of a bridge? Stranded, furiously pedaling the air. What sick sort of town?

She placed her hand against the precipitous slant of its cheek. Something, the coolness and cleanness of the touch, gave her Paula, who would have reached the Plaza Mayor by then, and, if the café was open, would have inquired of a waitress there if she had seen just such a man, just such a girl.

On his cinder blocks, her father leaned over his knees to keep the hard blue plastic out of the flesh of his backside. Various people had passed him. He had given a start to one woman on the arm of her husband. On another occasion he might have had to apologize. But the man had been upset with his wife and didn't seem to care if someone scared her to death. *Tonta*, the husband upbraided her for being so skittish, while, seated in his shadow, Ben tried to order his thoughts. He heard muffled voices, and he heard car and truck traffic and, he calculated, the last train. He heard the last of those people who'd come back to the *pueblo* going home. Then came a period of footfalls up and down the street, followed by the rattle of trash cans, closing windows, closing doors. Few cars drove this far into the neighborhood, and the last one passed him then. The last motorcycle.

His daughter had left the river and turned up a road and then another that swung her around the spur of a hill. On the town side of the road a string of small chalets was built, and Annie walked that road until the chalets ended and she came to a break in the foliage. At that point she had a dark, low-angled view into the town. She saw the river, the glimmer of the bird-fish-man hanging off a bridge; the church tower gave her the Plaza Mayor, the bridge that led to it and the avenue in. While she was standing there, a full moon rose over the hills behind her and the town changed mood. It took on the silver patina of old photographs, as if it were already a town behind glass.

At the bridge leading back into the plaza, Annie glanced upstream and down. She saw nothing. She heard the river, and if she heard men's voices behind it, they were voices that could just as easily have belonged to animals or birds, the sound of running water could do that. She crossed the bridge, passed through the silver membrane the moon had cast, and reentered the town.

A man in a large floppy beret stepped into the street accompanied by a couple. The couple might have been in their midtwenties. This time the beret reminded her father of what a Left Bank artist might wear, and Ben had to consider the possibility that these young companions were artistic disciples, that it was all a subversion of the established order of art. He stepped into the darkened doorway at his back and let the three of them pass. The young woman had a dazed, enraptured look on her face; the young man's eyes were narrowed judiciously, as if to make the difference between them clear. They reminded Ben of a photo he'd seen. In the photo the man had been more coldly calculating and the woman more wide-eyed and aware, but, essentially, the couples were the same. The man in the beret was saying something to them in Basque. His voice was level, instructional, leaving no room for doubt.

Artists never spoke like that.

Ben followed them at a distance of a block. At that well-lit intersection where the *pension* was located, they stepped into public view and their voices were jovial, typically loud, and their embraces came with an onrush of feeling.

Artists made spectacles of themselves and gave in to their feelings like that.

The young couple crossed over the river.

The man lingered at the intersection, as though considering the turn he might take. Then he continued down San Agustin, where numbers of people still strolled.

This time no one shied away from him. Perhaps it was the beret. Nor did anyone, seeking his favor, approach.

Ben fell in beside him, matching his stride. It was the same stride, no limp. They came to the same height.

In the Plaza Mayor the waitress at the café and a young boy had begun to bring the tables in under the arcade. Annie gave them time to complete the work, then, before the waitress could go back inside, where customers, all men, still stood at the bar, she took her aside. Yes, the waitress answered, a woman had just been there, speaking very good Spanish, a woman with red hair and . . . the word was *pecas*, freckles, yes just such a woman asking for a man and a girl, a girl such as Annie herself might have been. And the woman had been? Quiet, very quiet and still. As if she were looking at something very far away. Something that had already happened. The waitress shook her head.

"What is it?" Annie wanted to know.

The cute Basque waitress shook her head again. Her round eyes blinked on the slowest of shutters. "Very quiet and very still," she repeated.

"You didn't see us here today," Annie said.

"I see hundreds of people every day. Especially on Sundays. It's like a homecoming. But they're all the same."

"I'll never forget you, but you didn't see me."

The waitress kissed her on each of her cheeks. For a brief moment Annie was visited by the other woman's warmth, humid and very close in the evening's cool.

"Your friend is over there," the waitress whispered.

Paula was standing in the deeper shadows of what must have been a ball court. Where two high walls intersected she was quietly keeping watch. Annie crossed the plaza and stood beside her with the towering walls at her back, whose facing was peppered with scuff marks. They might have been marks of violence, a macabre scorekeeping of the spots where flesh had stood before concrete, and not the places where a ball had struck.

"You didn't call," Paula said. "I wasn't going to lose you both."

"He's here," Annie said.

"Yes, I know."

"He's very close."

"You've felt him?"

"Everybody's been here, now everybody's gone. We're the only ones left. Come with me, I want to show you something."

She gripped Paula by the softness of her upper arm, but Paula wouldn't be moved.

"It's a statue," Annie said. "It's another stranger in town, climbing up on a bridge."

With a nerveless equanimity in her voice, Paula replied, "I found you here. I'll wait for him here too."

Moving in their direction down *Kalea* San Agustin, Annie's father spoke courteously. "I'll only take a moment of your time."

The man striding beside him responded, "Speak to me in my own language and you can have all the time you want."

Speaking in English, Ben said, "It's about my daughter."

"Yes?"

"It's about my daughter and the Basque cause."

"Your daughter and the Basque cause?"

"Yes."

"What is your daughter's name?"

Before he could check himself Ben named his living daughter; then he took his living daughter back and offered his dead daughter instead.

"Michelle . . ." The man considered the name before declaring, "Michelle is not a Basque name. It's French." He turned to pass alongside the market. This was the passageway to the pedestrian bridge.

Ben called after him, "There are Basques in France."

"But not named Michelle."

"Is Sabino Arana a Basque name?" Ben asked.

The man turned back. His beret cast a diagonal shadow across his face, but this was as close as Ben would come to the man he'd seen on television talking passionately to anyone willing to listen, the man who could be quoted forever in the press.

Ben took his chance. "Armando is not a Basque name either."

"Armando?"

"Yes. Your name."

"You're confusing me with somebody else."

"I don't think so."

"Somebody who knows more about the Basque cause than I do."

"I know who you are."

"I can tell you this. The Basque cause requires a lifelong commitment. It is not an adventure you can walk away from."

"Yoyes," Ben replied, recalling in the moment the name, the nickname, of the woman who'd retired from the struggle to raise her daughter and whom ETA had killed before her daughter's eyes.

"Yoyes?"

Then he remembered the complete name. "Dolores Gonzales Catarain," he said.

"Who are you?" the man demanded.

"A father concerned about his daughter."

His living daughter had drifted out from the ball court. The waitress had gone back inside the café. A group of kids was gathered under the arcade, but they soon scattered. Annie heard footfalls in the plaza, made by people who had disappeared by the time she came to look for them. The town was quiet. If the Plaza Mayor was a stage, the stage was set, but it was too big a stage, too centered in the public eye, too resonant with historical occasions, too much a pour-in point for all the currents that made up the town, and she was not where she had to be. She stopped and listened. She heard the river, and she heard voices borne on the water. If voices got on the river they might be carried from one end of this mountain-rimmed town to the other, and she instructed her hearing until it was not apartment dwellers with their windows open and their nightly mutterings she heard but the voices of men relating matters of real import, real consequence, or voices relating their passion's blind folly. Those were the voices the river favored and those were the voices she heard.

Two men. One of them would be her father.

Annie was not a fool. If she heard the water making the sounds of two men talking, she heard what she'd come to this town to hear, she quite understood. But if those were the sounds the water made, and if one of the sounds was the voice of her father, what choice did she have?

She moved off toward the river. Paula called after her, and then Paula moved with her.

The man Ben had addressed as Armando Ordoki walked away, paused as though considering his course of action, and then walked partway back, so that the two now stood no more than five feet apart. The river ran below them. They were in a shadowy walkway that passed behind a string of offices and stores. The window just upstream gave them a darkened look into a gallery where pictures by local artists hung. Pictures of this river and these hills.

"I will take the time to explain something to you," the man announced with professorial forbearance. "Please listen carefully. I will describe to you a scene that all Basques know. When the *guardia civil* come to take your son or daughter away, they will march you and your wife and younger children outside into the street. More often than not, you will be barefoot, perhaps only half-clothed. They will insult you and threaten to beat you if you move. They intend to make an example of you. Your neighbors will not take you in because then the *guardia civil* will evict and beat them. You stand outside in the rain and cold and listen to your child's screams. When they finally take him away they will not let you back into your house. Not at once. First they will take all his possessions away, in big cardboard boxes, before your eyes. His books, his notebooks, his tapes, his posters, his clothes, his toothbrush and hairbrush and razor, everything, his childhood toys if he has any left. When they do let you back inside, you will find your house ransacked and no trace of your son left. Or your daughter. This is how the Spanish state functions. They are scrupulous down to the last detail. They will take your son or daughter to Madrid and for five days you will have no news of their whereabouts. You will not know if your son or your daughter is alive or dead. The one thing you can be sure of is that he—or she—will be tortured. Perhaps you have seen the photographs. . . ."

"Yes."

"You may have opposed what your son or daughter chose to do, but once they have done it you are part of the fight. Do you understand? You will never forget the night they came for him—or for *her*, for your daughter. They will have violated you too, in your innermost being. You think, what a pretty town. Most tourists think of our Basque towns as 'timeless.' Time here cuts deep. It is like a razor cut. It begins when they come for your child and you stand outside counting the seconds and minutes and hours. You will never know how many families have stood like that, exposed—"

"Armando Ordoki," Ben said.

The man stopped talking. He looked at Ben with an alerted curiosity, the flesh flow on his face come to a quivering halt. Ben remembered that Ordoki as a very young man had been taken away. It followed that Ordoki's family had stood outside.

"Why do you call me that? Armando Ordoki no longer lives in this town."

"I want to know if the cause is just," he said.

"It is just."

"In spite of the suffering. The torture and all the families that have had to stand outside."

"In spite of everything."

The man turned to go. At the grip of a hand on his shoulder, he turned back.

"My daughter," Ben said.

"Ah, yes, your daughter," the man recalled, in his voice a faint trace of scorn.

"In spite of her?"

The man removed Ben's hand from his shoulder. With his free hand he motioned back to the passageway they'd taken along the market to reach the spot where they stood. "Is that your daughter?" he inquired. "Is the woman beside her your wife?"

Annie saw two men talking at the entrance to the bridge. Two men dressed the same, roughly the same age, build and size. Beyond the man her father was talking to she saw the aluminum figure with the useless wings desperately trying to reach the safety of the bridge. She identified her father by his lighter skin, his finer and lighter hair, by the neck she'd held on to as a child, and the heavily sloped shoulders she'd ridden on when her father played horsey. Seen from the rear, he was immediately recognizable as the man who had tried to stand between her and the world's harm.

Her shield.

The man doing the talking wore a beret that shadowed his face, but he was as close a facsimile to Armando Ordoki as her father was likely to find. She saw the man turn away and her father place a hand on his shoulder to turn him back. Paula gave a gasp, a sharp intake of breath as if she'd been stung, and it was then that the man looked their way and raised his voice, asking if they were her father's daughter and wife.

It was an old trick, and with his eyes on the man before him, her father refused to be baited into turning around. In a show of solidarity, Annie refused to run to his side. Once that single gasp had escaped her, Paula stood quietly, as quietly—what had the waitress said?—as if she were looking at something very far away, something that had already happened.

"My daughter is dead," Annie heard her father say. "I have no wife."

"Dead? You did not say your daughter was dead."

"Three years ago there was an ETA attack on a *guardia civil* headquarters in Madrid. Before a park called Santander. Do you remember that?"

The man shifted his gaze away from her father and looked Annie directly in the eye. He did not look at Paula. Paula Ortiz did not interest him. Like her father, he had a fleshy face, but his was flesh growing off a scowling hardness so that at any moment it might gather itself for one more murderous assault.

She returned his stare. She was searching for the gleaming darkness she'd imagined at the bottom of his eyes, but in the inconstant light all she saw was the petty and impersonal shine of two eyes looking at her with their own petty and impersonal design. She'd seen their like before. It occurred to her that if this was Armando Ordoki, Armando Ordoki was not someone who deserved to be singled out.

There was no shortage of thugs.

"ETA," she heard him advise her father, "is not something you want to be talking about."

Whereas in a world full of fathers, she had only one.

Her father said, "My daughter was a student. She was running around that park. When you killed that lone *guardia civil* you killed her."

The man assumed an Ordoki-like bearing. Upright and righteous, he declared, "I did not kill your daughter." But at the back of his voice Annie believed she heard a faint stirring of sympathy, something like a quiet current running through his voice, which might have been the pacifying effect of the river running through them all. Armando Ordoki was said to have two children. A daughter of his?

"When you did not raise your hand to condemn the killing," her father made clear, "you might as well have set off the bomb."

"Raise my hand?"

"In the Basque parliament."

"I don't sit in the Basque parliament."

"I ask you again," her father said. "In spite of her?"

"In spite of her?"

"In spite of my daughter's death, is the cause just? The Spanish government takes your young men and women away. They torture them. They make inalienable enemies out of every Basque family. Does that give you the right to take my daughter's life?"

Annie saw the man do a remarkable thing, utterly un-Ordoki-like. He glanced back at her, as though including her, as though asking permission to act for them both. Then he raised his heavy-fisted hand and laid it on her father's shoulder. She might have said he laid it there consolingly. If he'd been anybody else, she might even have said fraternally. Her father stiffened. But the man did not remove his hand.

"If what you say is true," he allowed, "your daughter died an innocent death."

Her father stepped in closer to him and said something Annie couldn't make out, but whatever it was caused the man to step back. His hand remained on her father's shoulder, but his arm had gone rigid. He now appeared to be holding her father off. By the length of his arm, he appeared to be demonstrating the extent of his Basque apartness.

"That Civil Guard headquarters," he responded in a rehearsed and faintly wearied voice, but not lacking resolve, "was a legitimate military objective."

"But my daughter wasn't," her father reminded him, loud enough for them all to hear.

"Unfortunately, your daughter was within range."

"Her name was Michelle Williamson, and she was twenty-one years old."

Ben experienced it in the aftermath. The knife was in his hand and his hand was held before him, but the actual drawing of the knife was the click he heard afterward, and the leap of the handle into the palm and the fingers slipping into their grooves. He was not an agile man, but he'd once caught a pickpocket with his fingers nibbling in his hip pocket. He'd caught him by the wrist. In that instant he saw that boy's lean, startled face.

He and the man in the beret looked down at the blade, moonlight running cold on the stainless steel. That was his knife, Ben recognized it at once. He was astonished to find it in his hand.

One astonishment gave way to another: his daughter Annie had appeared at his side. She too was looking down at the knife. A third: moving up beside Annie, steadfastly, as though honoring a pledge, was Paula Ortiz. The four of them formed a close-knit group on the bridge, and Ben thought—the thought was presented to him, from the day's events, an image sprang to his mind—of the way families formed in this town.

Blood pairings.

The man leaned in, as though his eyes had deceived him. Which meant they all huddled closer.

"What are you going to do with that?" he said.

Ben advanced the point of the knife to the other man's midsection. Powerful tremors passed through his shoulder into his arm. To his left, close to his ear, he heard Paula Ortiz say, "The Goya, Ben. If you do it, you'll be stuck."

The Goya he saw was of two giants, colossi, mired to the knees in a mortal mud.

Obeying those tremors, the knife point found its way into the fabric of the windbreaker, the cotton shirt and the rubbery vicinity of the other man's flesh.

His daughter Annie reached out and removed the beret. Exposed, the face before them instantaneously changed shape; the eyes flared and widened, the forehead rose like a cliff. With a pallor that shone like the dusky sheen coming off the Icarus, or the fallen angel, or the bird-fish-man struggling to reach the bridge, the man threatened to become someone they'd never seen before.

"Who are you?" Annie said.

"Not the person you're looking for," he replied.

"Then you're nobody. Just another one of them."

"One of them?"

"Another Basque with a great big hard-on of a non-negotiable demand."

With the knife point pore-deep in his flesh, the man managed a grin. "This Michelle," he asked, "what was she to you?"

"A sister," Annie declared.

Ben heaved, then steeled himself and edged the knife forward.

"Don't," Annie said. "Please don't."

It was a test of nerves, Ben understood. The man could have broken and tried to run. The moment, which was as potent and rich with possibility as a dream, might have faded into the light of common day. Paula Ortiz said, "He's not worth it, Ben. It doesn't make any difference who he is, he's not worth it." His daughter slipped behind him and placed a hand on his arm, so that the tremors that ran from his shoulder to his knife point passed through her too. He flexed his arm; together he and his daughter fixed the point. He looked the man in the eye. He might have been looking out a window into the night. The man's eye was full of whatever Ben wanted to people the night with. It was up to him. He didn't really believe his daughter and Paula were standing on the bridge with him. They were night creatures too, phantoms he'd called to his side.

Family.

Armando Ordoki? With a phantom hand riding his arm, Ben suddenly advanced the knife so that the man who stood before him opened his mouth on a single soundless howl. Then, in a deliberate act of disengagement, Ben withdrew the knife. The blood on the blade shone blacker than red in the moonlight.

They all gathered around, inspecting the blood, as though admiring a rare jewel.

Then his daughter, the young woman at his side, handed him a large, floppy beret, with which he cleaned the knife. Ben offered the bloody beret to its rightful owner, whose pallor was even more pronounced and whose expression had formed around a scowling knot of disbelief. For a moment it seemed as though in a dizziness of disbelief he might fall.

There was only a trace of blood on the windbreaker, located around a small, blade-sized rip. Annie said, "If you didn't know where to look, you'd never know it was there."

What was the punishment for spilling Basque blood? From time immemorial, had a price been fixed? The man made an abrupt movement, as though he meant to lunge at them. Ben raised the knife, and the man fell back, brandishing his right index finger in that show of defiance Armando Ordoki was known for, a finger that ETA could always convert to the barrel of a gun. The man jabbed at them; one by one, he attempted to commit to memory the features of a face. But his concentration deserted him. He became distracted. His cheeks sagged, his bulging eyes clouded over and turned inward. Something had happened here, which he appeared to be puzzling out. There was a moment of quiet, of suspended animation, during which the river ran in a muted chorusing effect and a cow moaned from the hillside. When the moment had ended, the man seemed none the wiser. He looked as confounded as a dull-witted boy. His arm fell, and more to himself than to them, he muttered, *"¡Gora Euskal Herria!"* as though he were retaking an oath.

Ensimismado.

Ben lowered the knife.

In a poor imitation of a bear-like sway, Armando Ordoki—or just such a man—turned and walked off the bridge.

Ben Williamson threw the knife and beret over the rail.

Then he turned and walking in the opposite direction might have passed right by his daughter and lover if Annie had not reached out and hooked on to his arm. Paula took the other. Paula's whisper to him was urgent but curiously distanced, and very quiet: "Don't stop, Ben. I have my car. It's just up the street. We've got to get out of this town."

Annie said, "He really doesn't believe we're here. You don't, do you, Dad?"

He no longer smelled like her father. They walked him off the bridge and into that narrow passageway beside the market, and his sweat rose to her nose in a whiff of animal wildness that had Annie thinking of her mother, and then, of all things, of a field of popping goats. She bristled. Her mother was half a world away, which was where she belonged, and they were in Eskuibar, a name that sounded to her ear as willfully foreign as that poor misbred figure climbing onto their bridge.

The man at her side possessed a huge, slumberous fund of strength. At any moment he might swing his arms free and dash both Paula and her to the ground.

Annie coached him along, down *Kalea* San Agustin to the *pension*, to Paula's car, and the way out of town. "Dad, it was just a prick, a little flesh wound. You let the air out of him—that's what you did! The next time he gets up to make a spectacle of himself, he'll remember it and sit back down." And because men making spectacles of themselves could drive her sister into a cold fury, Annie added, "Michelle would approve."

Something passed through her father's body, a sort of questioning surge, and with all his weight he seemed to go on alert. Annie said, "I'm Annie, your other daughter, and that's Paula Ortiz, our dear, dear friend."

On her side, Paula murmured encouragement of her own.

They passed late-evening strollers on the street, and a couple of them bore a certain resemblance to Armando Ordoki themselves. Paula and Annie were two women out with their man, and these Ordoki-ites were such diminished little creatures that suddenly Annie's throat tightened and she discovered she wanted to cry.

But she was not a crier, she was a laugher. Laughing, not crying, was what she did.

Her father came around at the sound of it. "Annie, I didn't mean for you to come here," he said.

"Yes, you did, Dad. Yes, you did." Quietly she pleaded in his ear.

Reaching into her hip pocket, she brought out the Madonna-blue scarf, which she unwadded and tied to her father's arm. She would not have held it against Paula if she'd left the gold scarf back at the hotel, but she hadn't. Paula tied it to her father's other arm and said, "I don't think you realize how serious this is. If that was Ordoki, we may never get out of this town."

Annie shook her head. "He won't tell. This is a private matter. We're all sworn to secrecy here."

Up ahead, the *pension* curved into view, and in the streetlight Annie saw the plum-colored Renault, so tiny she couldn't imagine the three of them fitting inside. Not with her father the size he was now.

"Not too crazy, Annie," Paula cautioned. Then she spoke to Ben in a tone that caused Annie to feel both excluded and curiously privileged. She was being given a glimpse into the life Paula and her father shared, the memories they could appeal to, the veiled way they might grant and withhold their favors, really, in such a short time, a code of togetherness they'd created that Annie couldn't crack in a hundred years. Paula said, "We're almost there, *cariño*. If we were back on Castellana, it'd be like a short *paseo* from Cibeles to Gijon, really, no more than that. We'll be sitting there the next time Leslie and Garret come to town. We won't tell them about this, not this, but something, we'll make up something nearly as good...."

Her father strode down the center of the main street of this benighted Basque town, flying scarves of blue and gold, a woman on each arm and blood on his hands.

Had Annie been eager to see the blood flow? She didn't believe so. But the thing about blood was that once it began flowing it held your attention like nothing else, so that a drop could become a gallon while you stood there marveling that such dark beauty existed in the world. She'd placed her hand on her father's arm. Intending to hold him back, had she actually nudged him forward? And when her father withdrew the knife, as though severing a bond, had she resisted so quick an uncoupling? All she could say for sure was that it wasn't until his precious Basque blood had appeared on the knife blade that she'd come close to feeling anything for the man.

For Armando Ordoki.

Annie squeezed her father's arm. To her friend Paula Ortiz she made a silent vow: We'll both have him for a while, Paula. Then I'll leave you in peace. I'll take my scarf and get on an airplane and fly home. I promise. One day you'll look for me and I'll be gone.

I owe debts of gratitude to my editor, Fred Ramey, and my agent, Dan Mandel, for their belief in this book and their uncommon acts of editing and agenting.